Everything th[...] disappeared into [...] wild, kill-frenzied mania. His body contorted—he could feel that, and it hurt. He was changing again. He didn't know exactly what was happening to him, how it was happening to him, or why it was happening to him. He could feel it and experience it only for the first few moments, then any greater consciousness was replaced by the pure murderous impulses of the Bhaalspawned demon he had become.

Look for these fine titles
at your local bookseller

Baldur's Gate II

Shadows of Amn

Philip Athans

BALDUR'S GATE II
SHADOWS OF AMN

©2000 Wizards of the Coast, Inc.

All Rights Reserved.

Distributed in the United States by St. Martin's Press. Distributed in Canada by Fenn Ltd.

Distributed to the hobby, toy, and comic trade in the United States and Canada by regional distributors.

Distributed worldwide by Wizards of the Coast, Inc. and regional distributors.

First Printing: September 2000
Library of Congress Catalog Card Number:

9 8 7 6 5 4 3 2 1
ISBN: 0-7869-1569-2
21569-620

U.S., CANADA, ASIA, PACIFIC, & LATIN AMERICA	EUROPEAN HEADQUARTERS
Wizards of the Coast, Inc.	Wizards of the Coast, Belgium
P.O. Box 707	P.B. 2031
Renton, WA 98057-0707	2600 Berchem
+1-800-324-6496	Belgium
	+32-70-23-32-77

Visit our web site at **www.wizards.com/forgottenrealms**

This one's for The Group:

Gordon
Laura
Mike
Andy
Eric
Carl
and Julie

Chapter One

Late in the summer of the Year of the Banner, Abdel Adrian, son of the God of Murder, returned to Candlekeep a hero.

Gates that had been closed to him only weeks before were thrown open this time. A man he'd known all his life, a man who had accused him of murder, who had locked him up like an animal, who had all but handed him into the clutches of the Iron Throne, had embraced him with a smile of relief and confidence.

"Abdel," Tethtoril said, a tear coming to his eye, "Abdel, I'm so glad you've returned to us. I can only hope your stay this time will be a long one, and you'll—"

"Abdel!" a thin, reedy voice sounded behind him. Abdel turned to see a face he hadn't seen in—how long? A year?

"Imoen," Abdel breathed, meeting the slight girl's hasty embrace. "Imoen, you've grown into—"

"Don't say it, Abdel," she interrupted, a smile softening her voice and making her eyes dance.

"You're a sight for sore eyes, kid," he told her, and they embraced again.

She held him and said, "I'm sorry about Gorion. I'm so sorry."

Abdel's breath caught in his throat, and he forced a weary sigh.

1

"He didn't die in vain," Tethtoril offered.

Abdel looked up and was surprised that Tethtoril seemed to have moved farther away. The sky over the secretive bailey of Candlekeep roiled with green-gray clouds. Abdel could smell lightning but couldn't see it. He was delighted to be able to return to his home with his head held high, but there was a heaviness in the air and someone missing—no, more than someone—too many people. Where was Jaheira? She'd come with him from Baldur's Gate, surely, and there was Xan, but didn't he get lost somewhere along the road? Abdel remembered Xan arguing with the ghoul Korak, then something happened—

"Abdel," Imoen whispered, her breath cool against his bare chest. Abdel didn't remember taking off his shirt. Imoen shivered against him, and he looked down at her. He was easily a foot and a half taller than the girl. Imoen was beginning to fill out, her little girl's pronounced joints smoothing into her arms, her hips rounding, and her ribs fading into smooth, pale skin. Her hair was long, and it blew into Abdel's face, stinging his eyes. He breathed out a little laugh and made to gently pull her away, but she wouldn't let go.

Her small grip on his strong arms tightened and tightened some more when she whispered, "What's happening to me?"

He said her name again, then winced when one of her fingernails pierced his skin. Blood ran out of the wound, trailing down the top of her finger and past her wrist.

"Something's happening to me," she whispered, her voice deteriorating into a guttural, inhuman grunt. She actually snorted, spraying Abdel with freezing-cold spittle.

"Imoen," he said, and when she didn't respond, he pushed her away more forcefully. He might have been the only man on the Sword Coast able to push back against her suddenly superhuman strength, but he had no time to be pleased with his physical prowess. He hissed at the sight of this young girl's face. Her normally refined features were twisted and ugly, and her mouth was growing into a gaping, fang-lined abyss. A tongue, forked and long like a snake's, shot out and tasted Abdel's bare chest with a touch so chill it made the huge sellsword shudder.

The thing that had once been Imoen made a sound that made Abdel shout in return, as if he could launch the sound of his own voice against it in battle. Imoen's reddening eyes bulged to several times their natural size with a look as scared and confused as it was hungry and malign. A string of curses spat forth from her quivering mouth, already bleeding where the razor-sharp edges of her teeth pulled against the purple mass of her lips.

Abdel pushed her farther away, and the touch of her naked skin was freezing, and the texture was dry and rough, almost scaly. Abdel reached behind him and found the pommel of his sword though he swore he couldn't feel the strap across his bare chest. The sword came out with a shriek of metal on metal that harmonized with the Imoen-beast's keening wail. Abdel didn't think about what he was about to do to this girl he'd known since she was a baby, who'd put up with his sullen moodiness and occasionally cruel taunting through their cloistered childhood, a kid who wanted to follow him on his adventures and was pushed aside at every turn.

Abdel brought his sword down hard and fast. He cut off her head and screamed as it fell to the brittle brown grass of Candlekeep, and he was still screaming when he woke up, right into another, all-too-real, nightmare.

* * * * *

Abdel may have been a hero, but he had not returned to Candlekeep. He saw the light coming from the brazier first, then closed his eyes and felt the heat. The copper bowl full of orange-hot embers was too close to him. He tried to bend away from it, but his naked back moved only a fraction of an inch before it met a rough, cold stone wall. Abdel flinched away and adjusted again. Try as he might in those first few moments between dream and reality, he couldn't find the happy medium his body was demanding.

The unforgiving iron manacles chaffed his wrists, and the sound the chains made when he moved mocked him. Abdel growled, a low, animal noise deep in his throat, and clenched his fists.

He blinked his eyes open and saw a man enter the cell. He was short and fat, with a stinking abundance of body hair thick with sweat around the black leather straps of his simple girdle and harness. There were tools hanging from the straps, most of which Abdel didn't recognize. The strange man met Abdel's gaze and smiled, revealing a single tooth hanging yellow and jagged from his upper gum. The man's beard was uneven, broken by a rough burn scar that did nothing to add attractiveness or even character to his round face.

"You are awake," the man said slowly, careful to pronounce each word as if language was new to him, or at the very least difficult.

"Jailer . . ." Abdel started to say, then his parched throat closed on him, and his eyes watered. He sucked in a breath and started choking from the smoke from the brazier, dehydration, and the ache from a bruise he didn't remember getting.

"Dungeon master," the man murmured, looking away from Abdel, then pausing as if seeing the brazier for the first time. As he reached up to grab a poker hanging from a hook on the wall to Abdel's right, he said, "Dungeon master, not jailer. This is not a jail, it is a dungeon."

Abdel sighed, trying to meet the man's blank, glazed stare, but to no avail. The man was an idiot.

"What—" Abdel croaked as the man set the poker into the burning coals and held it there. "What is your name, Dungeon Master?"

The man smiled but didn't look at Abdel. "Booter," he said, "is my name. My name is Booter."

"Where am I?" Abdel asked, his voice beginning to really come back now. "How did I get here?"

"My boss's place," Booter drawled, scraping the tip of the iron poker against the bottom of the copper bowl. "My boss took you. I do not know where he took you from."

"Who is your boss?" Abdel asked, eyeing the poker suspiciously. He could feel the anger building, and though he was starting to remember trying to pull the chains out of the wall and failing, he kept his voice as level as he could.

"Who is your boss?" Abdel asked again as Booter pulled the poker out of the hot coals and dragged it across Abdel's chest. He screamed, smelling his own skin and hair burning and feeling every popping blister and seared inch of flesh in a pain that was almost a living thing on its own. His scream drowned out most of Booter's answer to his last question, but Abdel was sure he heard the man say "Shadow Thieves."

He couldn't be in Amn, could he?

* * * * *

Abdel had seen Jaheira murdered by Sarevok. As he went to spill his half-brother's vile blood, Jaheira was returned to the world of the living by the prayers of the priests of Gond at the request of soon-to-be Grand Duke Angelo of Baldur's Gate. It was fully a day after Sarevok's death that Abdel saw Jaheira alive again. She'd cried in his arms, and Abdel, drained of his ability to feel anything, just held her. They slept little, though the sense of relief was there. So much was over, but so much had been lost in the process. Instead of sleeping, they went on long walks through the dark streets of Baldur's Gate. Citizens, merchants, tradesmen, and soldiers alike recognized Abdel and tipped their chins to him in silent thanks. Word of Sarevok's deadly plans spread quickly through Baldur's Gate, a city, like so many others, that all but ran on gossip.

They were walking together again, that last night, neither of them speaking. Jaheira's hand draped limply in the crook of Abdel's elbow. He took one long-strided step for every two of hers, and though it hurt his battle-weary knees to walk that slowly, he was happy to stay alongside her. Every once in a while he would look down at her, and she would smile.

The men came out of the shadows in the manner of professional kidnappers. They were already surrounding Abdel and Jaheira before they made their presence known. It took only the blink of an eye for Abdel to realize what was happening and not much longer to draw his sword. In that same space of time, three of the kidnappers moved in.

Abdel brought his sword around, above his head, and was startled by the shrill sound of metal on metal, then a hard jerk that succeeded in taking the blade out of his hands. His arms were still moving forward fast and hard—faster now that the sword was no longer weighing them down—and it was a small thing to alter the direction of the swing enough to smash his heavy right fist into a masked man's face. There was a loud crack, and Abdel could feel the attacker's nose collapse under the blow.

Jaheira grunted, and Abdel looked over to see a black-masked man holding the half-elf in a painful headlock.

"I'll break her—" the man started to say, but finished with a hard exhale when Jaheira brought her elbow in sharply to his ribs. His grip loosened enough for her to wriggle out, and Abdel spared a glance behind him.

Another masked man was frantically unraveling a long length of black steel chain from around Abdel's heavy broadsword. Abdel took two long strides at him, and the man ducked the first kick with admirable speed. Slipping across the damp cobblestones to avoid Abdel's left fist, the attacker spun his chain out at his side and narrowed his eyes in warning.

The huge sellsword only smiled and feinted an attack. The masked man fell for it and twirled his chain up and across at Abdel's face, but it swished harmlessly short. Abdel punched the man in the ribs hard with his left hand, and all the air blew out of the masked man's lungs. The thug fell to his knees. Abdel put him down with a kick to the head.

Jaheira shot her elbow back and up this time into her attacker's face. This man, too, fell to the ground, and Jaheira smiled at Abdel and almost started to wink before another masked man grabbed her from behind.

"Enough of this," a heavily accented voice called from the shadows. "Just take them." The voice was commanding and impatient, but the masked men didn't seem to react to it at all.

Jaheira was pulled back and over by the much

bigger man who'd grabbed her from behind, and Abdel's blood boiled at the sight of it. Someone grabbed him roughly from behind, and Abdel bent forward quickly from the waist, throwing this attacker to the street with a crack, a curse, and a clatter of metal on stone when the dark-clothed man's dagger skittered out of his grip.

Abdel picked up one foot to stomp on the man, and a voice behind him said, "Bhaalspawn!"

Abdel's head spun almost as fast as his body did, and he made to face the man who had dared to use that name for him after all he'd been through to rid Faerûn of his own brother.

Something dry and surprisingly light hit Abdel in the chest, and there was a puff of powder in the air in front of him, powder so light it was almost smoke. Abdel breathed in to muster an appropriate curse, and he got a sharp, bitter taste in his mouth, and his eyes clamped themselves shut tightly.

"Abdel!" Jaheira called out.

Abdel growled, and his head spun. He shifted one foot out to his side to account for the sudden extreme list of the boat he was—but wait, he wasn't standing on a boat. . . .

There was another light thud, and Abdel's eyes rolled around to see Jaheira waving at a similar cloud in front of her face. She made to look at him, but her eyes just rolled up into her head, and she slumped back into the arms of a masked man behind her.

Abdel tried to growl again but just gagged. He felt someone touch his arm, knew it wasn't Jaheira, and tried to make a fist. His fingers wouldn't bend, and he had only one clear thought: That's strange, before his knees gave way, and he was out before he could see the cobblestones rush up at his face.

Baldur's Gate II

* * * * *

Abdel roared in rage, frustration, and bloodlust, but not in pain, even when Booter latched onto the second fingernail with his needle-nosed pliers.

"This will hurt too," the self-styled dungeon master murmured, then pulled hard, tearing the fingernail up and off in one swift, cruel motion.

Abdel held his teeth together tightly and swore to more gods than he thought might be listening that he would kill this "dungeon master" in a most telling way, and he would do it soon.

Chapter Two

Jaheira clenched her jaw tightly closed inside the iron band that held her mouth shut. She could breathe through her teeth and drink water, but she couldn't speak, and though they'd been there for what felt like at least two days, she wasn't able to eat. She'd been identified as a mage by her masked captors, though that wasn't quite true. A druid in the service of Our Lady of the Forest, Mielikki, Jaheira could call upon that divine power to cast the little miracles people called "spells," but she was no mage. Still, she had to admit that they'd been right to keep her from speaking. She could have warped the wood in the door that held them in this dark, stinking chamber, spoken to the roots weaving through the ill-kept stone blocks that made up the walls, or even just taken the rot and disease out of the stagnant, bitter water she had been given. She would have had to speak to do any of those things.

She remembered being jumped while walking with Abdel in Baldur's Gate and had assumed that she'd been brought to the same place as he, though she hadn't seen him since regaining consciousness in the cage. When she awoke, she met two others. Each of them had their own cage. They could see each other, and the other two could speak, but they were kept apart.

One of the others was an odd, stocky, well-built man

with long red hair and a patchy orange beard. He had
apparently taken some kind of small rat or large mouse
as a companion. Jaheira looked at the babbling lunatic
with a mix of fear and pity. She wasn't afraid that he
might harm her or try to take advantage of her—they
were in separate cages after all. No, Jaheira was afraid
that she might end up like him. Would she be locked
away, restrained, told nothing for so long that her
mind, like this poor fool's, might unravel?

"It's all right, Boo," the red-haired man muttered to
his rodent companion. He'd noticed Jaheira looking at
him, and before she realized she was making him
uncomfortable and turned away, she saw him tilt his
head down and to the side, revealing a jagged, still-
bruised scar running along the right side of his head.

A heavy blow must have addled him then, Jaheira
hoped. Maybe he wasn't left here too long.

"A fine group we have here, yes?" the second prisoner
asked her, obviously noting her discomfort with the
red-haired man. "The silent rodent, the madman, me,
and you."

She looked at him blankly, unable to figure out what
this one wanted her to say, even if she could speak. He
was a strange looking man, with features nearly like an
elf's but not really. She had seen only one other person
like him before: the woman Tamoko, lover of Sarevok.
Abdel had told her Tamoko came from Kozakura, on the
other side of the world, east of the endless Hordelands.
This one was a man, of course, but different from
Tamoko in other ways too. His face was rounder, softer,
as was his body. He seemed well fed but not fat, strong
but not muscular. He wore a simple black blouse and
loose-fitting black trousers, a uniform not unlike the
ones worn by her captors. Jaheira mistrusted this man
for that reason and for other, less concrete ones.

"If my name was Boo," the Kozakuran tried to joke, "I would be in a better situation, I think."

She tried to squeeze out a smile but realized it looked more like a sneer. Maybe she did mean to sneer after all.

"I want to get out of here, Boo," the red-haired man said to his little friend. The rodent didn't respond, but the Kozakuran man did.

"Indeed, Boo," he said too loudly, "get us out of—"

The lock drew back sharply, and the door vibrated, sending loud, almost painful waves of sound through the cramped chamber. The door swung open, and Jaheira blinked in the brighter light from the guttering torch in the narrow corridor. The same fat, soft-spoken half-orc in the leather harness who brought them their water from time to time shuffled in with something over his shoulder. The big jailer was obviously struggling with his heavy burden, and Jaheira quickly realized it was a man, then realized it was Abdel.

She wanted to scream his name but could only moan tightly under her iron chin strap. The jailer stopped and shifted his weight onto one foot, and Jaheira's eyes went wide at the sudden burst of motion. Abdel's hair was what she noticed first. Long, black, and matted with what looked like sweat and blood, it whipped up over his back. His set, determined face followed just as fast. The jailer started to fall backward at the sudden shift in Abdel's considerable weight, and Abdel pulled his shoulders back, bringing his chest away from the jailer's hairy shoulder while kicking his feet forward. The effect was to send the fat jailer tumbling onto his ample rump, while Abdel came solidly to his feet in a puff of dirt, rat droppings, and straw.

Abdel's hands were tied tightly in front of him, but Jaheira realized that wouldn't slow him down nearly enough to save the jailer's life. The burns and cuts blossoming over Abdel's body didn't register with Jaheira at first. He stepped back with his right leg and kneeled next to the jailer. Jaheira realized Abdel had been tortured and gasped as much at that thought as the sight of Abdel's hands coming up, his elbow falling past the jailer's head, and those two huge, godlike arms tightening around the still-stunned jailer's neck.

Why did Jaheira want Abdel to stop? She didn't know, she just didn't want him to kill, not out of anger, not when he didn't have to. Did he have to?

Abdel seemed to see Jaheira for the first time just before he started to twist the jailer's head. Their eyes locked, and Jaheira could see fire—literally a faint yellow glow—flare suddenly in Abdel's eyes. She realized he'd noticed the iron strap on her head. She had no idea what he'd been through, so she couldn't know what he was imagining she'd been through. She made her eyes wide and tried to shout at him with her mind. She wanted him to stop.

He couldn't hear her thoughts, but her face, smashed into the mask as it was, was plain enough, and Abdel stopped short of killing the jailer. He squeezed the man's neck, didn't twist it, and the jailer woke up just in time to try to take one breath, then pass out again.

"Jaheira," Abdel whispered as he strained at the ropes that held his wrists together.

She closed her eyes and jerked her head back once in hopes that he would understand. He stopped trying to get his hands free and moved to her. The burns on his chest and thighs were purple welts, and he was trickling blood from more than two dozen tiny cuts. He came to her cage and reached in. Without thinking she slid closer to him, pressing her body against the bars. A tear rolled down her cheek, and she had to close her eyes when he leaned closer to her. She felt his nakedness brush against her shoulder, and she heard the loud clatter of iron on iron as he fumbled with the lock on her mask, oddly ignoring the fact that she was still in a cage.

He cursed and pulled, wrenching her neck painfully. There was a whining sound and a crack, and the strap around her chin fell away. He stood quickly and moved to the locked door of the cage. Muscles bunched along his massive arms, and the cage door broke free with one hard yank. Bits of metal clattered on the stone floor, followed by the louder clang of the barred door Abdel easily tossed aside.

"Kyoutendouchi!" the Kozakuran exclaimed. "Now free the rest of us!"

Abdel ignored him, taking Jaheira's chin gently in his bound hands. "Did he . . . ?" Abdel asked, the yellow light returning to his intense eyes for half a heartbeat.

Jaheira opened her mouth to speak, and her jaw cracked painfully, but she managed to say, "No, no, he just left me here with these two. I don't know them."

Abdel looked at the other prisoners, then back at Jaheira.

"Get the keys," Jaheira said to Abdel. "Get the keys from the jailer."

Abdel smiled, said, "Dungeon master," and retrieved the keys.

He went to unlock the Kozakuran's cage but stopped when he passed near Jaheira. Abdel moved to embrace her, but she pushed him away.

She closed her eyes and said, "In the name of Our Lady of the Forest, by the will of the Supreme Ranger, by the touch of the daughter to Silvanus."

Abdel felt a cool nettling pass over him, and when he touched his own chest, the pain from the cuts had gone away—the cuts themselves had healed.

"I didn't know you could do that," he whispered, shocked.

"I haven't been calling on Mielikki enough," Jaheira admitted, blushing, "or listening carefully enough to her call."

"That's all very interesting, young miss," the Kozakuran said, "but I and my very dear fellow prisoner are still hoping to complete what I can only guess is a much welcomed escape."

Abdel looked at Jaheira, who smiled, then he unlocked the Kozakuran man's cage.

"Many and varied thanks, respected sir," the man said. "I am Yoshimo of the Faraway East, and you are my newest friend."

Abdel only grunted at the man, who stood on surprisingly steady legs, rising to a height nearly two feet short of the top of Abdel's head.

"Jaheira," the half-elf druid said, standing and stretching sore, hunger-weakened muscles, "and this is Abdel."

She didn't bother to watch for any reaction to either her name or Abdel's. She was too busy breathing, working her sore jaw, and stretching her cramping legs.

"It's all right, isn't it, Boo?" the red-haired man muttered over and over as Abdel unlocked his cage. The big sellsword was obviously taken aback by the prisoner's mad demeanor.

"Do any of you know the way out of here?" Abdel asked.

Jaheira had to shrug, and Yoshimo looked at the red-haired man as if sure he would have the answer.

The man shrugged, pointed to the only door, and said, "Through there?"

Jaheira allowed herself a laugh and made to follow Abdel and the red-haired man out.

* * * * *

They came out into an all-out melee.

The four escaped prisoners followed the sounds of battle, since it seemed the only thing to follow, through twists and turns in narrow tunnels that confounded even Jaheira's sense of direction. The red-haired man still seemed oblivious to anything but the rodent he carried cupped in his hands. He would ask the animal if it was all right to turn this corner, safe to go up that set of steps, wise to pass through some doorway. No one but him ever heard the thing answer, but he always followed the rest of the escaping prisoners.

They came into a wide, low-ceilinged chamber dominated by huge roselike growths of orange crystal. Black-clad men were locked in combat with other black-clad men, and neither side seemed to be winning. No one even noticed them at first and even when a few did glance their way, they were all too busy fighting to the death to do or say anything.

"I don't know if this is better than the cages or not," the Kozakuran said dryly.

"There!" Jaheira shouted, pointing to a door on the other side of the chamber.

"Is it all right, Boo?" the red-haired man asked the rodent.

"It's the only way out," Yoshimo said, putting a hand on the madman's shoulder.

"Boo says it's all right," the man said, addressing another human for the first time.

A man in black robes fell screaming to the ground only a dozen paces in front of them. The two assassins who'd killed him looked up sharply at the little group and came on fast, swords drawn.

Jaheira called on Mielikki, closing her eyes just after

seeing the still naked Abdel rush forward to meet the charging assassins. She took a tiny sprig of tree root she'd pulled from the wall in the chamber of cages and secreted under her torn, sweat-soaked blouse. The root grew in her hand, and she smiled at the feel of it in her palm. In no more than two heartbeats it was a sword of polished wood with a gleaming blade that showed its razor sharpness.

"Your side!" the red-haired man shouted just in time, and Jaheira dodged the warhammer coming at her from her left.

The wielder was a black-robed assassin with all-too-human eyes overcome with panic and bloodlust. She backed up two steps, which was enough time to recover, and brought her wooden sword up in time to parry another hard strike from the warhammer. She sliced her sword in low and scraped across the assassin's left knee, then his right, and the man went down like a sack of wet rice.

"You will learn the price of your failure, you . . ." a harsh male voice shrieked above the melee, the rest of his obviously enraged statement lost in the echoes of steel on steel.

Jaheira heard someone cast a spell just as another assassin came at her with a quarterstaff raised high. She threw her sword at him and kept her eyes glued to it. The assassin made to dodge the thrown blade but was surprised when the unlikely weapon stopped in midair and reversed its direction, striking for his throat as if it were being wielded by some invisible swordsman.

"We know our price!" a shrill male voice shouted over the general din. "Give us our payment, necromancer!"

The assassin parried each thrust from the goddess-given sword but was soon being pressed back into a stone-block wall. Jaheira had to concentrate on the blade, using her own will at this distance as she would have to if she were holding the blade.

She wondered what Yoshimo and the red-haired man were doing, what had happened to Abdel, and whether or not the other door really was a way out when the single word "Sleep!" shouted from somewhere to her right made her do just that.

* * * * *

Abdel knew that running into the green cloud would be a bad idea, but he'd already started in that direction when it suddenly appeared in front of him, engulfing the two black-clad men he was trying to defend against. The cloud had obviously been conjured by some mage mixed in among the assassins. The sound of murmuring voices had been part of the general cacophony the whole time. Abdel and the two assassins were overcome with the powerful stench of death and decay. They wanted to kill each other, but all they could do was retch. If Abdel had had anything in his stomach, he would have emptied it onto the floor beneath the cloud. Instead, he just stood there and coughed until a man crashed into his back, and he was pushed, pulled, nearly carried out of the cloud.

"I will destroy you all!" a strange man, a man Abdel couldn't see, screamed. "Your blood will serve me as your pitiful efforts could not!"

Abdel looked back through watering eyes in time to see Jaheira fall to the floor limply, Yoshimo standing impotently by her side, stepping back as two black-robed men grabbed for her. The man with red hair was suddenly standing next to Abdel and had what a more lucid Abdel might have described as a wholly inappropriate grin plastered to his face.

18

"Abdel!" a woman's voice screamed at him, thin and weak.

He was more confused that Jaheira seemed surprised to see him than that she could shout at all, then realized it wasn't Jaheira's voice.

"Imoen?" he gasped around another body-wracking dry heave. He looked up and saw a face he'd seen most recently in a dream but not in real life for many months. The impossibility of her presence washed over Abdel like a cold rain, and the sellsword was quite simply flummoxed.

"We have to go," the red-haired man shouted with an almost cheerful tone. "Boo insists!"

"We will kill you first, necromancer," a man screamed from somewhere in the middle of the battle, "then take what you owe us . . . take the son of . . ." The voice was lost again under the din of battle.

A wave of bright purple fire washed across everything, and Abdel was thrown across the rough floor. All throughout the underground chamber, people were being scattered. Chunks of orange crystal came out of the ceiling, the walls, and the floor. Weapons came out of hands, and at least one boot was pulled off a foot and hit Abdel in the face. Everywhere there were dangerous, heavy, sharp things flying through the air and people sailing upside down, crashing into the ceiling, walls, floor, and each other.

Abdel called, "Jaheira!" then, with a wild, yellow-eyed look of incomprehensible fate in his eyes, "Imoen!"

What was Imoen doing here? The last time Abdel had seen the young woman—barely more than a little girl—was behind the sheltered walls of Candlekeep. She was an irritating kid who didn't take Abdel seriously enough at all, was openly disrespectful and catty, and one of the few friends Abdel ever had in the monastery-fortress where he'd grown up. He couldn't begin to fathom what she might be doing in this place. She was a captive of these men who might be Shadow Thieves, but how, when, and why had they taken her from Candlekeep?

A handful of the warring assassins were on fire now in the wake of the bizarre, obviously magic-spawned explosion. There was a thick stench of smoke, burned hair, and blood. A few men were getting to their feet. Some crawled around searching for weapons. Others had started to kill each other already. Most of the room was blocked from Abdel's sight by a growing pall of smoke, but he started in anyway.

"Imoen!" he called sharply and was sure he heard her answer, though now there was a growing cacophony of steel on steel again ringing through the chamber. A piece of the ceiling fell in front of him, and he had to step back to avoid it. Someone grabbed him roughly from behind, and Abdel whirled with his right fist in front of him.

The red-haired man grunted and stepped back fast. Abdel was surprised enough that he missed hitting the madman.

"Gotta go!" the madman said. "Boo demands it! Boo demands—"

He stopped when he saw Abdel raise his fist again, and he flinched when it looked as if Abdel was going to punch him. Instead, the big sellsword pushed him down by one shoulder and saved his life in the process. A gleaming steel blade arced through the air where the madman's red scalp had been less than the blink of an eye before. Abdel had to bend backward an inch or two himself to avoid its singing tip.

Abdel waited the half second it took for the sword blade to finish its fast arc, then punched out with his left hand in one abbreviated movement that snapped the swordsman's neck back nearly enough to kill him. Losing blood from a viciously cut lip, the man went down hard, blinking all the way. As he fell, Abdel deftly slid the sword out of his hand, and just as the soldier hit the battered flagstone floor, Abdel had the sword up to parry another soldier's uncertain strike.

Soldiers wearing tabards Abdel immediately recognized as Amnian were flooding into the chamber from doorways the sellsword hadn't noticed before. In the smoke, screaming, and confusion, Abdel couldn't tell who was who, and neither could the soldiers, who just took on everybody in the place as they came in.

"Gotta go!" the red-haired man, now standing again in front of Abdel, said.

Abdel parried another swing from the confused soldier, who kept glancing down at Abdel's naked body and blushing. The son of Bhaal batted the Amnian's sword away and punched him in the face hard enough to send him down to join his friend on the floor.

"Imoen," Abdel said. He couldn't fathom how these kidnappers had managed to get Imoen out of Candlekeep. She had been an orphan who ended up in the care of Winthrop, an innkeeper well known and well liked in Candlekeep. Winthrop was an easier man than Gorion, less demanding, and Imoen's frivolous ways and casual demeanor were easy to explain. She was a good kid and didn't deserve to be here.

"Boo," the red-haired man said, kicking a black-clad assassin in the groin and taking his sword out of his hand as he went down, just like he saw Abdel do, "says 'Gotta go!' "

Chapter Three

Even a lesser vampire is strong enough to break a human's neck. This was proven three times in a single minute as two of Bodhi's thralls protected her from the rushing advance of the guards.

Bodhi looked through the smoke-filled chamber and sighed in profound disappointment. The Shadow Thieves had come, angry apparently at the handling of this Abdel person and the girl. She hadn't even seen this man Abdel. The Shadow Thieves had asked Bodhi and Irenicus to capture him, but Irenicus seemed as interested in him and this girl he described as Abdel's half-sister as the Shadow Thieves were. This is why they'd kept the prisoners longer than the Shadow Thieves wanted them too.

The response from the assassins was a testament to both their impatience and the level of desire they had for at least these two prisoners. Bodhi hoped that the guild of assassins she was gathering herself—on orders from Irenicus—would be as devoted.

Now the militia had appeared, attracted by what, Bodhi couldn't be sure. Maybe there was an informant among the Shadow Thieves. Maybe the noise and the shaking of the ground was something they could actually hear or feel on the surface. Maybe, Bodhi thought with a wry smile, the neighbors were complaining.

She tightened her grip on the girl's long, soft hair and kicked out at a running soldier, lifting him two feet in the air by his groin and laughing as he fell to the floor with tears streaming from his eyes and blood beginning to soak through his leather codpiece.

"Imoen!" a solid, deep voice called from somewhere in the confusion, and Bodhi looked up to find the source of the voice.

She almost allowed herself a gasp at the sight of the huge man, naked and straining against a red-haired man who was trying to pull him out of the room. He was beautiful, this naked one. He almost seemed to glow. Bodhi felt something she hadn't felt in a long time, since before she entered her state of undeath. The feeling made her smile.

"Abdel," the girl whose hair she was holding whimpered. This made Bodhi grin even wider.

"This is Abdel?" the vampire whispered, not caring that Imoen couldn't hear her over the sound of the melee.

A soldier slid to a stop in front of her, leveled a crossbow at her face, and shrieked, "Release the girl and step—" in a shrill voice cut off when one of her thralls stepped in.

The lesser vampire twisted the crossbow back into the soldier's throat. The steel tip punctured skin, and the soldier jerked, releasing the catch and sending the bolt slicing through his own throat with nearly enough force to behead him. The man coughed once, and the thrall opened his mouth, straining for the taller man's neck. The soldier's eyes rolled toward the thrall in abject horror, then blinked when a spray of blood covered his face. Bodhi's servant was feeding, and she let him.

She looked over to where a small group of soldiers were fighting with a pair of more skilled Shadow

Thieves. They fought over the prone form of a young woman—the one who had been captured in Baldur's Gate with Abdel.

"That one too?" Bodhi asked loudly.

Oh, yes, Irenicus's voice answered in her head, that one too.

Where are you? she asked him without speaking.

Gone from there, he answered, *as I suggest you do as well. These soldiers are as endless as raindrops and even more irritating. You could take days just killing them one after another.*

One in each hand, then, she thought with a smile, then said aloud, "Abdel, until we meet again. . . ."

* * * * *

Abdel wrenched free of the clutching hands of his friend and turned back into the chaos-filled chamber. He caught another glimpse of Imoen's face. Someone he couldn't see was pulling her by the hair. Abdel's head spun. What was she doing here?

He growled in rage and frustration when two soldiers drew arrows, pointed them at him, and one of them shouted "Just stop it! Stop right there!"

Abdel charged forward, trying to get in too close before the archers could react, but the lingering smoke made it hard to tell where he was, and the simple presence of Imoen threw him so badly he ended up just running into a deathtrap. He heard the bowstrings vibrate, and in the blink of an eye he felt one, then another jabbing pain in his chest. He took a deep breath, and the attempt made him flinch and cough, which only caused more pain. His foot slipped on a piece of broken crystal. He heard one of the soldiers laugh, then the other or maybe both grunt out all the air in their lungs. Abdel went down, twisting his ankle painfully, and he cursed all the way to the floor.

Abdel's head hit the flagstones, and the sound of battle was replaced by a shamefully hollow thud. There was a roaring in his head, and the light dimmed, then focused into a spot of hazy blur in the middle of his vision. Abdel tried to blink, but his eyelids actually hurt. He thought he might have groaned, but he couldn't be sure. Abdel was out cold.

* * * * *

The next thing Abdel was conscious of was the word "need," and the second was the pain. The roaring sound was still in his head, and there were specific points of agony flaring up as his body seemed to come back to life an inch at a time. The specific points faded in and out of an overall dull throb.

With his eyes still closed, Abdel tried to put a hand to his temple, but moving his elbow somehow made his head hurt worse, so he just let his arm fall, feeling the rough stone beneath him.

"I know, Boo," a strange voice said, "I know."

"Get up, my friend," another voice demanded. The order seemed entirely ludicrous to Abdel, who had every intention of staying exactly where he was for the rest of his life.

"Boo!" the first voice—Abdel remembered the red hair, the strong touch as this man pulled him away from something.

"Get up, now, get up!" The second voice was Yo-something.

"Yo . . . sho . . . yo . . ." Abdel murmured, the sound riding around the inside of his head on a little chariot of dull pain.

"Yes, sir, yes it is Yoshimo," the voice said.

It can't be, Abdel thought. They were pulling me away from Jaheira and . . .

"Imoen," Abdel said aloud and opened his eyes to a comfortable orange glow and the faces of the men who stopped him from saving the lives of two women he cared very deeply for. Abdel sat up, as unpleasant as it was, and started carefully planning the deaths of the two men.

"I am Minsc," the red-haired man said, smiling around blood that was oozing from a ragged cut on his right cheek, "and it is a pleasure to fight alongside you. Boo tells me your name is Abdel."

"Boo?" Abdel asked before he really even thought about it.

Minsc was wearing a simple, tattered tunic, which he held bunched at his chest with his left hand. He smiled and opened a fold in the dirty cloth to reveal a tiny brown and white rodent with eyes like black buttons. A pointed pink nose and whiskers twitched as it sniffed the air in front of Abdel.

"This is Boo," Minsc said with the smile of a pleased toddler. "He protects me with his stern intelligence."

Abdel ran quickly through several possible responses in his head before settling on, "Fine."

The big sellsword looked up for the Kozakuran, but he and Minsc were alone now in the intersection.

"Yoshimo!" he called, but there was no response.

"If you say so, Boo," Minsc whispered, then said to Abdel, "He must have already gone. I mean, Boo thi— says he's already gone."

Abdel sighed and brushed grit and the dust of shattered orange crystals from his body. He was suddenly aware that he was still naked, but he didn't bother to blush in the presence of the madman.

"Boo says this way," Minsc told him, then started off down one of the passages.

"That's the way back?" Abdel asked, determined to find Jaheira and Imoen.

"I'm afraid not, my friend," Yoshimo's voice came from the darkness of a side passage.

"Yoshimo?" Abdel called, his sword at the ready. The Kozakuran emerged from the darkness, smiling contentedly.

"Indeed it is I, sir," Yoshimo replied. "I have found the way out."

"I don't want to get out," Abdel stated flatly. "I need to get back to where we left Jaheira."

"If that were possible, my friend," Yoshimo said, "I would applaud your courage and send you on your way. But alas, that passage collapsed just as we passed through."

"Boo says this way," Minsc repeated.

Yoshimo ignored the madman and looked Abdel up and down. "You are not in a condition that will help you to help her," he said to Abdel. "Perhaps we should get out of here, regroup, and come back for your friend. I knew her for only a short time, but it was my opinion that she will be able to care for herself for at least this nearly as short time, no?"

Abdel clenched his teeth to bite back an angry response. He hated more than anything to admit it, but the Kozakuran was right. Yoshimo nodded and turned back into the dark passageway. Abdel got up and followed him, having no better idea which way to go.

* * * * *

It was possible that the learned men Abdel grew up around in the library-fortress of Candlekeep had a name for this peculiar feeling of recognition, but if they did, Abdel didn't know it.

"There's a dirty picture scratched into the railing at the end of the ramp," Abdel told Minsc and Yoshimo. They both just looked at him quizzically.

They'd come up out of the tunnels by climbing rusted iron ladder rungs into a dusty, empty room as big as a barn. There were wide doors on the two short ends of the rectangular building and a normal-sized door on one side. The little door was closer to the wooden trap-door they'd climbed out of, so they went out that way into the hazy light of early evening.

There was a straight wooden deck outside the door. A low wooden rail wrapped around it and led down the scratch-planked ramp to the hard dry dirt the warehouse was standing on. Around them was the subdued bustle of a city well into the process of settling down at the end of the day.

Minsc, sighing with a shaking fatigue, ambled down the ramp and looked at the spot on the railing Abdel had pointed to.

The red-haired man smiled, showing yellow teeth turning gray, and said, "How'd you know that?"

"I've been here before," Abdel said, looking around and having to squint even in the dim light. "I guarded this place once with a man named Kamon who I later had to kill."

"You know where we are then?" Yoshimo asked him.

"Where are we?" Minsc asked the little rodent he was carrying.

Abdel answered for the animal, "Athkatla. We're in the city of Athkatla—in the realm of Amn."

Minsc looked up and chuckled, said, "You're naked." He looked back down at the little animal and said with a laugh. "He's naked, Boo."

Abdel sighed and looked down at his grimy, bruised body. The arrow wounds had not only stopped bleeding but had begun to close and didn't hurt at all anymore. He looked at the two fingernails that had been torn off and saw, with no small surprise, that they had both begun to grow back. Abdel was only now feeling like he had any time to think, and he wondered at the sudden speed with which he seemed to be able to heal.

"We shall have to find some clothes for you, my friend, and maybe find some help," Yoshimo offered.

"Help?" Abdel asked absently, then turned his gaze over a city he remembered as rough and unforgiving but still ruled by law. "Good idea."

* * * * *

Abdel tried a number of different hand postures, various walks, or a combination of both to try to cover the fact that he was walking down the street stark naked, but eventually he just had to resign himself to the fact that, regardless of where he put his hands, he was walking down the street stark naked.

The streets weren't very busy, and as they proceeded, Abdel started to get his bearings. He'd visited the city more than once. They were north of the Alandor River, which cut through the middle of the city to the Sea of Swords, flowing from some mountain source to the east. The warehouse was set against the wide strand in what the locals called—with typical Amnian imagination—the River District. Most of the activity in the city, even this time of day, would be concentrated around the terraced marketplace called Waukeen's Promenade. That was across the river. Abdel wanted to find some clothes before he tried to go there. As he thought back to his days guarding the warehouse, he remembered a local dive not far to the east, on the way to the single bridge that spanned the river between the River District on the north bank and the appropriately titled Bridge District to the south.

"There is a tavern not far from here," Yoshimo said.

"The Copper something?" Abdel asked.

"The Copper Coronet," the Kozakuran replied. "You know it?"

"I know taverns," Abdel admitted.

Chapter Four

"Good," the pale woman said quietly as she dragged Jaheira and the other woman through the storm drain, "he likes long hair."

Jaheira struggled against the woman's viselike grip but succeeded only in pulling out some of her own hair. She stumbled and grunted in pain when her head was jerked up, but she found her feet again and fell more than walked along the round stone tunnel. It was difficult to believe that this woman could manage to drag another woman, let alone two women, by the hair through a tunnel she couldn't even stand up in, but this stranger was doing just that. Jaheira tried to trip her on more than one occasion, but the woman avoided her feet easily, not even seeming to notice the attempts.

The other prisoner was a pretty young woman, maybe not even twenty years old. Her face was stained with dust and tears, and her eyes were sunken and exhausted. She was hanging just at the edge of consciousness, as if sleepwalking. Like Jaheira, the other captive's hands were tied behind her with rough, scraping rope.

"Who are you?" Jaheira asked the powerful woman for the third time since she'd regained consciousness in the stranger's less than tender care.

"Silence," the woman said.

Jaheira was vaguely aware that someone was following them, but she couldn't turn her neck enough to see behind her.

"Why are you doing this?" she asked, ignoring the woman's command.

The pale woman laughed—not an unpleasant sound, surprisingly—and said, "I can rip your tongue out of your mouth and feed it to my rats, if you'd like."

"Just—" Jaheira started to protest, but stopped when the woman's powerful hand came away from her hair, and she stumbled to the slimy, damp stone. The woman slapped her hard across the face with the back of her hand, and Jaheira fell back. Her head spun, and she was aware of a spreading numbness on her face and a cold wetness soaking into her tattered shift.

Someone with ice-cold hands grabbed Jaheira roughly from behind. His hands found her breasts, and she stiffened at the coldness of his touch. He hoisted her to her feet to face the glowering woman. Jaheira turned her head to try to see the man who was holding her this way, but he shifted his grip, pushing her forward. She heard a ringing click in her right ear like bone snapping against bone.

"No!" the woman said sharply, and Jaheira realized she was speaking to the man holding her.

"But this one is so warm," the man said, his voice low and sibilant, cool against Jaheira's neck, "so sweet."

Jaheira gasped and looked at the woman, who caught her eyes and smiled in a way that made Jaheira blush.

"She is at that," the woman said, "but I need her for more than blood . . . for now."

"Will I have her then?" the man asked eagerly.

"No," the woman said, letting her eyes trail up and down Jaheira's body, "I'll want her for myself, I think."

The word "vampire" appeared in Jaheira's head like

an explosion, and she gagged at the feeling of the thing's cold breath on her.

"Where are you taking us?" Jaheira heard herself ask. She'd never felt this powerless but couldn't make herself submit.

The woman smiled, seemed almost charmed by Jaheira's defiance. "Your friend is very special," she said. "I suppose you know that."

Jaheira looked at the woman, still hanging by the hair in the slim vampire's iron grasp, and said, "I don't know this woman."

"I wasn't talking about her," the vampire said.

It wasn't a difficult thing for Jaheira to realize she was talking about Abdel. Being the son of Bhaal, the killer of Sarevok, and the enemy of the Iron Throne, Jaheira didn't have much trouble believing that Abdel had enemies even he didn't know about, but why this vampire, why the Shadow Thieves, she couldn't fathom.

"He got away didn't he?" Jaheira asked, finding a flicker of hope. "He got away from you."

The vampire took a deep breath in, and Jaheira was surprised when the vampire's ample bosom moved out and up, was surprised that the undead thing really took in air or needed to breathe at all.

"Will he come for you?" the vampire asked her, though Jaheira could tell by the look in her eyes that she already knew the answer.

"He will," Jaheira said simply.

"And if not for you," the vampire said, glancing down at the young woman now passed out on the damp stone at her feet, "he'll come for this one."

"Who is she?" Jaheira asked, then breathed in sharply when the man grabbed her tighter, hurting her, arching her back against him.

The vampire woman hit her again with the back of

her hand, and the sound of the blow rang through Jaheira's head with a snap that warned of a broken jaw. The half-elf's eyes blurred, and she felt as if she was falling, though the cold man was still holding her firmly.

As she lost consciousness again, she heard the vampire say, "I will drain you slowly, bitch."

The man behind her sighed, and the vampire woman said to him, "You know what to do. I have other places to be."

* * * * *

It was called the Copper Coronet, and it looked as bad, and smelled as bad, as Abdel remembered. He'd been there several times but had made no friends. He had not a single coin and nothing to barter with, so he knew he'd have to rely on something that was always in short supply in a place like this: charity.

"Oy," a drunk old man sitting near the door exclaimed when Abdel strode confidently into the tavern with Minsc and Yoshimo in tow, "whatta we got 'ere?"

"Hey, now," the bartender barked, a look of stern disapproval crossing his distinctly ugly face, "what kind of place you boys think this is?"

"We were waylaid," Abdel said, looking the barkeep directly in the eyes. "They stole everything."

"You ever learn how to use those muscles?" the old man asked incredulously, then coughed out a series of guttural grunts that might have been a laugh.

Abdel ignored the old drunk but nudged Minsc when the madman started talking to his pet again. The red-haired man looked up, but was curious, not embarrassed.

"Alas," Yoshimo broke in, speaking first to the old drunk, then to the dark, swarthy barkeep, "our enemies had muscles too, and the aid of more than one *wu-jen*."

"I need clothes," Abdel said, clearing his throat uncomfortably. "I need clothes, maybe something to eat, and some water, and I need to speak with Captain Belars Orhotek as soon as one of your boys can fetch him here."

The barkeep looked at the sellsword blankly for a long time, so long in fact that Abdel narrowed his eyes to peer at the man, checking to see if he was still alive or had died, staring, on his feet.

"Did you—" Abdel started to say but was stopped by the barkeep's loud whoop of laughter. Tears streamed out of the man's eyes, and he quickly lost the rhythm of his breath and started gasping between body-wracking guffaws. This did not make Abdel happy, but short of strangling or pummeling the bartender, he had no idea what to do.

"Indeed," Yoshimo started to say, "it is amusing, but—"

"Easy there, stranger," the barkeep said, glancing back and forth between Yoshimo and Abdel. "Word travels faster in Athkatla than you do, boys, and the three of you are hard to miss. Her name's Imogen, right?"

Abdel's jaw fell open, and without thinking he said, "Imoen."

"Imoen, then," the barkeep said. "Anyway, I know where she is and who's holding her, but information costs in Athkatla."

Fire rose in Abdel's blood, and his head throbbed. The barkeep's eyes went wide, and he took a step back, suddenly not confident that the bar would keep him safe from the massive sellsword.

"I need to make a living," the man said, "and your lady friend has made some very, very powerful enemies. If they know I sold them out, they'll be . . . unhappy with me, if you know what I mean. I might need to pick up stakes, right? Make a fresh start in a new town."

"How could you possibly—?" Abdel started.

"I suggested this place for a reason, my friend Abdel," Yoshimo interrupted. "This man is Gaelan Bayle, and there is little that might go on in—or under—this city that escapes his notice. He demands a stiff price, because his information is always correct."

Abdel glowered at Yoshimo and said, "I'm no fool, Kozakuran. What's going on here?"

"Yoshy-boy brought you here because he knows I know what's going on around here, Abdel Adrian, Son of Bhaal, Savior of Baldur's Gate, friend of the missing Imoen who was taken by Shadow Thieves who were none too happy about your late half-brother's bandying their not-so-good name about the Gate . . . oh," he said, "does that sound like I might know what I'm—"

Abdel was over the bar and standing in front of the barkeep in less than the time it took for Yoshimo to blink. Abdel's hand was coming up toward the startled man's face, and before Gaelan could duck, Abdel pulled the punch short.

"You can tell me who you are now and what you want from me," Abdel snarled, "or I'll do something I've been trying not to do so much of lately."

Gaelan just nodded. "Listen," he said, "I'm just a guy who keeps his ears open and knows people who know people who know people. I can tell you where she is, not because I'm a swell guy but because you're going to pay me ten trade bars—fifty thousand gold pieces—for the information."

Abdel had to laugh, but the force of it made his already aching head sting. "Look at me," he said, "and ask yourself if you think I have that kind of treasure at my disposal, you gutter wretch."

"Hey," Gaelan said, smiling nervously, "you seem capable enough. Your little miss is alive and will be for long enough that an enterprising young man like yourself could scrape up the coin."

"But fifty thousand . . ." Abdel said. "I could buy a ship for that."

"Just what I had in mind myself, truth be told," Gaelan admitted.

"It does seem a bit much, Master Bayle," Yoshimo offered.

"Who asked you?" Gaelan grunted, then turned back to Abdel and said, "Take it or leave it, son."

"Holy snakes and eggs!" a woman's voice exclaimed.

Before Abdel could even glance at her, he blushed and tried to turn around and cover himself. This made the bartender laugh even harder, and a red-faced Abdel hoped the man would choke.

"I think she saw everything, Boo," Minsc muttered. "Not that it's hard to—"

"Minsc!" Abdel roared.

"What are you boys . . . ?" the woman asked. Abdel heard her soft footsteps approaching. She'd come in from behind a curtain that led into a dark storeroom in the back of the bar. The bartender's laughing was beginning to settle down, and the old drunk was in the process of passing out. "What kind of place do you think this is?"

"Boy says he was robbed, Bodhi," the bartender said, rubbing his pink, watering eyes.

"Were you now?" she asked Abdel's back.

"Yes, ma'am," Abdel answered quickly. "I need clothes, food and water, and word sent to Captain Orhotek. Please."

"I'll give you some of Gaelan's clothes," the woman said, ignoring the beginnings of a protest from the barkeep. "You can work for some food, but I doubt Captain

Orhotek himself will be coming to your rescue. Maybe you just need to sleep it off tonight?"

"I need to speak with someone," Abdel insisted, "there are Shadow Thieves about."

The bartender Gaelan chuckled at this and said, "No foolin'?"

"That'll do, Gaelan," Bodhi said. "Go get him some clothes."

"Like this one, eh, girl?" Gaelan grumbled as he passed through the grease-stained curtain into the room behind the bar.

"I must go," Yoshimo said suddenly. Abdel looked at him, but the Kozakuran wouldn't return his gaze. "I will find you if you need me, my friend. Best of luck."

"Boo says to ask if I can work for some food too," Minsc said.

Abdel said, "Minsc . . ." but stopped when he wasn't sure how to chastise the madman. When he turned back to where Yoshimo had been standing, the Kozakuran was gone.

"What have you got there?" the woman asked and stepped forward toward Minsc. Abdel caught a glimpse of her before he turned away again to keep his back to her. She was a tall, thin young woman with a serious face that clashed with her revealing, almost silly dress. Her pale face and flaxen hair were clean, and Abdel couldn't help thinking she was older than she was trying to look.

"This is Boo," Minsc told her. "He helps me."

"Does he now," she cooed, humoring him. "Is he a mouse?"

"Boo is a hamster," Minsc said. Abdel sighed at having at least one question answered.

"Where did you find him?" Bodhi asked.

"Oh, Boo found me. Didn't you, Boo?" Minsc answered.

"He comes from space. His kind are actually quite large, but he is smaller than most."

"Space?" the woman asked, obviously never having heard the word before.

"The place of the crystal spheres," Minsc explained conversationally, "up in the air beyond the heavens."

Bodhi laughed lightly and said, "Well, Boo, so you're a miniature giant space . . . ?"

"Hamster," Minsc provided.

"A miniature giant space hamster," she said, "and a cute one at that."

"Boo likes you," Minsc said dully. "Can we work here for food and stuff?"

"Oh, for—" Abdel started to say, but stopped in order to spend all his energy trying to turn around. Bodhi had stepped in front of him. Her eyes were cast down, and a knowing smile curved her lips.

"Well, now . . ." she whispered.

"Excuse me," Gaelan said. Abdel hadn't heard him come back behind the bar. He tossed Abdel some dirty, ragged clothes, which the sellsword caught happily.

"We could use a busboy," Bodhi said.

"I can't stay here," Abdel told her, ripping his way into the too-tight trousers. "I left someone behind. I need to—"

"I wasn't talking to you," Bodhi said.

Abdel looked up at her, and she nodded to Minsc.

"Oh, come now, Bodhi," Gaelan objected, but she cut him short with a disapproving glare. "Fine, then, he can start by throwing out the captain."

"The captain?" Abdel asked, for some reason thinking Gaelan was referring to him.

Gaelan tipped his head to the old drunk and said, "Captain Havarian."

"One of the more notorious pirates of the Sword Coast," Bodhi said with a laugh in her voice.

Philip Athans

Two men stepped through the door and paused at the scene in front of them. Abdel was dressed now, though he was still hardly an ordinary sight. Minsc was cradling Boo in one hand and reaching for the now loudly snoring pirate with the other.

"Evening, good sirs," Gaelan said to the newcomers, "step right in."

The men moved to the bar, and Abdel turned to watch Minsc trying to pull the deadweight old man out of his chair with one hand.

"You'd make a better bouncer," Bodhi said to Abdel.

The sellsword looked at her, forced a smile, and said, "I'm not mad."

"I know," she told him, and he believed her, which surprised and worried him. Any normal person would have thought him mad.

* * * * *

Irenicus let the smile drop off his face and slid his iron-cold gaze along the length of steel chain that strung him to the prisoner in front of him. The chain was attached to a heavy manacle around his left ankle. The manacle around his right ankle held a chain that strung back along the floor like a coiling snake, ending at the ankle of another prisoner. Behind him was a third, then a fourth, a fifth, and a sixth.

Irenicus shuffled along with the rest of them and kept silent. He didn't give the guards an excuse to strike him. If he had given them an excuse, and they had struck him, he would have had no choice but to destroy them in a blaze of power and indignation that would have revealed him too early and thrown his plan, at least temporarily, awry. Still, part of him hoped it would go that way, hoped he could just start killing and not stop until they were all dead. That would be satisfying on some level—on some level important to who Irenicus was—but it would have only brought him farther away from what he really wanted. Irenicus didn't always remain focused, but this time he forced himself.

The string of prisoners was led through a wide doorway, and Irenicus examined the rusted iron spikes that made up the bottom of the portcullis bars they passed under. Someone screamed loudly from down the long, wide corridor, and another person laughed loudly in answer. A voice clearly called out "Stop me!" from some space many walls away. A low sound of moaning that sometimes became a melodic hum pervaded every nook. Irenicus didn't recognize the tune, but he took note of it.

The prisoner behind him said, "Please," in a voice so pitiful Irenicus wanted to kill him. The guards didn't respond in any way, though Irenicus expected at least one of them to at least sigh impatiently. Irenicus would have.

The trip down the corridor took a long time, and though Irenicus didn't relish it, he made as much use of it as he could. He noted the way the bricks were mortared together, the iron banding on the doors that occasionally led off from the wide corridor. He noticed the straw scattered on the floor and the stains on the flagstones that might have been blood, or food. He saw a spider in its web in the corner ignoring what was going on around it, waiting for its web to quiver with fresh food.

At the end of the corridor, he counted the clicks as the guard turned the big iron key in the elaborate lock, heard another lock click open on the other side of the door, memorized the squeak of the tired old hinges, saw the way the double doors pulled apart from each other,

Philip Athans

opening inward. These doors were meant to keep people in, not out. They were sturdy but not sturdy enough. He knew he would have to do something about that eventually.

One of the prisoners behind him hesitated when the guards prodded them though the doors, and a flash of anger crossed Irenicus's otherwise passive face. He resisted the temptation to speak or strike out, but one of the guards noticed his expression. He looked at Irenicus curiously, his body tensing in blind anticipation, like a squirrel caught in the middle of a yard by the neighbor's cat.

Irenicus smiled and said, "Three buckets of hot water, Momma. Three buckets of hot water," just so the man would think he was an idiot.

It worked. The guard looked away, prodding the man in front of Irenicus with the rounded end of his slim oaken cudgel. As they crossed from the straw-strewn flagstones to an expanse of polished marble, one of the prisoners started to weep openly, inconsolably, with the wild abandon of madness and despair. The sound made Irenicus smile at the same time it made the hair on the back of his neck stand on end.

"Welcome, tortured souls," the man standing in the middle of the otherwise empty room said in a voice of practiced calm. "This will be your home for a very long time. You will be treated well. You will not be allowed to harm yourselves or others. You will rest, you will meditate, you will heal, or you will not."

Irenicus didn't smile. He kept his face blank and stared hard at the man, who didn't seem to see any of them.

"I am the coordinator here," the man continued. "You will refer to me simply as 'Sir.' Is that understood?"

None of the prisoners responded except one, who

42

said, "This is madness," in a voice full of insult.

The coordinator smiled in a condescending, fatherly way, and said, "Quite."

Irenicus continued to stare at the coordinator, who was looking each of the ragged prisoners up and down in turn. When he got to Irenicus, their eyes finally met. The coordinator seemed surprised by Irenicus, by the look in his eyes, or the color, or the depth, or something. The coordinator didn't look away.

Irenicus said, "I am very happy to be here," in a slow, careful way.

"I'm . . ." the coordinator started. He seemed confused—was confused—by the look in this prisoner's eyes. Irenicus knew the man was looking for what he always saw, either madness or fear. Irenicus knew the coordinator saw neither of those things in his eyes.

"I want us to talk," Irenicus told him, "you and me."

The coordinator smiled feebly, and a drop of sweat started a slow crawl down the side of one high, bald temple. A small man, round from years of inactivity, the coordinator dressed well but simply and carried no weapons but what he obviously thought to be a superior will.

"We can," the coordinator said, matching Irenicus's cadence and tone. "We will."

"Coordinator?" one of the guards said. Irenicus was surprised at the guard's perception and felt a passing reluctance to kill the man.

"He's fine," Irenicus said, not looking at the guard but keeping his eyes firmly fixed on the coordinator. "Aren't you, Sir?"

"I'm fine," the coordinator said, his voice creaking. The drop of sweat made it to his softly rounded jaw and hung there, catching light from the four torches that lit the room.

Someone far away screamed three times in exactly the same way each time.

Irenicus smiled and said, "Everything is going to be just fine here."

Chapter Five

Of course he was going to go back for them. What else could he do?

Abdel had found pity at the Copper Coronet—clothes, food, and a place to part ways with Minsc—but when he allowed himself the minutes it took to eat the chicken they gave him and drink some water, he could feel his mind clear. He came into the tavern exhausted, still reeling from what had been a long period of unconsciousness. He'd demanded to see Captain Orhotek, and though it seemed perfectly reasonable at the time, now he had to admit to himself that he didn't actually know the man, had heard of him but had never met him. Abdel looked mad and told stories that were difficult to believe at best. He knew he'd left Jaheira behind, and he wasn't even sure if she was alive or dead, but he wasn't so sure anymore that Imoen had been there too. It sounded like her, looked like her, but how could it be her?

Abdel put his head in his hands and felt the grease coating his fingers mingle with the dried sweat and grime that covered him. His head lolled, and he almost fell asleep. Knowing he couldn't possibly leave Jaheira to the Shadow Thieves—or whoever their captors were—for as long as he knew he'd sleep if he let himself, Abdel struggled to stand. His head spun, but when he got to his feet, he actually started to feel better. Minsc walked by, holding a tray full of empty flagons and dirty dishes. He caught Abdel's eye and smiled. The little hamster peered at the sellsword from a pocket in Minsc's already dirty apron.

Abdel tried to return the man's smile but couldn't. He turned and went through the door in the back wall of the barroom he'd seen several of the patrons pass through. It led into a space off the alley where two barrels of water stood open to the warm night. Abdel went to one of the barrels, and after splashing a handful of water over his face, he grew frustrated and simply dunked his head into the lukewarm water.

He scrubbed at his face and hair, scratching his itchy scalp, then pulled off the too-tight shirt he'd borrowed from the barkeep and let it drop onto the alley floor. Abdel washed himself aggressively, using the action to wake himself up. He had no plan and still wasn't thinking well enough to try to form one. All he knew was that he didn't want to fight with the light long sword he'd taken from the soldier. He had one of the swords, and so did Minsc. The red-haired man seemed to have found a place to settle, so Abdel figured the madman wouldn't be needing his sword. Maybe Abdel could trade the two blades for one decent broadsword, but he knew he'd have to wait at least until morning to do that.

His own weapon and armor might have been left in Baldur's Gate for all he knew, but they might also be down somewhere under that warehouse with Jaheira. Before he did anything else, he'd have to go back there.

"You should sleep," a voice behind him said, and he didn't bother spinning. He turned slowly and saw Bodhi standing in the doorway, leaning casually against the doorframe.

"I have to go back there," he told her and turned back to the barrel.

"To find your wife?" she asked. He heard her light footsteps approaching him from behind.

"She's not my wife," Abdel told her simply. "I don't care if you don't believe me."

She came up next to him, and from the corner of his eye, he saw her smile. "In the morning I can take you to see someone from the militia or someone from the council, maybe."

He knew she was trying to humor him, and he only grunted. She smiled again in answer to that and stepped up to the barrel. She dunked her head into the water and came back up quickly, letting it cascade over her shoulders and onto the light fabric of her dress.

"That does feel good," she said quietly, running her fingers through her hair, her eyes closed.

The wet dress began to stick to her, outlining small details of her body that drew Abdel's eyes as they would any man's. She noticed him noticing her and glanced down. Abdel was too tired and too worried about Jaheira but most of all too disappointed in himself to blush.

"You can touch me," she said. "I want you to."

He sighed and took one step back. "I have to go."

"In the morning," she said, stepping toward him, stopping less than an inch away from his bare chest. "Please."

"I love her," he told her.

"She could be dead," Bodhi said too bluntly, and Abdel restrained himself from backhanding her across the alley.

"That's why I have to go," he said instead.

Bodhi didn't follow him when he took three steps away from her and bent to pick up his shirt.

"She must be very beautiful," she said.

Abdel didn't feel the need to answer.

"I can help you." He looked at her with a wrinkled

brow, and she continued, "You need gold, don't you? Gaelan knows where she is. He knows things like that, but he's serious about the gold. You can kill him if you want to, but he won't tell you anything unless you pay him first. It's what he does."

"What are you asking me to do?" he asked her.

"Aran Linvail," she said, "have you heard of him?"

"No, should I have?"

"He deserves to die," she said, "and there is a price on his head."

"Am I an assassin now?"

She smiled, and Abdel looked away, so he wouldn't return the smile. "You can be a bounty hunter. Linvail is the assassin—a very prolific one."

Abdel figured he'd have to take her word for that. The shirt ripped again as he tried to put it on. It was too small for him, and now that he was wet, it didn't seem like he'd get it over his chest. He was only half listening to her.

"I know someone who will pay thirty thousand gold pieces for his head," she said. "They've got the coin, Abdel, and they will pay it."

He stopped, gave up on the shirt, and looked at her sternly. "You want me to kill for gold?"

She smiled again, and Abdel was struck by how pretty she was. Her dress was still wet, and she wasn't making any attempt to hide herself from him.

He turned away, moving to the door, as she said, "Can you afford not to? You've got a pair of my brother's old pants and a stolen sword, Abdel, and that's all. By your own account, you're not even from here. I like you, but not everyone will."

He sighed and turned away. If he hadn't been so tired, and didn't have somewhere to go, he might have hit her after all.

* * * * *

Jaheira had a vague memory of the sound of water, and there was the motion that made her think she'd been on a boat. She was outside—or had been—and it had been night, but she couldn't see any stars.

It took her three tries before she actually regained consciousness. Her eyelids opened only with great difficulty, and one side of her face was awash in a dull, throbbing ache.

"She's alive," a voice said. It was a young woman's voice, tired and unenthusiastic.

Jaheira turned toward the voice, and something hurt her neck. She winced, and that made her face hurt. She closed her eyes, which filled with tears, but tried to keep her breathing steady.

"Where am I?" Jaheira asked, her voice scratchy and uneven.

"A cave," the voice replied.

This time Jaheira opened her eyes and saw the girl who had been dragged with her through the storm drain by the vampire woman. The girl was chained to the wall by a wide leather collar fastened tightly around her neck. The pain in Jaheira's own neck came from an identical strap. The half-elf tugged at her bonds, but they held fast, anchored firmly into the wall.

There was a torch hanging in a crude wall sconce guttering out a smoky orange light from maybe twenty feet above Jaheira's head. The ground she was sitting on was smooth, uneven stone. Above her hung stalactites of varying yellow, gray, and dull brown. It was a natural cavern, probably carved by an underground stream. The ceiling was high, but the walls were close on two sides. The cavern went off into the thick darkness on either side as if they were in a tunnel or natural corridor.

"My name is Jaheira," she said to her fellow prisoner, looking up to catch the young woman's surprisingly steady gaze.

The girl was dirty, disheveled, and tired, but still undeniably pretty. Shoulder-length auburn hair framed a smooth-skinned face with a high forehead and full lips. Her dark eyes sparkled with intelligence even as red with exhaustion as they were. Her body was slender and tightly well-proportioned. Her tattered blouse covered modest breasts and narrow hips. There was something about her that looked fast, like a gazelle, but somehow more dangerous.

"Imoen," the girl answered. "Nice that you came around. I'm happy for someone to talk to."

"How long have we been here?" Jaheira asked, determined to settle some facts of her situation, so she could have some chance of escaping it. The question seemed to upset Imoen.

"I have no idea," she answered. "Hard to tell in a cave, actually. I fell asleep for a while, I think. Maybe a couple of days."

"Since the storm drain?" Jaheira asked.

"Storm drain?"

"We need to get out of here," Jaheira said simply, not entirely surprised that the girl hadn't been conscious of that part of their journey.

Imoen smiled pleasantly and said, "Gee, think?"

The girl's tone made the fine hairs behind Jaheira's gently pointed ears stand on end.

* * * * *

"I am your friend," she whispered in a voice as solid as bedrock. "We can help each other."

Abdel tried to think of Jaheira, but this woman's

presence was overpowering. He closed his eyes and turned his head sharply to one side. She seemed sad but confident at the same time, hopeful and consumed with sorrow. He wanted to reach out to her, but he took two steps backward instead.

She took two steps toward him, keeping the distance between them constant. Her eyes were a pale gray that Abdel couldn't possibly ignore.

"I can get you weapons," she said quietly, "armor maybe, too, but you'll have to kill him. You just have no choice."

Abdel's brow knitted, and he sighed.

"You've killed for gold before, Abdel," she said, even quieter now. "I can see that on your face, in the lines of your arms, on the backs of your hands. You can do this. You can get the gold you need to pay Gaelan to tell you where your—"

"That's enough," he said, turning away.

She stepped closer still and touched his shoulder. Her fingers were cold, but soft. He wanted to flinch away from her touch, but he didn't.

"He's a Shadow Thief," she said. "Aran Linvail. He's an assassin for the Shadow Thieves. He kills for gold every day. Shouldn't he die that way too?"

"I don't do that anymore," Abdel said, not turning around. "I've changed."

"You can change back," Bodhi whispered, "if you love her enough."

Abdel knew what Jaheira would say if she were there. She would remind him of how far he'd come since he watched Gorion die. He wasn't a hired thug anymore. He didn't kill out of anger anymore.

But Jaheira wasn't there.

She was being held prisoner, was being tortured maybe, or worse. Abdel didn't know what was happening to her. If it was the Shadow Thieves who'd taken them in Baldur's Gate—and that seemed easy enough to believe—then maybe killing this Aran Linvail was a form of justice after all.

Abdel knew he was fooling himself, but he had no choice. He could beat the information out of Gaelan Bayle, but would that be better than killing a Shadow Thief assassin? If he knew where Jaheira was, wouldn't he gladly kill any number of Shadow Thieves to rescue her? So, Aran Linvail would be one of those.

"I'll need a broadsword," he said quietly to Bodhi, "and chain mail, but nothing fancy."

She smiled. "You're doing the right thing, Abdel," she said reassuringly. "You don't seem to believe it, but when this is all done, you'll know you did what you had to do to save her and left the world a better place— without Aran Linvail—in the process."

"A broadsword," he repeated, "as heavy as you can find."

Chapter Six

She knew everything. She was right about everything. Every door. The sliding panel behind the bed in
the third room at the left at the top of the stairs. She
knew where the key was hidden behind the loose mortar.
(Could a professional assassin be that stupidly naive?
Apparently.) She knew exactly how to get him in there.

Abdel had been set up before. As a sellsword, he
spent most of his life being set up in one way or another.
He was paid to do the dirty work for this merchant, that
trade guild, or the other petty principality. . . . This was
a setup, this assassination of the assassin Aran Linvail,
and Abdel knew it, but he had no choice.

There was no part of his body that hurt anymore.
Only a few hours had passed since he'd been tortured,
beaten, burned, shot with arrows, and he was fine now,
but he was broke. He was in the middle of a city that
didn't give a sewer rat's ass about anyone, especially
him. Hours ago he'd been wandering around naked
with two perfect strangers. He hadn't slept except that
period of time he'd been unconscious. His head felt
heavy and thin at the same time.

He took a deep breath and exhaled with a whisper,
"One more time."

The air in the closet smelled of perfume and moth
powder. It wasn't as cramped as most closets. This Aran

Linvail had made a lot of coin killing people—more than Abdel ever had. The closet was full of expensive Kara Turan silks, wool from the highlands of the Spine of the World, and soft cotton from exotic Maztica. There was a suit of leather armor hanging in there that was so perfect, so flawless in its execution and upkeep that it must have been magical.

Somewhere outside the closet, outside the townhouse's tight bricks walls, the sun must have been coming up over Athkatla. In the bedroom beyond where Abdel stood ready, Aran Linvail was making frivolous love with a girl who was obviously no stranger to frivolous lovemaking.

She called him "honey," which made Abdel wince. She was insincere, but Linvail didn't seem to care. To the assassin's credit, the play went on for what seemed to Abdel to be hours on end. He was hiding in the closet because he didn't want to kill the girl. He wanted Aran Linvail alone.

Abdel settled down in a squat and tried to stretch his muscles as best he could. He tried to clear his mind and found that he could a bit more easily than he'd expected. He didn't want to be where he was, didn't want to do what he was going to do, but at least he was doing something.

Some time later they finally stopped, and Abdel heard Linvail say, "Just move."

The girl said something Abdel couldn't hear, but her tone was gruff and insulting. Her response was answered by a loud slap. She squealed, and there was the sound of something heavy falling and the dull squeak of furniture being shoved across a wood floor. That was all Abdel had to hear.

The closet door came off its hinges, and Abdel stepped out, bringing his broadsword out and in front of him in a fluid motion. Aran Linvail looked up at him, and so did the girl. She was young—not too young but young enough. She was pretty. Her hair was a dull red color, and her skin was freckled all over her slim body. She was holding the left side of her face, but she wasn't bleeding. She looked surprised.

Aran Linvail had suffered a terrible injury some years before. His face was horribly scarred—it was a mass of scars. One eye was closed, gone all together. He looked up at Abdel with his one good eye from where he stood crouched over the girl. He was wearing loose-fitting breeches and nothing else. There were other scars on his chest, stomach, and sides. Abdel charged at him, the girl squealed, and Aran Linvail turned and ran.

Abdel actually missed a step. The assassin didn't just evade the first attack, he flat out ran away, and he ran fast. The girl was confused. Abdel spared her a glance, and for some reason he would never be able to figure out, she shrugged.

Abdel followed Aran Linvail out an ornately carved mahogany door and into the townhouse's upstairs hallway.

"Who are you?" the retreating assassin called over his shoulder.

Abdel didn't answer. Linvail got to the top of the stairs still three or four steps ahead of the tip of Abdel's broadsword. The assassin let himself fall down the stairs as much as he ran. Abdel followed at a slightly more controlled pace.

"Who sent you?" Linvail called back again.

Abdel ignored him again and kept on coming. Linvail hit the floor at the bottom of the long, narrow staircase and spun around with one hand on the knob at the end of the banister. The foyer was tastefully decorated, and Abdel grunted in frustration. The front door was only steps away. If Linvail made it outside, Abdel would have to withdraw back into the house and sneak out the way he came as Aran Linvail raised whatever hue and cry he might be inclined to raise in the surely busy morning street outside.

Oddly, though, the assassin made no move toward the door.

"Are you just going to kill me, then?" Linvail called over his shoulder as he ran down a short hall parallel to the stairway.

Abdel followed, finally gaining a step on the fleeing man. Linvail passed through a swinging door at the end of the hall, and Abdel burst through behind him. The knife slipped between two of Abdel's ribs and tore through flesh, muscle, and some soft tissue the big sellsword might have needed to survive.

Linvail had made it to his kitchen, and as Abdel sagged into the knife, he had to acknowledge Linvail's speed in not only getting to the kitchen but also in grabbing a large knife with such a quick, fluid motion that he could thrust it into the blindly pursuing sellsword without missing a step. This assassin was good after all.

As fast as Linvail was, Abdel was at least as fast. He clenched his tight stomach muscles around the blade and bent forward, drawing the knife painfully farther into his guts even as he pulled the handle out of Aran Linvail's hand.

"Who are you?" the assassin asked again.

Abdel grunted in pain and brought his sword up. Linvail slid under the attack, and Abdel could see the assassin's good eye register the reverse and anticipate Abdel's following attack.

Avoiding a slash that should have taken his head off, Linvail ducked in and grabbed the knife still sticking out of Abdel's abdomen. The blade came out with no little blood and even more pain. Abdel let himself curse loudly, but the assassin wasn't stupid enough to take the time to gloat. He tried to stab Abdel again right away, but the big sellsword managed to get his new broadsword in and down fast enough to swat the blade away. It was a good knife and didn't break, but Linvail grunted as the force of the parry obviously sent a painful vibration up his arm.

He hacked down at Abdel's hand—a cowardly sort of attack Abdel should have expected from this man.

From upstairs the girl called "Aran? Aran, are you all right?"

Linvail brought the knife down hard, and Abdel stepped to one side, avoiding it even as he stabbed hard and low at the assassin. Linvail proved faster again, though, and not only avoided the big broadsword, but hacked down again with the big knife, taking off the first finger of Abdel's left hand with a sickening snap.

Abdel roared in rage and pain, more embarrassed than injured really. The finger hit the wood floor of the cramped kitchen with an almost inaudible *splat!*

"You can't kill me, big man," the assassin mocked, obviously happy with his petty dismemberment. "I've killed more—"

Whatever he was going to say ended up as a bloody gurgle. Abdel sliced in so fast and so hard he surprised even himself. He nearly cut the assassin in half at the midsection. He put one foot on the assassin's chest and pushed him down. Blood was everywhere instantly.

"That's . . ." the assassin managed to say around a mouthful of blood, "that's too bad."

Aran Linvail died on the floor of his own kitchen.

"Aran?" the girl called again. "Aran, you're scaring me. Who was that?"

Abdel grunted again and searched the floor for his missing finger. Drenched in blood, Abdel bent and retrieved the severed digit. He'd seen parts of people amputated one way or another on any number of occasions in his life and knew the simple rule that if you loose it, it stays lost unless you have a lot of gold and a very good priest. Abdel wasn't actually conscious of placing the finger back on the end of the little bleeding stump, but he did. It mended almost immediately, though it still bled. He held it in place for a few deep breaths, and when he let go, it stayed there.

"Bhaal," he breathed, knowing all too well the source of his ability to heal. So, he thought, maybe there's some advantage to this cursed blood after all.

"Aran?" the girl called, her voice quavering. "Aran, this isn't funny."

Abdel almost considered going back upstairs to tell the girl what happened, reassure her that she was better off, and send her on her way with a couple pieces of gold. He didn't have any gold, of course, and really didn't want the girl to see him covered in the blood of her lover.

He kneeled in the puddle of blood still growing rapidly around the inert form of Aran Linvail.

"One more," he said. "Last one."

He cut the assassin's head off because he had to. It was worth a king's ransom in gold to him—a druid's ransom at least, and Abdel knew Aran Linvail wouldn't be the last Shadow Thief he'd have to kill to get Jaheira and Imoen safely out of wherever they were.

A thin, lightly constructed door led off the kitchen into the cellar and Abdel went through it. There was a trapdoor in the floor of the cellar that led to the sewer, which led to an alley, which would take him in relative safety and anonymity back to the Copper Coronet. At least, that's what Bodhi had told him, and she'd been right so far.

"Aran?" the girl called from upstairs. "Aran, that's it. I'm coming down."

Chapter Seven

Bodhi was getting nervous, with dawn approaching, though she was well underground and out of any danger of exposure to the sun's killing rays. Still, she had to get up to the surface to get back to her resting place deep in Irenicus's island asylum. She could travel rather quickly in the form of a bat, but getting back to the island would still take time. She had no idea what might be taking Abdel so long. Could he have failed? Aran Linvail was a practiced killer, but surely he could be no match for this supposed son of a god. Had Linvail managed to turn him? Is Abdel working for the Shadow Thieves by now?

She was only seconds from contacting Irenicus again, having decided to move on to her contingency plan and return, when Abdel burst into the room, panting and shaking in barely concealed rage. He sat heavily on the floor, tossing his broadsword aside casually.

"Well," he said, "I'm back. In more ways than one."

Relieved to see him, but still concerned about the coming dawn, Bodhi went to him quickly. The sellsword shook his head a little and held up a hand to keep her away, keep her quiet, or both.

"Abdel," she said, letting the real relief at seeing him again make her role all the more convincing. "What happened?"

Abdel smiled at her and laughed. "You owe me thirty thousand gold pieces."

She smiled, too. His laugh sounded good to her. The sight of his smile had an effect on her she hadn't experienced in a good many decades.

"I'm glad to see you," Abdel said sincerely. "Is that odd?"

"And I'm happy to see you," she replied and only partly because she was told to do so. She leaned in and kissed him.

He flinched away from her at first, but she pressed in, and he responded. His lips were surprisingly soft, and Bodhi tried not to be drawn to the warmth, knowing Abdel would feel only coolness in return.

When she pulled away, his eyes were clouded and confused.

"Jaheira . . ." he said.

Bodhi shook her head, and his eyes met hers. She focused on the blackest point of his pupils and held his gaze in a grip as real and as tight as any vise. She released a slow, steady exhale, and her will drifted out from her eyes to his. She saw a brief flash of yellow light in his eyes, and it almost broke her concentration. She didn't allow herself the luxury of wondering what that light was. Half god or not, this man could come under her spell like any other, and she could feel any resolve he might have had fade away.

"You've done well, Abdel," she whispered, and he nodded with an almost imperceptible tilt of his chin. "You can rest now . . . from everything."

Abdel's face fell, then he forced a smile and made to stand. Bodhi shifted on her haunches and helped him up with a strong, firm grip around his back. He let himself be drawn into her. She could tell he wanted to say something. Bodhi didn't have time for Abdel to go through any soul-searching. She pressed another kiss and used her tongue, a shift of her hips, the brush of a breast against his chest, and an anticipatory breath to force a reaction.

Even Bodhi wasn't ready for the reaction she got.

* * * * *

Abdel never made the conscious decision to betray Jaheira and take Bodhi—still a stranger—as his lover. Like most things over the last few days, it just happened.

He let the tension slide out of his hands and arms, to be replaced by the smooth feel of her linen dress and her cool, soft skin under it. She held him in arms stronger than any woman had ever held him in. Bodhi's mouth closed on his, and her breath tasted of the earth. It was a primal smell—more a feeling that a scent. Her lips were cool, almost cold, and the chill they sent down Abdel's spine made him feel more awake than he had in days. His body burst into full life. The blood that coursed through him carried different signals, went to different places, but was powered by the same super-human passions that drove his fighting arm and his ability to kill without hesitation. It was less an ability than a need, like the need to breathe.

When their tongues met there was no going back for Abdel. His eyes burned in his head, and he surrendered to the strange woman's rhythms the same way he surrendered to the clanging-steel rhythms of an opponent. They came together in the same kind of hesitant, exploratory dance of two swordsmen parrying blows and searching for weaknesses and openings. Her dress came off like an opponent's shield being batted away, and he shed what limited clothes he wore himself in the same way he would remove any encumbrance that might interfere with his sword arm's range of motion.

The feel of the floor was cold and rough, but Bodhi accepted most of it at first. It scratched her, and she flinched away from it—flinched into Abdel, who responded to the weakness by pulling her up and to him. They were moving completely without thought, pretense, or plan now. They were completely together in a single, crystalline moment. It was the sort of moment Abdel had never experienced, even in his most intense blood frenzy, or his most violent, kill-crazy melee. This was no tavern wench or camp follower, and the transaction they made was one that went to the blood, not just the purse.

It was at the beginning of what both of them knew on a silent, accepting level, was the end of it that her face slipped to his throat. Her cool breath brushed against his corded neck. Abdel heard a hollow, popping crack that in an even semi-lucid state he would have recognized as a joint dislocating.

There was a warm wetness on his skin, and he took a deep breath as Bodhi pressed her face into his neck. Her body convulsed once so violently they almost came apart all at once. Abdel held her tightly, and her back seemed to pop under his grip. She was breathing fast and hard through her nose with a rhythmic *hiss-hiss-hiss* and made a guttural, animal sound in her throat. Her chest, pressed as flat as her chest could be pressed against his, vibrated with the sound.

Her body quivered through a series of spasms that made it seem as if every muscle in her body had been granted individual will, and every one was fighting for escape or supremacy. Abdel's own release came as this passionate frenzy began to subside, and Bodhi's face came away from his neck. Abdel's vision blurred, and his head spun. She pressed a cold-fingered hand to his neck and held it there hard while Abdel almost swooned like a widow at a summer funeral.

* * * * *

This was no man.

He was right, Bodhi thought. By the darkest layers of the Abyss, Irenicus was right. This was no man. No man at all.

She was afraid, rightfully so, that Abdel would kill her if he realized what she'd done. She'd tasted only a little—well, maybe more than the little she intended. She was curious, but now that it was over, she realized she had been hoping Irenicus was right about Abdel. He was so very right.

She'd fed on hundreds of men, maybe thousands, from all walks of life. She'd tasted the blood of shepherds and princes, generals and pikemen. She'd fed on the fey blood of elves, the bitter humors of orcs, and all manner of the Underdark's primitive shadow-stalkers. The taste of blood, to her, had become like the cuisine of the living. Some was good—prepared well by a good, wealthy, comfortable life—some was left to its own devices, left to rot or congeal in its destitute chef's muddy veins. Abdel's blood was like nothing she'd ever tasted before.

To the blunt sensitivity of her tongue, Abdel was the strong young man he appeared to be. When it seemed like her head was going to explode in a shower of frenzied light, the simple taste stopped being important. When her whole body pressed into the experience then burst into flowers and starbursts and every explosion of red, whirling hell, she stopped being the predator and became a sort of worshiper, begging for the favor of a fickle but generous god.

Philip Athans

She wanted to do it again so badly she made herself crawl away from him. She'd been alive for centuries, and it was that experience that kept her from going back for more. She'd already taken enough blood from him to make him light-headed. That worked, luckily, in her favor. Abdel couldn't tell he'd been bitten. He lay back on the flagstone floor and let the wash of the experience pass through him. She'd done a good job of stopping the bleeding, but when her vision finally cleared enough to look back at him and see something more than a bright-burning deity, she saw that the wound was already healing. He should heal fast but not quite that fast.

She wiped the blood from her lips and chin with the palm of her hand, then licked the blood off her hand hungrily, her naked back turned to Abdel, so he couldn't see her in this feral moment. He started breathing deeply and regularly, and she knew he would be up and looking at her soon, if he wasn't already. She scrambled for her dress, found it, and with hands trembling like a schoolgirl's, she slipped it over her head and did her best to smooth it around her hips without having to stand.

She didn't think she'd be able to stand.

* * * * *

Abdel's neck tickled and when he scratched it, it hurt just a little, but he didn't pay it any mind. He propped himself up on one elbow, and though he was sure he would see Bodhi next to him, he didn't see her at all. From behind him came the rustle of cloth and he turned slowly, his head heavy and his body sluggish. She was there, smoothing her wrinkled red linen dress over her soft round hips. Abdel couldn't help but smile, though he knew he must look like a love-struck fool.

64

He didn't know what to say, so he just stared at her until she turned one cheek to him to sneak a glance. Abdel wasn't sure how to feel about her obvious reluctance to face him. He suddenly felt very naked and grabbed for the trousers slumped on the floor next to him.

"I didn't hurt you," he said quietly, hopefully.

"No," she said quickly, part of a long, sibilant breath.

He pulled on the trousers, cursing under his breath at the trouble he had pulling them on. His hands were strangely weak, shook a little, and the pants were just so tight on him.

"Where will you go?" she asked him, her voice— louder now—echoing in the empty stone chamber, the cellar of the Copper Coronet.

Abdel didn't answer for what seemed like too long. He had to figure out what she meant. He'd done a lot of thinking on his way back from killing Aran Linvail and had come to some conclusions.

"You know where I need to go," he told her, "don't you?"

"You killed him in his house?" she asked, her voice tight.

He stood slowly, his knees stiff, and went to the stairs. He looked back at her once, his eyes heavy, clouded, somehow dull, then he went up the stairs and reached around for a burlap sack soaked in blood. From the top of the stairs he threw the sack at Bodhi's feet. When Aran Linvail's severed head rolled out of it, Bodhi took a deep breath and tried not to smile.

"I don't need to kill someone else for the other twenty thousand, do I?" he asked.

"Do you know the madhouse?" she asked him.

Abdel tipped his head to one side like a dog. It was an odd question.

"Madhouse?" he asked, coming down the stairs to face her, avoiding the blood as he walked.

She turned to look at him, and in the dwindling lamplight, he thought she might have blushed.

"She's being held there," she said. "They're both being held at Spellhold. It's a madhouse . . . an asylum for the insane."

Abdel sighed. His head was beginning to clear, and he was just so tired. His mind was a confusion of a million emotions and thoughts that made no sense to him. He knew he was being manipulated by this woman and her friend Gaelan Bayle. He knew he was being targeted by the Shadow Thieves for something Sarevok did—ridiculous enough. He knew somehow a young girl from his past—a past that seemed so distant it was like another life all together—was caught up in all of it. He didn't care anymore whom he had to kill, who wanted how much gold, or what had to happen. The only thing that made sense to him was finding Jaheira and Imoen and making them safe again. So they were in a madhouse, a prison, a dungeon, wherever. He knew there would be more strings attached to anything else Bodhi told him, but those were strings he'd have to cut once Jaheira and Imoen were safe.

"Where is this place?" he asked Bodhi.

"One of my brothers is there," she said.

"What does that have to do with me?" he asked. "Should I kill him too?"

"No," answered Bodhi, "he's on our side. His name is Jon Irenicus."

"He's mad?" Abdel asked, not bothering to point out that he wasn't sure he and Bodhi could ever be on the same "side."

She looked at him sharply this time and turned away just as fast, but Abdel could see the unmistakable flash of anger in her eyes.

"I'm sorry," he said quickly. He needed to know what she knew.

Bodhi's shoulders slumped, and she said, "He was falsely accused—manipulated by the Shadow Thieves, who control the asylum. They took him there to get him out of the way, to torture him, to make him witness the great evil they're going to make."

Abdel swallowed in a throat suddenly dry.

"They've got Jaheira and Imoen there too," Bodhi said. "I can get you there and get you in." Bodhi looked up at the ceiling, not looking at him. "It must be near dawn up there."

Abdel glanced up at the ceiling himself and found no answers there.

"I have to go," she said.

"If Jaheira and Imoen are being kept at this madhouse as you say," Abdel told her, "nothing could keep me from going there."

"And will you help my brother?" she asked.

Abdel sighed. He'd been manipulated into all of this but . . . "Of course," he promised.

"I have to go," she whispered, tracing something into a scatter of sawdust on the floor. "You will see this mark on a wall at the base of the tallest tower on the island. As quickly as you can, say the word *'nchasme'* or you will be burned to cinders. A way in will be opened for you."

"Wait," he said, an edge he didn't like still playing havoc with his voice. "Stay with me—I mean . . . go with me."

She moved slowly to the stairs and put one foot on the bottom step. He took a step toward her but knew he couldn't go any closer.

"I can't," she said simply. "It's almost . . ."

"Bodhi," he said.

"The captain can get you there," she said, her voice loud and clear. "There's only one madhouse. It's on an island. You'll need a boat. I beg you . . . I beg you to go there. And remember the word—"

"*Nchasme*," he repeated, glancing down at the sawdust. She'd traced two wavy, parallel lines like water, with something that might have been an eye between them on the right-hand side.

Her eyes red and her face drawn and weary, she looked back at him. With a tight, forced smile, she ascended the steps, opened the door, and passed quickly through it.

ChapteR EiGht

Having taken the form of a bat, Bodhi flew with all her still considerable strength to race the lightening sky to the asylum's jagged, unforgiving towers.

She alighted on a high minaret and turned her face to the east. The sky was a deep blue that became both lighter and more blue as she transformed into a woman again. Hanging sixty feet from the ground in a slim, shuttered window, Bodhi sneered at the patch of crinkled gray-brown horizon that would soon enough explode into a light that would fry her to ashes with its first tentative reawakening. Bodhi hated the sun, despised the light. Every day mocked her, showed her that as long as she lived—through century after century of supreme immortality—she still had a weakness.

She looked down at the waves crashing over the rocks below and thought of Abdel. A surge of power, riding on the god's blood even now coursing through her own brittle veins, passed over her, and she smiled, letting her long, graceful canine teeth slip from the protective wrap of her gums. She hissed at the sun as the first sliver of it broke the line of the horizon.

The light touched her hand as—still hissing her impotent defiance—she backed into the window and went to draw the shutter behind her. Where the light touched her there was an uncomfortable heat, just on the edge of pain. Bodhi drew the shutter closed all the way and held her singed hand in her other, examining it closely. The sun's light had touched it. It should have all but burned off, but instead it was barely kissed with red.

She smiled and drew in a breath, almost considering throwing wide the shutters to spit her challenge at the hated sun. Instead, she moved to the door leading to the stairs down, which led to more stairs down, which led to a little locked room where sat an old, weathered casket.

Abdel, she thought, Son of Bhaal.

* * * * *

In the days since Minsc started working at the Copper Coronet, the place had never been so clean. After a full night of working, the red-haired madman always stayed through the morning to clean up and wouldn't go to sleep until the miniature giant space hamster he carried with him told him it was all right. No one was happier about this than Abdel, who returned to the tavern exhausted, still crammed into his borrowed trousers, and in need of a boat.

When the big sellsword came up the stairs from the cellar, Minsc greeted him with a smile and said, "The big man, Boo, it's the big man!"

"Minsc," Abdel said, "I need your help."

Minsc smiled and looked down at the little animal sitting contentedly on his shoulder, nodded, and said, "Anything you want, if you help me move the captain."

Abdel stepped into the common room, a dark space that smelled noticeably better now than it did the last time Abdel was here. There were no windows, and though the sun was bright outside, Minsc was working by the light of a single candle. In a particularly dark corner was a grizzled old man, passed out and snoring loudly.

"The captain?" Abdel asked, vaguely recognizing the old drunk.

Minsc nodded, still smiling, and crossed to the old man. "Let's go, Captain Havarian! Closing time!"

Abdel smiled for the first time in a long time and tried to think of a god to thank. "This man has a ship?" he asked Minsc.

Minsc shrugged, lightly tapping the old man's face, and said, "He's supposed to be some kind of big pirate captain, but he's been here—alone—every night since I've been here."

"I need him awake," Abdel said, glancing around the tavern until his eyes stopped on Minsc's wash bucket. "I need a ship."

Abdel picked up the bucket and threw the full load of water square into the old man's face. Havarian burst into blustering consciousness, roaring a word that made even Abdel blush before barking out, "We're scuttled, lads, we're hard aground!"

Minsc laughed loudly, and Abdel put a hand on the delirious pirate's shoulder in a futile attempt to steady him.

"What in the name of blue-green Sekolah . . ." the pirate sputtered, then finally fixed blurry eyes on Abdel.

"I need a ship," the sellsword said, close in to Havarian's face.

The captain laughed—a gravelly, almost choking sound—and said, "Passage costs, lad, but I can take ye as far as Luskan, if yer need be."

"I won't need to go that far," Abdel said.

"Good," the old man said, "but it'll cost ye wherever ye're goin'."

"I have nothing to pay you with, old man," he admitted, "but perhaps we can work something—"

The old man coughed out a laugh and managed to stagger to his feet. "Poor son of a . . ." Havarian growled. "I'm going home."

"I can lend you some coin," Minsc said. Both Abdel and the captain whirled on him. The act of whirling made the old sailor fall heavily on his rump, eliciting another grumbled curse. "How much do you need?"

Abdel looked at Havarian for an answer. Rubbing his bruised rear, the old pirate asked, "How much ye got?"

* * * * *

"I thought you had a ship," Abdel said, scowling at the still-drunk captain and against the glare of the sun from the sea.

From where he sat sprawled in the bow of the little dinghy, Captain Havarian belched resoundingly and said, "Yer friend with the mouse couldn't afford a ship. Besides, I didn't charge ye for the clothes."

Abdel grunted and let the subject lie. He concentrated on rowing, keeping to the course the captain had set for them. Havarian seemed to know all about the island asylum, though he wouldn't tell Abdel any specifics about it. He just kept saying, "Bad port, that one, bad port."

The captain had given him clothes that fit reasonably well. Abdel wore a simple white sailor's blouse and sturdy though short trousers under the chain mail tunic Bodhi had arranged for him. The heavy broadsword hung from a simple thong sling he'd made himself waiting for Havarian to get the boat. He felt awake, alert, and ready for battle for the first time in a while. He hadn't slept, but it didn't matter. His finger and other wounds, including the nasty puncture to his gut, had healed completely.

Havarian fished around in the bottom of the boat and smiled when he came up with a stout earthenware bottle sealed with a cork. He popped the cork out between his ragged, gray-yellow teeth and downed a huge swallow of whatever was contained inside. When he took the bottle from his lips his eyes bulged dangerously, as if they were going to pop out of his head, and he seemed to be either trying to take a deep breath in, or scream.

"Havarian?" Abdel asked, momentarily concerned.

The old pirate finally let loose a huge, phlegmy cough. Spittle and mucus trailed off his chin, and his body convulsed through a series of deep gags.

"Are you all right?" Abdel asked.

Havarian managed a laugh and said, "Smooth . . ."

Abdel sighed and threw his back into the rowing. He couldn't get there fast enough.

* * * * *

Abdel didn't study the island asylum very carefully at all. He could spot the tallest tower easily enough and made straight for it. The building did generate a kind of dull foreboding, and Abdel had to work to keep it out of his mind. He didn't want to think too much about what he was doing. He didn't want to think that he was intentionally breaking into a place that no one would ever want to see the inside of.

Abdel shook his head and rowed faster.

"Ease up, kid," the old pirate grumbled. Havarian looked up at the towers and battlements of the fortress-like asylum and went pale. "Ye sure yer'll wantin' to be in such a hurry?"

"I need to get to that wall, there," Abdel said, ignoring the old man's question, "below the tallest tower."

Havarian scanned the rocky shoreline and pointed at a collection of boulders that made something like a miniature harbor. Waves crashed all around, but there was a small place of relative calm no more than a few yards from the base of the tower. The smooth brick wall rose up from the jumble of boulders, just at the edge of the island.

"I can get yer in there nice enough," Havarian said, taking the oars, "but I won't be hangin' around this rock, boy. Yer passage was one way, hear?"

Abdel smirked and nodded impatiently. Havarian turned the dinghy into the shelter of the boulders and nodded once to Abdel when he thought it was shallow enough for the sellsword to get out of the boat.

"Don't die in a place like this, boy," Captain Havarian called after Abdel, who was wading toward the boulders at the foot of the wall. "It's a bad place to let yer soul loose in."

Abdel nodded again, only glancing at the old man long enough to see him already rowing quickly away from the island.

It took Abdel only a few minutes to find the odd glyph Bodhi had traced for him.

He said "*Nchasme*," in a loud, confident voice and was rewarded with the sound of stone grinding on stone.

A cluster of bricks pulled back into the wall slowly, shedding dust as they moved. A door barely big enough for Abdel to squeeze through opened into darkness. Abdel thought he heard a man screaming from somewhere far away, and he looked back at the little harbor. There was no sign of Captain Havarian.

Abdel forced a smile and ducked into the opening.

* * * * *

The man was missing both his legs, but that wasn't his most obvious handicap. Abdel took another small step toward him, the big sellsword biting his bottom lip in puzzled indecision. The madman with no legs was weeping inconsolably and occasionally barking out a strangled, desperate, "Where are you *going*?"

Unfortunately for Abdel, he was doing this in the open doorway that was the only exit out of the straw-littered room. The place smelled so strongly of urine it was all Abdel could do to hold his stomach down. He could have simply pulled the man away and passed, but there was something about the grimy, crawling skin and the gnashing, ground-flat teeth, the flying spittle, the crawling lice, the smell, and the insane, unpredictable nature of the man that made even Abdel more than a little reluctant to touch him.

Abdel cleared his throat, but the madman gave no sign that he noticed the sellsword or any one of the handful of asylum inmates in the room.

"I need to pass," Abdel said, in a clear, unwavering voice that still sounded weak somehow.

The madman didn't look up, but he did sob loudly once and squeak out, "Come back, come back, come . . ."

"Oh, 'e ain't movin', swab," one of the other inmates, a vile-smelling man in the garb of a sailor, drawled with a wink and a smirk.

Abdel looked at the sailor and sighed. Looking at him made it clear to Abdel that it wasn't the straw on the floor that smelled so bad—it was the sailor.

"That one ain't moved since . . ." the sailor said, obviously not sure how long the crippled madman had occupied this inconvenient resting place.

"I need to get through there," Abdel told the sailor, as if that would help.

The sailor laughed, showing more empty space than

teeth, and said, "Why'd ye e'er set that course, swab? That away leads *in*."

"In?" Abdel asked.

The sailor nodded, smiling broadly.

"I need to go farther in," Abdel told the sailor. "I need to go all the way in."

"Ye're mad, then," the sailor said.

"So I've come to the right place," Abdel replied, drawing his broadsword and taking three confident steps toward the man in the doorway.

" 'E won't like that," the sailor warned. "The coordinator, 'e don't want nobody to kill nobody."

Abdel stopped and turned, glancing at the blade and realizing he didn't want to kill this poor wretch anyway. "What are you talking about?"

"The coordinator," the sailor said, his tone at once condescending and afraid. "The captain o' this nut house. Big time lord mage type, this one. 'E'll rip ye apart . . . seen that one do it, too, I 'ave."

"The coordinator?" Abdel asked.

"Aye."

"Take me to him."

The sailor smiled and said, "Name's Mal Cheirar."

Abdel narrowed his eyes. He'd seen dozens of this type before. Pirates, cutthroats, scalawags, whatever you called them, they weren't to be trusted, not even tolerated. Abdel had ended up killing as many of them as not.

"Take me to him, now."

Mal Cheirar stopped smiling and nodded curtly. He sized up Abdel quickly, then smiled again. "Ye'll 'ave to move that one after all, mate."

Abdel turned to the man in the doorway and lifted the broadsword high, holding it as if to behead the raving lunatic.

"I need to get through that doorway," Abdel said slowly.

This time the man looked up, revealing a bruised, pockmarked face.

"All . . ." he croaked out with a voice deeper than his earlier plaintive wails would ever have hinted at, ". . . you . . . had to . . . do was . . . ask."

Abdel sighed, not enjoying being played for a fool. "Just move," he demanded.

The suddenly lucid inmate scuttled out of the doorway and Abdel wasted no time stepping over his slowly receding form with Mal Cheirar in reluctant tow. He passed into a narrow corridor, lit by guttering torches that made the place smell of smoke. There was a faint breeze that kept the smoke from getting too thick, but the air in the corridor was heavy and hot just the same.

Abdel looked at the pirate, who pointed, smiling, in one direction. Abdel was tempted to start off in the opposite direction, but after a moment's indecision, he followed the man's lead. Abdel had to hold his breath when the pirate passed, and as they continued down the corridor, Abdel intentionally fell behind, hoping some space would lessen the stench.

"Ye're sure about this?" the pirate asked, his voice echoing in the tight, windowless space. "Ye're sure ye wanna meet the coordinator?"

"You're sure this is the way?" Abdel asked, ignoring the pirate's question. He tried to breathe only through his mouth. Mal Cheirar passed out of sight briefly as the corridor took a sharp turn to the right. Abdel took the opportunity to take a breath and rub his eyes.

"Aye," replied the sailor, "aye, that's the way . . ."

Abdel came around the corner just as he took his hands away from his eyes.

". . . deeper into my asylum," a clear, resonant voice

Philip Athans

sounded from a doorway off one side of the torchlit passage.

Abdel looked up at the door and saw a well-groomed, handsome man who by virtue of his very cleanliness appeared out of place here.

The reeking pirate made a jerky, hesitant bow and sputtered, "Co-co-coordinator."

ChapterR NIne

"Awoke" probably wasn't the right word for what Abdel did. He felt sort of as if he was waking up, but there wasn't really any word that might have covered it. He felt strange. His head was numb; he couldn't feel his body, and he had a kind of tunnel vision—blurred around the edges with a sort of bluish haze. He couldn't see everything and even had trouble thinking clearly. Something was terribly wrong.

He could see the corner of a room, a stone wall, flagstone floor, some cobwebs—there was more detail coming into focus now. His vision swung to one side without his intending to move his eyes or his head, his neck, or his body. It was more like the world swung around him. Someone was lying on the floor.

It was a big man, with powerfully muscled arms and legs. He was wearing a chain-mail tunic similar to Abdel's own and, like Abdel, had long, dark—almost black—hair. He was lying facedown.

His vision swung suddenly forward and down, and Abdel could see the man on the floor being turned roughly over by a pair of hands that couldn't be Abdel's— they were too small, too dirty.

The man on the floor was limp—dead. The man's face came into view, and the features were as recognizable as the body. Abdel was looking at himself.

So he was dead, then. He was dead and floating above his own body. He'd heard of something like that before—had heard that this happened.

He was surprised by so many things. He wasn't sure what order he should put those things in. He was dead and couldn't feel anything about that. How do you react to being dead? If he was disappointed in anything it was that he didn't get Jaheira and Imoen out. He never got a chance to say good-bye to Jaheira and never knew why Imoen was here—what these people would want with her or who these people were in the first place.

So that was it? All this Son of Bhaal this and Savior of Baldur's Gate that, and here he was floating above his cooling corpse in some godsforsaken madhouse on an island no one bothered to even name? And people—smart people like Gorion and Jaheira—thought he had some greater destiny. He felt like a fool, but worse, he felt like he'd made a fool of them.

His memory was starting to clear even as he continued to watch his own body being dragged by the feet across the rough flagstone floor. He remembered his last sight of Jaheira—and Imoen—Imoen was there.

He thought back, and the events that had transpired until this moment played back in his mind, as if he were watching them for the first time. . . .

* * * * *

Someone jumped him from behind. It was Mal Cheirar. The coordinator smiled at the sight of it, and Abdel was sure he heard laughter as he stumbled forward. The blow to the back of his head would have killed any normal man, but Abdel not only survived, he managed to remain conscious.

"Very good," the coordinator said cheerfully enough.

Mal Cheirar swore incoherently at the same time.

Abdel turned, and Mal Cheirar hit him again. The sellsword managed to roll with this blow, and it was considerably less painful. He punched Mal Cheirar dead center, smashing the pirate's nose. Blood sprayed across Abdel's forearm, and the pirate staggered back one step, then another, but managed to stay on his feet. From behind him, Abdel heard the coordinator saying something, but the words made no sense. Abdel had time only to form the words "a spell" in his mind before he felt two fingers touch him on the small of his back.

The fingers were cool and dry, and Abdel wondered how he could feel them so well through the chain mail he was wearing. The touch grew rapidly colder, spreading across Abdel's back in a frigid wave. He turned again, and his chest seized up. His knees shook, and his jaw clenched painfully. His right knee almost gave out, but he stepped toward the coordinator and brought his sword up.

The strange man stepped back and smiled. The chill continued to tense Abdel's muscles, and he thought if he could just open his mouth his teeth would start chattering. As it was, he was afraid his jaw would break from being clenched so tightly.

He brought his sword up despite the stiffness in his muscles and sliced it down hard at the coordinator. Stiff, frozen muscles or not, the sword came down fast enough that he should have split the man in half. Instead, the sword pinged off some obstruction in front of the smiling mage. He had some kind of invisible shield around him, and as the sword slid down its impossible surface, Abdel got the feeling it was a sort of elongated dome, as if the man was encased in a glass bell jar as strong as steel.

The cold was gone all at once, and Abdel's jaw came

open, and a breath escaped. His arms still stiff, but considerably faster now, Abdel spun his sword through loose fingers and brought it back down at the coordinator—much harder this time. The invisible barrier held, and the sword bounced off it. Abdel heard one footstep behind him and didn't realize that Mal Cheirar had come up close behind him until the sword flipped back past his head and slid down the middle of the sailor's right eye.

Mal Cheirar screamed, and Abdel shrugged, happy to have this tiny bit of good luck in what was becoming a frustratingly long run of bad luck. The half-blind sailor staggered back and dropped his dagger, letting it clatter on the bloody flagstones.

This made the coordinator laugh even louder, and he laughed louder when Abdel tried to slash him again and was frustrated when the sword was deflected once more.

"Damn it," Abdel growled, "who are you?"

"I'm the coordinator," the man laughed, making it clear that he thought the title was ridiculous.

Abdel struck again, and this time there was something different about the way the broadsword bounced off the barrier. Abdel was sure the blade came just a little closer to the coordinator.

Their eyes met for just the briefest moment, and the coordinator actually winked at him, a wicked, mischievous twinkle in his eye. This made Abdel angry.

He growled again—it made him feel better—and stepped in closer to the coordinator. He slashed at the barrier at the coordinator's waist level, and the blade came a good three inches closer to actually cutting the man. The coordinator shrugged and stepped back once, twice, then turned and took four quick steps and passed through a door. Abdel followed so closely behind that he barely had room to swing his sword at the rapidly crumbling magical barrier.

They crossed a thin, dimly lit corridor, and Abdel hung back half a step as the coordinator passed into another room. Abdel needed more room to get a good slash in and finally take the barrier down the rest of the way. He needed enough room to cut this smug bastard's head off.

What Abdel saw in the room made him pull up short.

"You are not a very smart young man are you?" the coordinator said.

Abdel knew he'd eventually kill this man, so he gave himself a second or two to make sure he wasn't imagining things. They were in a room with a ceiling easily three times Abdel's own considerable height. Hanging from the ceiling was a series of heavy black iron chains. Suspended from some of those chains were cages no bigger than coffins. Iron maidens, Abdel had heard them called. They were simple steel cages, about half a dozen of them. Two of them were occupied.

"Abdel!" Imoen called from one of them. "Abdel—what are you doing here?"

"What am—?" Abdel started to ask, then looked over at the second cage, where Jaheira was standing. Her face was covered in another one of those terrible steel masks that kept her from speaking—or casting spells. Her eyes told Abdel enough: she was happy to see him but still afraid.

"You came right to me, Son of Bhaal," the coordinator said. "And they told me you wouldn't be so easily manipulated."

Abdel sighed and hefted his sword. He glanced back at Jaheira one more time, then shot a quick smile at Imoen.

"Take his head off, Abdel," she cheered.

She always had so much confidence in him.

The coordinator laughed again and said, "Oh, yes, by all means, Abdel. Take my head off."

Abdel brought his sword up, took stock of the unarmed man, and feinted once to make it seem as if he was going to oblige both the coordinator and Imoen. The coordinator barely flinched. Anyone—even a trained fighter—would have reacted to the feint in some way. It was the whole reason Abdel even tried it in the first place. The coordinator's reaction to the fake attack would tell Abdel how he'd react to a real one, and tactics could be devised accordingly. The only thing Abdel wasn't expecting was for the man to have no reaction at all.

"I'm over here," the coordinator said sarcastically.

So be it. Abdel returned the odd man's smile and set his heavy broadsword swinging in front of him. He stepped toward the man, bringing the blade in and around in fast figure eights. The coordinator's eyes twisted in his head, following the blade, but he made no move to cast a spell. Abdel knew enough from the freezing touch and the invisible barrier that this man was some kind of mage. He was unarmed—not armed with physical weapons—but that didn't mean he wasn't deadly. Still, in Abdel's considerable experience, he knew that spells were always preceded by some amount of muttering, waving about of hands, and the handling of odd bits of this and that. The coordinator made no such attempts.

It struck Abdel that though they were confined to the iron maidens above, here he had both Imoen and Jaheira. This man meant nothing to him now—alive. All he could do, at best, would be to explain why the women were here, why he'd manipulated Abdel into coming here to aid them. Abdel felt a certain measure of confidence that Jaheira would know at least the answers to some of those questions, and even if she didn't, Abdel didn't really care. It was good enough to assume that this coordinator—whoever he really was—was next in a line of various evil geniuses bent on world domination who, for whatever reason, thought Abdel's peculiar parentage might help him become Emperor of all Faerûn.

All things considered, Abdel decided to just kill the man and get it over with.

Abdel stepped in fast and held closed his eyes in anticipation of a sudden splatter of blood. The blood never came, and Abdel felt his brow furrow. The coordinator, still smiling, was simply leaning back away from the whirling tip of Abdel's heavy blade. In response, Abdel spun the blade faster, extending the arc lower.

Still smiling, the coordinator backed up, replanted his feet, almost danced backward across the smooth stone floor of the huge room, managing to keep his body always half an inch from the blade. Abdel had never seen anyone move that fast. A flash of yellow passed in front of Abdel's vision, and by sheer force of will alone, he made the sword move faster, until there was nothing but a vaguely gray fog in front of him.

A look of concern was made plain on the coordinator's face, and Abdel took heart. The man's lips parted, and he must have only said one short, simple word, and he was just gone.

"Behind—" Imoen shouted.

Abdel spun so fast he almost took off his own head. He let the blade decelerate just enough so he could see better, and there was the coordinator standing at the opposite end of the big room, little more than an outline in the wavering torchlight.

"—you!"

In the space of time it took to blink, Abdel looked up

at Jaheira, back at the coordinator—who was just standing there—and made a decision. He started running at the coordinator, his sword spinning at his side and making a gentle, keening hiss in the air. He glanced up at Jaheira again, and her eyes betrayed confusion but also a level of trust he suddenly hoped he'd be able to earn.

"That's right," the coordinator said, his voice echoing in the big room, "come and get me, thug."

Abdel hopped once, then again, and the coordinator's brow furrowed. The sellsword leaped high into the air about midway to where the coordinator was standing. The strange man let out a single barking laugh and came running at Abdel, obviously intending to meet him somewhere in the middle.

Abdel hit the bottom of Jaheira's iron maiden hard enough to make it swing. Jaheira bumped into the cold iron bars with bruising force, and Abdel hung on with his left hand, letting the sword come to rest in his right. The coordinator was almost underneath him when he started mumbling through some incantation.

Ready for anything, Abdel dropped his arm back and changed his grip on the sword. He looked up, fixed the iron maiden's swinging padlock in his mind, and everything went black. He pulled up short so fast that a muscle in his shoulder twisted painfully. He couldn't see the lock and couldn't risk a blind swing at it. He could injure, even kill Jaheira.

"That was easy," the coordinator's mocking voice drifted up from below.

Knowing he was only about eight feet off the ground, Abdel simply let go of the cage and dropped. He hit the floor on his feet and kept his sword in front of his forehead, blade parallel to the ground to block any attempts to split his skull. The darkness was absolute. He couldn't see the blade that must have been a hand's span in front of his face. He couldn't see his feet—couldn't even see the bridge of his nose.

"Abdel . . ." Imoen shouted. The sound of her voice—perturbed, impatient, immature—made him feel very nostalgic for the simpler days in the safety of Candle-keep. What was she doing here? "Abdel, I can't see you!"

A muffled sound came from above, and Abdel got the idea that it was Jaheira trying to say the same thing. She might have been telling him to risk hurting her if there was a chance of getting her out.

"You came here exactly when I wanted you to," the coordinator said, his voice echoing too much for Abdel to get a decent fix on his position in the absolute dark-ness. "You can swing your sword around all you want—even break the ladies free of their maidens—but you can't kill me, and you can't get out of here. You will serve my needs, even if we have to play for a while before it happens. I have a little time, at least."

It was three years before, in Roaringshore, when Abdel joined a merchant caravan headed for Khel-drivver. He was tasked with guarding a wagon filled with fine wine. It was easy enough work—who would steal wine between Roaringshore and Kheldrivver. Well, the caravan master had failed to mention a cer-tain group of priests of Selûne from whose temple the wine had been stolen. The priests descended on the car-avan on a high pass across the Troll Hills. One of the spells they'd used that day seemed familiar to Abdel now. A globe of darkness had descended over the wagon. That day, Abdel had managed to stumble out of the globe of darkness, which ended—luckily for Abdel—a few inches from the edge of a steep cliff. Assuming this spell was at least similar, and the whole room wasn't dark, Abdel picked a direction and ran.

Over the sound of his own footsteps, Abdel heard the coordinator say, "Come on and die then. You're not the only one. I know you're asking yourself why—why Imoen."

Abdel stumbled, almost stopped short, but kept on. He came out of the darkness all at once, and the coordinator had moved farther away.

Abdel stopped then, adjusted the grip on his sword and asked, "More lies?"

The coordinator shrugged, smiled, and motioned to the iron maiden in which Imoen still stood trapped.

"What's going on here, Abdel?" the girl asked impatiently.

The coordinator laughed and said, "You're not the only one, boy. She has the blood too. She has the blood of Bhaal, and all I need is one of you. Though I'd prefer both."

"That's a lie," Abdel said without actually wanting to. He couldn't help but look up at Imoen, who was simply confused, tired, dirty, and afraid.

"Abdel?" she asked quietly.

The coordinator said something Abdel thought might have been "out of the vessel," whatever that meant, but the rest of it was gibberish. Knowing the man was casting some spell, Abdel had no choice but to run at him and hope he got there before the spell went off.

He was close.

* * * * *

Whoever was dragging Abdel's body was stuffing it into an iron maiden.

Sound was starting to become clearer, and Abdel could hear a muffled voice that might have been Jaheira—still masked. He'd failed her. Oh, how he'd failed her!

The man who was stuffing his body into the cage seemed to be standing behind the point in space where Abdel's immortal soul was floating. Abdel tried to speak but couldn't find anything that felt like a mouth. He saw blood dribble from behind him onto his dead body.

The cage was closed over his corpse, and Abdel wondered why anyone would be bothering to lock a dead body in an iron maiden. The hands didn't belong to the coordinator. They were too rough, and too dirty. The blood dribbled some more, and Abdel thought this man must be Mal Cheirar, still bleeding from the eye Abdel had sliced open.

If it was Mal Cheirar, Abdel thought his soul must be floating somewhere just on the smelly pirate's chest.

The hands shifted to a chain and began hauling on it slowly, obviously struggling with the weight. The iron maiden was being drawn up.

"You can hear me, Abdel," the coordinator's voice sounded. He seemed to be speaking from the bottom of a well—or was Abdel at the bottom of the well? "I'll put you back in your body soon enough, Son of Bhaal. You'll need to be whole to serve me. You'll need to feel every precious sting."

Chapter Ten

Imoen's otherwise normal, reasonably happy life had become, over the last tenday or so, a sort of hell that alternated between boring, painful, and horrifying. The latter was the case now.

Abdel had appeared rather suddenly, and when he did, the relief she felt was almost orgasmic in intensity. She'd certainly been waiting long enough for this so-called "Hero of Baldur's Gate" to come and save her. His new girlfriend was of little use but as a model for how to grow up haughty and ineffectual. The "coordinator"— he called himself Irenicus, a name he obviously made up himself—was a raving lunatic with a decent command of magery, but he had an ego so out of control and delusions so deeply implanted in his worm-ridden psyche, it was a wonder he could manage anything but a slow, twitching drool.

The iron maiden hurt, as had the leather collar, the chains, the ropes, the grabbing, and the cold-fingered hands of one vampire after another. They were rarely fed, and when they were, it was gruel obviously prepared by a chef suffering from some combination of head injury and sense of humor.

Abdel had come in sword literally blazing, but had managed to get himself killed. He made it a few steps out of the circle of darkness, then was dropped in his tracks by another spell. Imoen had seen a couple people die before. Reginald of Wide Girth, a monk she knew in passing, dropped dead of heartstop seconds after walking in on her while she was bathing. She always took that personally. Yorik—another monk—fell off the top of the Shrine of Oghma, though no one knew why he was up there in the first place. All attempts to restore life to his broken body failed, leading many in Candlekeep to assume Oghma wanted him dead for some reason. That one was kind of a mess.

Abdel's death looked a lot more like Reginald's than Yorik's. His body just up and quit.

Imoen sobbed when she realized he was dead. She began mourning him right away with half her brain and railed against him with the other half. This was Abdel the mighty? Sellsword par excellence who defeated Sarevok, Son of Bhaal, and saved the Sword Coast from years of bloody war? Irenicus was obviously a mage, yet Abdel just ran at him, swinging his sword. Imoen had to admit, at least to herself, that Irenicus actually went easy on him. It was obviously some death spell. Wizards had more creative, more dramatic, more painful, more lingering, and more humiliating ways to kill someone.

Yeah, he was lucky.

Then Irenicus told Abdel's dead body that he wasn't dead after all and had his reeking henchman lock Abdel in his own iron maiden.

This gave Imoen another ray of hope, though this time it was rather less fulfilling. He'd be locked up like her and Jaheira, but if Abdel was alive, they'd at least have some chance. She'd seen him bend metal that was stronger and thicker than the bars of the hanging cages. Powerful as his spells may be, Irenicus wouldn't stand a chance if Abdel managed to get close with either fist or blade.

Then there was all this stuff about her being Abdel's secret sister—or half sister. Not that she needed any more proof that Irenicus had gone mad a long time ago, but here was a delusion that made no sense at all. Granted, she always knew she was adopted, that the kindly old innkeeper named Winthrop wasn't her real father. Candlekeep had a lot of orphans—it was something the monks just did.

She'd heard that Abdel was the son of some dead god, but what . . . that means every orphan was? That would make Candlekeep demigod central, wouldn't it.

Besides, if she was a daughter of some dead god, wouldn't she have some powers? She should have at least been able to seduce women—gods do that, don't they? She should be able to lift boulders, withstand the breath of a dragon (thankfully, she'd never had an opportunity to test that one), or do at least one thing that was beyond the normal abilities of mortal humans.

Imoen was mortal enough.

She'd stopped trying to ask questions a long time before. Irenicus almost never answered at all, but when he did, it was usually some sarcastic quip that told her nothing and seemed designed to either make her more curious, or make her feel bad about herself. Imoen was neither curious, nor would she ever feel bad about herself, so the exercise had quickly become tiresome.

Things had changed suddenly though, and she just couldn't help it.

"When are you going to bring him back to life?" she demanded. "Do it!"

Irenicus stopped and looked up at her. Their eyes met, he winked, and he went on about his business. Men, Imoen thought. Bastards.

* * * * *

Imoen watched the preparations for the ritual with only minimal interest. This strange man was going on about his strange work—work that would certainly end in her death. Memorizing the details, ins, outs, and nuances of it wouldn't help her escape or keep her alive, so she opted to spend her last hour or so trying to find a way out of the hanging cage.

The room was lit by torches, then candles were lit, then more candles, then braziers of hot coals that made it so hot in the room sweat was pouring off her. She could see the other woman—Abdel's woman—also looking for weak spots in the bars or floor of her cage and not finding any. She was sweating too. Abdel, naked now and slipping in and out—mostly out—of consciousness was sheeted with sweat. He never opened his eyes, and when Irenicus's people moved him, he let them, oblivious to what they must have in store for him.

When the chanting started, Imoen was more irritated than afraid. It wasn't an entirely pleasant sound. It went on for what seemed like days, was surely hours. They moved her cage, and all she could do was twist in it, trying to stay out of their reach and unbalance the cage at the same time. She wasn't very heavy, so she couldn't unbalance anything. The men who were helping Irenicus were mad—every last one of them just raving lunatics—and they smelled awful. Some of them looked at her with undisguised lust in their eyes, and she couldn't help but be impressed with herself that she managed to keep from vomiting.

They put her close to Abdel—close enough that she knew if he'd just wake up, he'd be able to save them all. She was aware of the first few minutes of the ritual. There was a sound—chanting, mumbling, muttering, and murmuring—and light, heat, and rending, searing pain. Imoen remembered hearing herself cry out, then she burst into laughter, then collapsed into tears.

Irenicus said something like, "It's happening. It's really happening."

Imoen's vision blurred, turned yellow, then became more acute. She saw details in the stone but couldn't understand what she was seeing. It was a crack in one brick in the far corner of the room, or some enormous canyon seen from miles in the sky. Irenicus laughed, and her vision went yellow again. She heard Abdel roar, and her body flushed and turned warm, wet, then tightened.

All sense disappeared all at once, and she was aware of only one thing. She wanted to kill. She lusted for it. Death. Murder. Pain.

She wanted to find the one person most valuable, most beloved to all people, and she wanted to kill it—kill him—kill her. She wanted to make someone cry. She wanted to feel hot meat twist in her fingers while the victim—her victim—screamed and writhed in her grip. She wanted blood to spray into her face, into her mouth, across her breasts and all over her body. She wanted to submerge herself in gore and bathe in screams.

She screamed herself into an impenetrable darkness behind her eyes. It was one word, a word that had never meant anything to her: "*Father!*"

Her voice was all wrong; her body felt all wrong. She heard something that might have been a lion or a dragon or the God of Murder scream in incoherent rage and agony next to her, and the sound empowered her. Her hands were bigger now—everything was bigger now, and the cage couldn't contain her—she didn't even remember she was in a cage.

A man's voice said, ". . . too much," then ". . . too fast, I can't . . ." and there was a series of wet popping sounds that made Imoen sigh in twisted, evil pleasure, and she raged out of her cage with speed she knew she couldn't really be capable of.

A tiny voice like a child's coo in the wilderness came to her, and she recognized it as her own.

"What have I become?" she asked herself, and the thing that she had become set that question aside to instead savor the taste of an asylum inmate's head. The brain exploded in her mouth, and it was good.

Through the wild yellow haze, she saw a flash of light, then heard someone say, "He left us! He—" and she was feeding again, and the blood was hot and perfect, and she wanted more, more, more!

Chapter Eleven

Jaheira sat in a corner and tried to stop screaming. It took her nearly an hour.

She had seen things like that before—subtle variations of spells that change the shape, the essence or appearance of a person. She herself had undergone similar transformations, taking on the shape of animals as part of her training as a druid. Spells did not shock her. The unnatural unsettled her but rarely surprised her. She'd been witness to rituals before as well, had been schooled in the religions of Faerûn and knew of the many ways in which people honored the many gods. When the ritual started, she knew what to expect: anything. But what she saw, she could never have been prepared for.

Gods had walked the very real ground of the world around her. She herself had visited some of those places. Gods were real. She felt Mielikki's power course through her on many occasions and knew how to call upon the will of the goddess to do amazing, beautiful things.

What she witnessed was neither amazing or beautiful. It was simply wrong.

Abdel and Imoen had been turned into monsters.

Jaheira didn't like that word: monsters. It was disrespectful. What made one creature an animal and

96

another a monster? Were monsters animals that were new, threatening, or dangerous to people? Monsters behaved like animals, didn't they? When they were hungry, they ate. Calling something a monster made it easier to kill. She hated calling anything a monster, but that was what Irenicus had created in this underground hell of his. Monsters. These creatures were abominations—things outside nature.

He'd done it on purpose, Irenicus. The ritual was designed to transform them. He'd done it on purpose, but Jaheira could see—even Irenicus's own insane henchmen could see—that he had gone too far somehow. He'd made these things out of Abdel and Imoen, but he couldn't control them.

Animals kill everyday, to eat or to protect themselves or their young. It was part of Mielikki's grace—the natural order of things. This was different. These things killed out of the pure joy of it—an evil sort of pleasure nothing natural could ever experience.

So Irenicus made these things and watched in surprise when they escaped their cages and killed his servants. He'd mumbled a quick spell and disappeared seconds before the thing that had been Abdel could rip him apart.

They killed the madmen, then started to turn back to their normal selves. It didn't happen all at once. The evil force relinquished control slowly and with great reluctance. Jaheira knew she was alive only by sheer luck. She knew Abdel loved her and would never willingly see any harm come to her, but he had been completely transformed, and that love couldn't have protected her—it couldn't have been that. It had to have been luck.

When they came back to normal and got her out of the cage, the first thing they did was get out of the room. They were in a madhouse on an island off the coast of

Athkatla—Abdel told them that much—but the place was a seemingly endless maze of passages and rooms, chambers and corridors, and they were lost right away. It was the worst place Jaheira had ever been and even with a restored, normal, though tired and confused Abdel at her side, she was afraid of what she might find around every corner.

The only thing she could think of besides that fear was a simple question: why not me? Irenicus had transformed Abdel and Imoen but why not her too? Maybe she was next, and Irenicus had been scared away before he could get to her. Abdel and Imoen had been turned with the same ritual though, so why not her too? Two at a time? Was that a limitation of the ritual spell? Or was there something else? Abdel had the blood of the dead God of Murder in his veins. It was easy enough to assume that had something to do with it, but what about Imoen?

What was going on, and why was this man doing all this? Why would anyone make some monster even he couldn't control? Why?

* * * * *

"I was hoping you would know," Abdel answered.

Jaheira almost laughed and looked away.

"I just want out of here, all right?" Imoen said, holding her own shaking arms close to her quivering body.

"I don't even want to know what's going on here anymore," Abdel admitted. "I don't want to know what he was supposed to gain from doing whatever he did to us. If we find him, I'll kill him myself. If we don't, that's fine with me as long as we get out of this madhouse and back to Baldur's Gate. I want to live some kind of life eventually, damn it."

"Yeah," Imoen mumbled, "that'll be possible."

Abdel scowled but didn't say anything.

"This Irenicus wants something," Jaheira said as they rounded yet another corner in a seemingly endless string of corners in the twisting labyrinth of the madhouse. "We can't just let him—"

Something hit her on the head, and Abdel saw her spin around, fight briefly to remain conscious, then fall into a doorway and onto the floor of a dark room. Imoen squealed and stepped back, bumping into Abdel. The thing that had hit Jaheira jumped out into the corridor from the room and grabbed for Imoen. She evaded it out of sheer instinct, and Abdel was close enough to grab its arm.

Abdel punched the thing in the face and connected with a flat, porcine snout. He could feel the rough skin and the edge of a thick ivory tusk. It had been a while since Abdel had had the opportunity to punch an orc in the face, and all things considered, it felt good. The thing went down, and a straight-bladed broadsword clattered out of its grip onto the floor. Abdel scooped it up.

The minotaur attacked him the second Abdel crossed the threshold into the dimly lit, cramped room. It attacked low, at Abdel's stomach, but the big sellsword deflected the bull-headed giant's battle-axe blade easily with the orc's broadsword. The defense forced Abdel a bit farther forward than he'd wanted to go, and the minotaur took advantage of it by recovering with surprising speed and coming in higher at Abdel's neck. The sellsword hissed a sharp exhale and twisted back and to the side, painfully wrenching a tight, tired muscle in his back. The minotaur made to stab him through the heart, and Abdel had to parry with more desperation than he was used to. Spiraling his elbow around uncomfortably loosened his grip on the sword enough to allow the minotaur to grab the hand guard and actually twist it out of Abdel's grasp.

Though Abdel couldn't prevent his opponent from disarming him, he did pop his elbow hard and fast into the minotaur's chin. The blow staggered the creature, and the blade came out of his hand too. The sword clattered onto the floor.

Abdel continued the same movement, bending forward and grabbing for the fallen weapon. The minotaur, unable to grab it himself, kicked it fast enough to send it sliding with a shrill metal-on-stone sound. It came to rest less than an inch from Abdel's fingertips.

The sellsword swore and had to abandon the blade in order to roll out from under a downward slash from the creature. The minotaur kicked again, and the sword slid under a sheet that was hanging off some kind of bedlike table.

Abdel scuttled away, and the still partly stunned minotaur let him have the distance. The sellsword scanned the cramped room quickly and was as unsettled as he was confused by its contents.

Strapped to the table in one corner of the room was a naked man. He was conscious but obviously delirious. A tight leather strap was wrapped around his mouth. His eyes were dull and vacant. He made no attempt to struggle against the bonds that held him down. Around his temples and forehead was a steel crown from which ran a thick, ribbonlike band of copper. The copper band crossed half a dozen feet to a huge glass tank that took up more than half of the room. The tank was filled with green-tinged water that smelled sharply of brine. Dark shadows like thick, stubby snakes swam in lazy, slow circles, occasionally nudging against the side of the tank.

"What is this place?" Imoen asked.

"Another one of Irenicus's little play rooms, I guess," Abdel answered as he eyed the circling minotaur, trying not to look at the sheet behind which the broadsword had come to rest. "I don't have any reason to fight you, minotaur."

The minotaur exhaled through its nose, sending a hissing noise echoing through the chamber. It closed its eyes as if to dodge Abdel's words, then lifted its sword high and came at Abdel fast, on its toes.

Unarmed, Abdel wasn't terribly confident that he would survive this attack. He waited until the minotaur was close, almost close enough to kill him, then simply sat back fast and hard onto the stone floor. The minotaur couldn't stop and couldn't get its axe down fast enough to hit Abdel, so it kept going. It put its foot up onto Abdel's shoulder and launched itself into the air, walking up the wall behind the big sellsword, its feet continuing up and around over its own head. The minotaur's toes tapped the ceiling as it spun around, twisting in the air and hitting the floor a pace to Abdel's left. Abdel might have been the only human on Faerûn big enough to allow the minotaur to use that move.

Even as the minotaur's foot came off his shoulder, Abdel launched himself forward and slid along the floor in the direction of the sheet-shrouded table.

He stopped short of being able to reach the sword and swore loudly just before the minotaur stabbed him deep in the left calf. Abdel sat up onto his knees and came backward, trapping the blade still protruding from the thick, corded muscles of his lower leg. Abdel knew he was lucky the blade had come down at that angle. If it was turned the other way, the wide-bladed axe would have severed his leg easily enough. He swore loudly again and growled more than screamed from the pain. The force of Abdel's pinching the blade in his knee made the axe come out of the minotaur's grip. The blade vibrated in Abdel's leg and sent a wave of sensation up through him that caused him to actually gag.

The minotaur struck him hard against the face, and Abdel rolled with the blow, succeeding in getting the axe farther from the creature's grip. Abdel spun, wrenching his back again and tore the axe from his leg.

The minotaur abandoned the battle-axe to Abdel and rolled on one shoulder toward the table. It shot out a hand and came up with the broadsword in a single, fluid motion. Abdel ignored the blazing pain in his leg, kept his footing in the blood now pooling on the stone floor from his wide, deep wound, and hopped to his feet, sliding the battle-axe in front of him fast enough to meet the minotaur's attack. A spark shot out from steel meeting steel. The force of Abdel's parry was enough to force the minotaur back a step. The minotaur collided with the table, and the man strapped there flinched.

Abdel feinted in, hoping to scare the minotaur back farther, but the creature turned its shoulder into the sellsword's midsection and pushed off with both feet.

Abdel let the creature push him back, concentrating on the minotaur's axe.

The minotaur took the broadsword in both hands and made to stab downward into Abdel's chest. Abdel dropped the battle-axe and grabbed the minotaur's wrists in both hands, falling back in an effort to flip the creature over backward. Abdel forgot about the big tank, though, and instead of pulling the minotaur over him in an arc, the creature's sword dipped into the water, and its head struck the glass with enough force to send a hollow ringing sound echoing in the room. The sword pierced one of the swimming eels, and the minotaur's body jerked harshly, and so did Abdel's. The sellsword had felt a similar sensation when a doppelganger had used the power of some enchanted ring on him in the basement of a warehouse in Baldur's Gate. It was as if every muscle in his body tensed and cramped, seeming to lock up with a force beyond its normal strength. The same thing was happening to the minotaur, and the man on the table gave a curious whimper through his tight gag.

Abdel's head spun, and the minotaur's hands came away from the broadsword, which fell into the water with a resounding splash. The minotaur fell backward and stared at Abdel with bulging, dry red eyes. Abdel's vision blurred, and he fought hard not to lose consciousness but wasn't sure he didn't. He heard footsteps but could see the minotaur sitting, shaking, incoherent on the floor.

Abdel was aware that someone had come into the room, but he couldn't do much more than sit and watch things transpire for what felt like forever. The intruder was huge, bigger than Abdel, and came into the room fast. The door swung into the huge sellsword and sufficed to block him from the view of the newcomer.

Someone else came into the room, and Abdel, realizing he wasn't alone when he started this fight, said, "Imoen?"

"Abdel!" Imoen called, but her voice was too distant, still out in the corridor. He could hear the sound of steel on steel and knew that Imoen was fighting someone out there.

Abdel looked around at the person who'd entered the room. The big man was easily eight feet tall and a mass of corded muscle. The top of his head was strangely flat, and he moved slowly but deliberately, with the gait of a brute more than a trained fighter. Abdel, still stunned, thought he must be a half-ogre.

From the corridor outside came Imoen's voice. "They're

trying to kill the minotaur," she said. "The orcs are trying to kill the minotaur!"

The minotaur faced the half-ogre with a dazed sneer. The bull man only started to flinch—unable to dodge or block—when the half-ogre threw a punch and connected with its face with a cracking, meat-on-meat slap. The minotaur went down hard, eyes twitching closed. The way it hit the ground, it might have been dead.

Why Abdel thought he had to defend the minotaur who had been so bent on killing him mere moments before, he wasn't sure, but he stood—the deep wound in his calf already hurting less—teeth clenched, and came at the half-ogre with determination. The aftereffects of whatever the eels had done to him was fading fast, and as he stood, he caught the glint of steel from the corner of his eye.

Sensing the movement behind him, the half-ogre whirled on Abdel, leading with a ham-sized fist. Abdel stopped his forward motion and dropped to one knee to retrieve the battle-axe. The motion sufficed as a dodge. The half-ogre's fist flew over Abdel's head close enough to ruffle the sellsword's long black hair.

Abdel's fingers curled around the axe handle, and he rolled to avoid a slow but strong kick. He spun around on one shoulder and was only dimly aware of deciding on a target. He dragged the simple but serviceable axe across the back of the half-ogre's knee. When the blade came away, it was followed by a scream and a lot of blood. The half-ogre's knee gave way, and he fell. Abdel had to roll again to avoid the falling brute and came up onto his feet with his back to the door.

He didn't see the man who came in next but could see enough in his peripheral vision to take a guess as to the position of the second intruder's face. Abdel

threw his right elbow back fast and hard, letting it
snap more than follow through. He felt rough, sweaty
skin and the texture of a tusk under a lower lip. The orc
he hit made a quiet grunting noise and fell with a clatter of wood on stone.

Abdel looked down and to the side, curious about
whom he'd just hit. It wasn't a prudent course of action,
or so he realized when the half-ogre's rough-knuckled
fist drove up hard into his chin, sending a burst of colored lights sparkling across his vision. He remained
conscious by sheer force of will alone, but the blow
elicited some kind of too-late reflex action that made
Abdel drop the battle-axe.

Shaking his head clear, the sellsword avoided a second
blow from the slowly standing half-ogre and kicked out
fast with his right foot. His toes caught the half-ogre's
damaged knee, and he dug them into the gaping wound.
The half-ogre screamed in rage and pain, then fell backward. The brute took one step back, tried to catch himself,
but ended up just extending his fall back by a pace or two.
He spun as he fell and ended up sprawled across the
chest of the man strapped to the table.

Abdel looked down for the battle-axe and saw the minotaur, his face set and determined, grab for the weapon.
Both the sellsword and the creature gasped when a
long length of rusted iron chain seemed to appear out
of nowhere, wrapping itself around the battle-axe. The
weapon was yanked away after it just barely brushed
the tips of the minotaur's fingers. At the other end of
the chain was a gaunt, green-skinned orc wearing only
tight breeches and a parti-colored kerchief wrapped
around its head. On the orc's face was a crudely ren-
dered tattoo of a mermaid. A pirate, this one, Abdel
thought.

The orc pirate yanked hard on the chain and whipped

the axe back. Abdel, having just regained his footing, lunged at the pirate. The motion startled the tattooed orc and sent his chain flipping wildly through the air over his head. It looked as if he'd meant to take the battle-axe himself. Instead, the weapon came out of the chain and dropped into the eel tank with a splash.

Two of the eels startled, and the man strapped to the table reacted instantly. His chest and back convulsed so sharply and with such strength that the half-ogre—who must have weighed as much as four hundred pounds—popped off the bound man's chest and fell, grimacing, to the floor. The motion made the inmate's head jerk again. One of the half-ogre's fingers had fowled in the leather gag and when he fell, the gag came off the restrained man's face.

Abdel crossed to the tank. Though he was still not sure what sort of power these stubby black eels contained, he knew that the only two weapons at his disposal were both at the bottom of the thick-glassed tank. He lifted one hand, tracking the motion of the eels and looking for the shape of the broadsword in the murky green water. His fingers almost touched the water when he heard something click off the wall in front of him. Less than a second later he was hit in the right eye by something that must have been a stone. It felt heavy and rough and was moving fast. The pain wasn't the half of it. Both his eyes slammed shut, and tears flowed freely.

"What the—?" was all he managed to say.

Abdel looked up with one blurry eye and saw a short figure dart into cover in the doorway, then his attention was drawn to the pirate with the chain. The skinny orc was whirling the rusted chain in fast circles around his head and advancing on an alert minotaur. The creature stayed on his toes and let the orc come in too close. The pirate brought the chain down, but the minotaur was able to slide out of the way.

Abdel turned, momentarily forgetting the weapons in the tank. He held one hand over his wounded eye and was blinking tears out of the other when another stone hit him in that eye.

"Bhaal damn you to . . ." Abdel cursed, now blinded all together.

"Got her," Imoen called.

Abdel forced his eyes open and saw the blurred shape of Imoen move away from the door. He looked over his shoulder and thought he saw the minotaur dodge a second attack from the chain-wielding orc pirate. The orc switched tactics and brought the chain whipping down low. The minotaur hopped over it and came up high enough that when it straightened its right leg sharply, its foot smashed hard into the sailor's tattooed face. The pirate's nose exploded with a red smudge that must have been blood. Abdel closed his eyes again. He heard a jagged spur of bone pop out of the orc pirate's nose and bounce onto the stone floor. It hit just before the rest of the unconscious humanoid's face did.

The sellsword felt the minotaur brush past him, and he opened one eye. It hurt, but he could see. He was momentarily curious about why it hadn't hurt more when the minotaur had brushed past the leg he'd wounded so severely.

The minotaur hopped up onto the edge of the tank, and a small stone clipped his ankle hard enough to push his foot off its precarious perch. The creature fell into the water with a resounding splash that seemed to contain an odd sizzling noise.

The man on the table quivered, hissed a sharp breath out, and said quietly, "One good a was that."

Abdel looked back in the direction of the stone's flight and saw the short figure a bit more clearly. It was a female orc—not at all attractive, even for an orc—wearing a simple white cotton shift. She was carefully wrapping a small stone in a leather sling. She was an odd sight, but she was good with her chosen weapon.

The minotaur came up out of the water and screamed. The sound was pained and sincere, and it made Abdel turn to face him. Abdel was aware of the sound of the sling whipping through the air, and he turned in time to see the stone launched but not in time to avoid it. The rock hit him square in the groin, and all the air left Abdel's lungs in a ragged burst. He wanted to fall to one knee, but all he could do was stand there.

The battle-axe spun over Abdel's head and came down with a glinting clamor on the stone floor in front of him. Abdel looked down at it, then back up at the orc. Abdel smiled. The orc smiled back, then turned and ran, fast.

Abdel leaned down to get the axe and took a couple shaking steps to the door. He looked in both directions, but there was no sign of either of the orcs.

"Help me," the minotaur gasped behind him.

Abdel turned and saw the minotaur roll out of the tank and fall to the floor with a thud. He was holding the broadsword but made no move to attack. His fur had taken on a curious gray-black hue, and he was shaking uncontrollably, gasping for air on the floor. If Abdel had wanted to kill him, this would be the time.

"Abdel?" a voice behind him asked softly. "Abdel, are you all right?"

The sellsword turned and saw Imoen standing in the doorway, holding a hand to a huge flowering bruise on one side of her face. A simple, rusty short sword she must have taken from an orc hung from her other hand.

"Jaheira?" Abdel asked, his eyes still blurry and painful.

"She'll be all right," the girl said impatiently. "And I'm fine, thank you."

"Please," another voice said. Abdel turned back to the man strapped to the table. In a voice heavily accented and muddy from a swollen tongue, the asylum inmate said, "Now this of out me get someone can?"

Chapter Twelve

Jaheira pressed her hands to her temples and held them there tightly. She'd eventually have to stop taking blows to the head, she knew, or there might be permanent damage. Abdel was next to her, though, and holding her now in his strong arms, so she was already feeling better.

She looked over at the minotaur sitting on the floor in the little room. A chill ran down her spine, and as much as she thought she trusted Mielikki's varied creations until they proved untrustworthy, she was afraid of the huge creature.

"I get knocked out for two minutes," she whispered to Abdel, "and you make a new friend."

The sellsword smiled and said, "Any port in a storm."

Imoen was helping the odd naked man on the table into a sitting position. The man seemed dizzy and more than a little demented.

"We need to get out of here," Imoen told him.

"That we do," Abdel said, looking between the madman and the minotaur. "We don't have to fight, do we?"

"Sir, fight a up put won't I," the madman said.

Abdel looked at him blankly, and Jaheira let out a breath that might have been a tired laugh. Abdel helped her to stand, and she looked at the minotaur.

"The coordinator," she said, "a man named Irenicus, do you know him?"

The minotaur nodded, the gesture obviously reluctant.

"You can speak," Abdel said to the creature.

"Crazy we're thinks he," the madman said to Imoen, a gentle smile on his face. "Me ask you if one crazy the he's."

"I can speak," the minotaur said, ignoring the madman. Imoen gasped at the sound of the creature's gruff voice.

"What is all this about?" Abdel asked simply.

The minotaur grunted and shrugged. "I was made to inhabit this place. Your Irenicus had plans for this labyrinth beyond peopling it with the addled of your kind."

"But he's gone?" Jaheira asked the huge bull-man. "He's fled this place?"

The minotaur nodded.

"His of woman vampire that with Underdark the into went he," the madman mumbled, nodding.

"Vampire?" Imoen asked him. "Did you say vampire?"

"He went into the Underdark with that vampire woman of his," Jaheira translated. "Why?"

"Does it matter?" Abdel asked, not expecting an answer. "Good riddance. He belongs down there."

"His plans are for Suldanessellar," the minotaur said, and it was Jaheira's turn to gasp.

"Well as say I riddance good," the madman said, laying back down on the table. "Fed been have should they way the eels the fed never he."

"Suldanessellar?" Jaheira asked. The minotaur nodded, and she said, "That can't be."

"Suldanessellar?" Abdel asked.

"What's that?" asked Imoen.

"Us about care really didn't he like was it," said the madman. "Me with fine just be it'll him kill and him find you if, anyway."

"Suldanessellar is an elven city," Jaheira explained. "It's no surprise you've never heard of it. It's one of Faerûn's best kept secrets. It's the home of some of the few elves who have yet to join the Retreat to Evermeet."

The minotaur nodded, and Abdel asked, "What could that possibly have to do with us?"

"I have no idea," the minotaur said. "You fought with me against the snortsnouts, and I owe you enough to part ways with you peacefully. I've told you all I have to tell."

"We could use your help . . ." Jaheira said to the huge bull-man.

The minotaur nodded, but said, "Your quest is not mine."

"At least tell us how to find them," Jaheira insisted.

"Do we need to?" asked Imoen. She turned a questioning gaze on Abdel.

The big sellsword sighed and said, "I guess we do. We can't let this go on. I owe him one for that ritual anyway and for the odd kidnapping here and there."

"Easy is down way the," offered the madman, who was busy replacing the copper band on his head. "It over hanging skull a with door a to come you until turns left three first the take and right the to corridor the follow just."

"Are you getting this?" Abdel asked Jaheira. The druid nodded, listening intently to the madman's directions.

"One that want don't you," he continued. "It over nailed bat dead the with door the through go and that by pass. Ramp a to lead that'll."

"You know what?" Imoen said. "This isn't making me feel better."

"Right the on door third the find and, goes it as far as down that take," the madman went on. "Down way long a be it'll."

"I can image," Imoen quipped, and Abdel shot her a stern look, which she ignored.

"Underdark the to get you when," the madman concluded, "It know you'll."

"One question," Imoen said, looking directly at Jaheira. "Is this Suldanessellar place worth it?"

"I spent time there," Jaheira said. "I learned to be a druid there."

"I'll take that as a y—"

Imoen was cut off when the madman yelped and seemed to hop up off the table.

"Imoen!" Abdel shouted in warning, but the girl was already in the process of jumping backward.

The madman hadn't jumped off the table—he'd been pulled off. Ropelike tentacles covered in a viscous slime hung from the ceiling and wrapped themselves around the suddenly stiff, unmoving inmate. Abdel, Jaheira, Imoen, and the minotaur all looked up at once and saw the source of the tentacles. The minotaur growled something in some guttural language.

Hanging from the ceiling, upside down over the madman's table, was a huge wormlike beast made of fleshy, spherical sacks. Its head was shaped like an onion, and from it sprouted a blossom of tentacles.

"What in all Nine Hells is that?" Imoen said, stepping quickly backward to get out from under the thing.

"Carrion crawler," Abdel, Jaheira, and the minotaur all answered simultaneously.

Abdel was surprised by, of all things, the height of the ceiling. Thinking back, the minotaur had jumped over him. The creature was eight feet tall, and Abdel seven, so the ceiling must have been far above them. He could see a hole in the wall near one corner of the gloomy ceiling where the giant beast had obviously come through. He'd heard of these things. They scoured the deepest caverns and dungeons cleaning up the remains of dead carcasses and the aftereffects of battles. This one had obviously mistaken the madman for a casualty.

"Me," the madman grunted, his jaw tightening around the words, "help."

The minotaur jumped onto the table and brought its battle-axe around in a long overhand arc. One of the tentacles dropped onto the table with a wet smack, and the minotaur deftly avoided being splashed with any of the paralyzing poison that coated it. The carrion crawler let out a hiss and withdrew into the dark opening near the ceiling, dragging the paralyzed madman in with it.

"I won't need your help," the minotaur said. "Go on about your quest."

The bull-man didn't wait to see if Abdel and the women complied. It jumped up, grabbed the edge of the opening with one hand and was through it before Abdel could even get to the table.

Jaheira stopped him from following with a hand on his arm. "Suldanessellar," she said. "Irenicus."

Abdel looked at her and nodded, then looked once more at the dark opening, and said, "You understood those backward directions?"

"I didn't," Imoen admitted.

"I think so," answered Jaheira.

"Then let's go," said Abdel.

Chapter Thirteen

The creatures intended to eat them alive, Abdel knew that much for sure. What he didn't know was what exactly they were or how he was going to kill them.

"What are these things?" Imoen shrieked. "And how are we going to kill them?"

The girl nimbly climbed to the top of a smooth stalagmite, deftly avoiding the snapping jaws of the bizarre beast that was chasing her.

Abdel was only paying marginal attention to Imoen's predicament. He was in one of his own. One of the creatures lunged at him, and Abdel dodged to the left, bringing his hand up fast and catching the monster under its snapping bottom jaw and pushing it away before it could bite his face off.

The monsters had come upon them during one of their short, infrequent rest stops as they continued to follow the winding, seemingly endless tunnel deep underground. The things looked like snakes or thick-bodied worms, but to all appearances they were made of stone. Their odd skin was hard—Abdel's broadsword barely chipped at them the few times he'd managed a successful strike—and had the color and texture of the surrounding rock. Though they moved in a snakelike undulation, they appeared to get most of their mobility from two vaguely humanlike arms that sprouted from their serpentine bodies just past their nublike heads. Cold black eyes—two of them—gleamed in the light of Imoen's makeshift torch. Below the eyes was a proportionately huge mouth lined with triangular teeth. Abdel could tell by the way the light glinted off those fangs that they were razor sharp.

Jaheira's voice echoed loudly through the cavern. Abdel understood only the occasional word. He glanced at her as he spun around to toss the rockworm away from him, and he could see her standing still, eyes closed, chanting what must have been some prayer to her goddess. Abdel turned away from her just in time to see the creature snap at his heels. He jumped up fast enough to avoid it but came down on the thing's rounded form. His foot slipped off, and he splayed his arms out to break his fall. The monster twitched away as Abdel hit the stone floor. His ears rang, and he wasn't sure if Jaheira had stopped praying or he'd gone deaf.

He looked up, and Jaheira had opened her eyes. Another of the monsters snapped at her, and she twitched away. There was something about the movement that looked wrong to Abdel. Jaheira moved just a little faster than he'd known her capable of in the past, and the monster seemed to move more slowly than his companions. Abdel didn't have time to mull over this strange feeling. His own monstrous opponent was coming at him again.

Abdel rolled to the right, and the thing shot past him as if it were suddenly struck blind. Abdel smiled at the thing's show of weakness and hit it hard on the top of its head with the pommel of his sword. The thing let out a shrill whistle that Abdel instinctively knew was a sign of pain. He took advantage of this opportunity and jumped onto its back. The thing was as long as Abdel was tall, and when the sellsword wrapped a strong arm around it, he could feel no warmth. The thing was actually made of living stone.

There was a pained, all-too-human scream from behind him that sent a chill down Abdel's spine. One of his companions had fallen. The scream had an edge of panic in it that Abdel recognized all too well. Whoever it was was sure she was dead.

"Imoen!" Jaheira screamed, then grunted when the worm she was still just trying to avoid lunged at her again and almost found its mark.

Abdel dragged the blade of his broadsword across the rockworm's eyes and was happy to see them burst open and pour out a dark gray, watery putrescence. A sharp, tangy smell pervaded the tunnel, and the thing convulsed hard once in Abdel's grip. He let it buck him off and made use of the momentum to get some distance from the thing. He hit a warm, wet spot on the floor and slid a bit farther than he wanted, but he recovered in time to see the thing blindly lunge at him. Abdel fed the creature the length of his blade and was satisfied when the shower of charcoal blood was followed by the rockworm's final death spasm.

"Abdel!" Jaheira called sharply. "Mine!"

The sellsword burst to his feet, yanking the sword out of the dead creature's gullet and turning in the direction of Jaheira's voice. She was backing away, nimbly dodging the rockworm's leaden strikes. Abdel rushed it and slashed with a backhand motion in an effort to take its head off. The worm twisted, anticipating the attack, but didn't move fast enough to avoid it. The prayer Jaheira had offered up was the obvious source of this welcome advantage.

Abdel's sword lodged into the rocky flesh of the creature's bottom jaw. It too shrieked in pain, and Abdel grunted, smiling, as he sawed into the thick hide. The rockworm's lower jaw came off with a pop and a torrent of gray fluid.

It tossed its head back and to the side, and Abdel, overextended for the cut, couldn't get out of the way in time. The thing's bleeding head smashed into Abdel's broad chest and knocked him back hard.

Abdel, dazed, looked up and saw nothing but a dim yellow haze. Something seemed to pop in his chest and a wave of pain shook his body.

"Imoen," Jaheira said quietly, her voice quavering with concern.

Abdel stood, his vision starting to come back, and stepped over the twitching, jawless rockworm as it finished dying. He ran and stumbled at the same time to Jaheira's side, coming around a stalagmite. He could hear more of the rockworms skittering in the darkness.

Next to the base of the stone column, Imoen was lying, gasping for breath like a drowning woman. Jaheira knelt over her and began praying. She held the tiny rock she always kept close to her in one hand, and her other hand slid deftly across the wound, smearing bubbling crimson blood over Imoen's shredded chest.

"By the black gods," Abdel muttered, "she's been . . . half . . . eaten."

Imoen's eyes stared up at the darkness above them in mute, twitching agony. Jaheira's voice lifted in a songlike prayer, and Abdel thought he could see a thin, blue-gray glow around the fingers of the hand she now pressed hard into the wound. Another wave of pain made him stagger backward. Jaheira didn't look up at him. He stepped back, then fell back and rolled away from the women. In the darkness no more than a few paces from him, rockworms began to gather.

* * * * *

Jaheira pulled her hand up suddenly with a shouted last word and her prayer was over, Imoen pulled in one rattling, deep breath and made to sit up. Jaheira, her hand covered in the girl's blood, gently pushed her back down.

"You'll need to rest," Jaheira told her.

Imoen rested her head on a smooth stone and smiled. Jaheira returned her smile, then looked at Abdel and said, "We'll have to stay here for at least a few hours," she said, "but by Mielikki's never-ending grace, she'll . . . Abdel?"

She spun, realizing in a wave of nauseous dread that she'd lost sight of him in the darkness.

"Abdel?" she called again.

She was answered by an inhuman roar that echoed deafeningly in the confines of the cavern and made the half-elf throw her hands up to her gently pointed ears to keep them from bursting.

"Abdel!" Jaheira screamed, her voice drowned out not only by the ringing in her ears but by the clatter of rockworms—all around her—moving in fast for the kill.

She saw Imoen mouth, "It's happening again."

* * * * *

Everything that was the essence of Abdel Adrian disappeared into a roiling vortex of rage, bloodlust, and wild, kill-frenzied mania. His body contorted—he could feel that, and it hurt. He was changing again. He didn't know exactly what was happening to him, how it was happening to him, or why it was happening to him. He could feel it and experience it only for the first few

119

moments, then any greater consciousness was replaced by the pure murderous impulses of the Bhaalspawned demon he had become.

He could see the rockworms clearly now when all there had been before was darkness. His perspective had shifted decidedly upward, though he didn't have the capacity to understand why. He grabbed for one of the creatures, all thoughts of something as puny and ineffectual as a broadsword forgotten, and held it easily in one huge, firm grip. When he squeezed he could feel the rocklike skin puncture, and the thing's blood bathed him. He roared in idiot pleasure and turned his attention to another rockworm, then another.

He tore through their stony bodies as if they were made of tissue paper. When some of them turned to flee in the face of prey that had turned predator, the Abdel-thing moved quickly behind them. He grabbed one by the tip of its tail and spun it into the others. The rockworms started biting at him, but their teeth just tickled around the edges of what used to be his thighs but were now closer to his ankles.

He killed them for the pure joy of it and let not one single rockworm escape alive.

When the last one lay twitching at his transformed feet, pouring its charcoal blood onto the cold floor of the cavern, Abdel screamed again.

This time, his voice sounded more like his own, real, human voice, and his body convulsed through a single body-tightening cramp that made his vision blur and flash yellow again. He fell to the floor of the cavern, and his eyes cleared enough to see his hand, and it was starting to look human again. He tried to call out for Jaheira, but his throat was tightening, changing back to something with human vocal chords. He sputtered a ragged cough.

"Abdel!" he heard Jaheira call, her voice echoing from quite a distance.

He looked up, and with tears streaming down his face, he saw the dull blotch of Imoen's torchlight. It took him several minutes to stand on shaking, cramping legs, but he eventually made his way back to the light.

* * * * *

Worms made of rock, giant beetles, and the things that looked like stalactites that occasionally tried to drop on them from the ceiling of the tunnel aside, Abdel couldn't imagine how any thinking being was able to live in the Underdark. There was no passage of time, save for the rhythmic drips of water or the occasional fall of pebbles. Abdel had no idea how long they'd been down there. They'd made torches from the hard stalks of giant mushrooms and scraps from their own dwindling clothes. They would stop to rest and occasionally sleep. As soon as one of them awakened, he or she would rouse the others, and they'd start moving again. It was a blind existence, and the toll it took on all of them was intense.

The nature-worshiping Jaheira just seemed tired all the time. She prayed to Mielikki, and her prayers were answered, though it was an unlikely place to feel the touch of the Lady of the Forest. Still, Jaheira was as moody and quiet as Abdel, and though they walked side by side for mile after endless mile, they hardly spoke.

Imoen was as uncomfortable underground as any surface dweller. Even before she was nearly killed by the rockworm, she was always looking over her shoulder, sensitive to every random noise or shift in the cool subterranean breeze.

They rested again, and Imoen, who had been able to

walk only with the help of either Abdel or Jaheira, had
fallen into a deep sleep. Jaheira gathered mushrooms.
Only she had some idea which might be edible and
which deadly poison. Abdel scoured the area for signs
of the rockworms or any other unpleasant denizens of
the Underdark. He saw a few pinpoint reflections in
the darkness. Abdel took them to be the eyes of the
ever-present rats that always kept out of the pool of
torchlight. He took some odd comfort from the presence
of the furry scavengers. Rats he knew what to do with.

When he came back to the big stalagmite Jaheira
had told them not to move Imoen away from, he saw
that the half-elf had collected a good sampling of the
native fungus. Abdel grimaced at the collection of gray
mushrooms and thought for the hundredth time about
trying to kill one of the big rats. Jaheira held a mushroom out to him with a weary but understanding smile,
and he waved it off.

"I can't live on those damned things much longer," he
told her.

She shrugged, took a bite of the mushroom, and
chewed it with an uninterested expression.

"That necromancer—or whatever he is—did something to me," Abdel said. "I'd be happy to let him go
wherever he's going in peace—at least if it meant I
could climb out of this hole once and for all—but he—"

"He has plans for you," Jaheira told him with obvious certainty. "He must have plans for you both. If he's
going to attack Suldanessellar for some reason, maybe
he intends to use you as a kind of weapon."

"But you said he couldn't control us, me and Imoen,"
Abdel said, nodding at the sleeping girl. "What does he
mean to do . . . get me to go there, then get me angry?
Let me ravage the place in the form of some . . . whatever it is?"

Jaheira shrugged, her face a dark mask of fear. "That could be enough." She shuddered visibly and added, "You couldn't believe what . . ."

Abdel forced a smile and said, "My father's legacy again, I guess."

Jaheira nodded.

Abdel sighed and took a reluctant bite from a mushroom. "Why Imoen?" he asked. "And how? If this . . . thing, this force or whatever it is, is in me already, I guess I have to understand and believe that, knowing what I know about myself, but Imoen?"

"You may have to accept that Imoen shares that blood with you, Abdel," Jaheira said quietly.

Abdel sighed. It was an easy enough connection. If the monks of Candlekeep had brought one of the offspring of Bhaal into their midst to watch over him, why not another? Why not a daughter? Winthrop was no more Imoen's father than Gorion was Abdel's.

"You never told me how you found us," Jaheira said. "How did you know to come to that madhouse?"

"It was Bodhi . . ." Abdel blushed and turned away. He hadn't considered . . . but that had just been a dream, hadn't it? He hadn't really touched Bodhi that way, been touched that way by . . .

Jaheira looked as if she was going to say something, but Abdel looked at her in such a way that made her keep quiet. Jaheira could see that Abdel was thinking deeply about something. He could see her recognize this, and her face changed, softened somehow even as the corners of her mouth drew down.

"Vampires have certain powers, Abdel," she said. He shook his head in answer, but she continued, "You weren't necessarily—"

"Stop," he said, too loudly. "Please."

"We should take advantage of Imoen's need for rest,"

she said, not looking at him, "and rest ourselves."

Abdel nodded, but neither he nor Jaheira moved for a long time.

Chapter Fourteen

"Your skin," Bodhi said, her eyes sliding slowly along the drow's lithe body, "it's so . . . May I touch you?"

The drow woman smiled and shrugged. Bodhi brushed the back of one finger against the drow's cheek, and the woman leaned into the touch, smiling. Bodhi recognized the subtext of that smile. She'd offered it herself in the past, usually right before she made a vampiric thrall out of someone.

"Satisfied?" the drow Phaere asked playfully.

"No," Bodhi replied, taking her hand away, "but there are other . . . priorities tonight."

"Is it night?" Phaere asked playfully, lightly, but with the understanding that something terrible could happen any second.

"Force of habit," Bodhi admitted. "My apologies."

The drow woman crossed the dimly lit chamber, her slippered feet whispering on the fine spidersilk rug. She uncorked a decanter of wine, picked up a glass and tipped it toward Bodhi, who only shook her head.

"You're not afraid of me," Bodhi said.

"Should I be?"

"I'm a vampire," Bodhi said directly. "That unsettles people."

Phaere laughed, the sound tickling Bodhi's ears in a way that was at once pleasurable and disturbing. "I'm not 'people,' Bodhi. I am drow."

"You say that like you're the only drow."

"And you speak as if you're the only vampire."

Bodhi nodded in conciliation and sat in a deep arm-chair upholstered in a strange, soft leather. She touched the leather in the same way she'd touched the drow's ink-black skin.

"Halfling," the drow offered. "Very expensive."

Bodhi knew she'd passed another not-so-subtle test by not recoiling from the fabric.

"You have the pieces of the lanthorn," Phaere said, changing the subject.

Bodhi nodded and said, "My brother will hold up his end of the bargain as long as you do."

"I'm drow," Phaere said. "We're all about bargains. I'm a decoy, aren't I?"

Bodhi laughed and nodded, shrugged, and said, "And you'll get what you want in the process, Phaere."

The drow smiled, her violet eyes twinkling.

"I like it here," Bodhi said, her eyes caressing the richly appointed room, lingering on the tall window over-looking the subterranean city. "The sun never shines here."

"Vampire paradise," Phaere murmured.

"Drow paradise," Bodhi replied.

Phaere looked at her sharply and said, "We weren't always down here."

Bodhi returned the drow's stare and said, "You'll get what you were promised if you do what you have promised."

"The mythal," Phaere said.

"Power," Bodhi concurred. "Enough to destroy your mother, yes?"

Phaere smiled and turned away. "I won't expect you to understand the subtleties at work. It's not just matricide."

"Of course not," Bodhi said quietly, though she knew that's exactly all it was.

* * * * *

It started with mist.

They'd been underground for some unmeasurable length of time and had fallen into a sort of routine, the three of them. The Underdark held certain surprises, but each was dealt with in turn. They persevered and continued on. They found traces of Irenicus and someone else at odd intervals—enough so they knew they were on the right track.

The mist, at first, was just the next oddity in the long string of oddities that defined their adventures in the Underdark. The mist was cool, not too thick, and didn't even really seem unnatural. It wasn't too hard for Abdel to believe that even the Underdark could have its variations of weather.

They continued on, maybe a little more cautiously. The three of them tried to keep closer together so as not to become separated in the mist.

"I find it hard to believe," Imoen said, "that this is just some random thing."

She'd recovered from her nearly deadly wound but not completely. Her face was drained of color, maybe a bit gaunt. She seemed gray and was tired almost all the time. Jaheira prayed over her, and it helped a little but always fell short of what might constitute a "cure."

"I have to admit," Jaheira replied, "that this is a little out of my field of expertise, but I don't think we have to panic."

Abdel drew his broadsword and smiled. "I'll try not to panic, but if something's using this mist for cover . . ."

"It can be dangerous down here," an unfamiliar voice echoed out of the mist.

Abdel stopped, planting his feet, ready for anything, even though the voice was obviously a young woman's and not terribly threatening on its surface.

"Over there," Imoen said and pointed into the swirling heart of the mist.

It was a girl in her late teens. She was pretty and blonde, with features so perfect she looked like some Netherese statue—the kind people said were actually petrified slaves made perfect by magic, then frozen as stone for all time. She was dressed in a simple white silk toga, and a fine silver chain wove through her almost white hair. Her eyes were crystal blue and glistened in the feeble torchlight.

"You don't have to be afraid of me," she said. "My name is Adalon."

"I'm not afraid of you," Abdel told her, "but I find it hard to believe that a girl like you could just happen to be wandering around down here alone, cloaked in mist, casually strolling through the Underdark like—"

She cut him off with a laugh that implied a wisdom greater than her age. "Not much gets by you, does it Abdel Adrian, Son of Bhaal, Savior of Baldur's Gate?"

"Why do people keep calling me that?" Abdel asked. It was his way of asking how she could possibly know him.

"You work with Irenicus," Imoen assumed aloud.

A look of impatience crossed Adalon's pretty features for half a heartbeat, then she smiled and said, "Not in a million years, Imoen."

"But you know us," Jaheira said. "You're here waiting for us. Tell us what you want."

"I want to help you," she said.

Abdel sighed and stepped closer to her, his sword

still in his hand. She didn't seem the least bit afraid of him.

"We're not even sure how to help ourselves," he said. "Who or what are you, and what do you want with us? What does Irenicus want with us?"

A flash of yellow light passed in front of his eyes, and somehow the girl seemed to notice it.

"Calm yourself, Abdel," Adalon said. "He's changed you. He's brought out what was inside of you—what you, with Jaheira's help, have managed to keep deep inside of you. Your father's blood powers his avatar, and you will lose yourself to it if you let yourself."

"Why?" Jaheira asked.

"You'll have to ask Irenicus that," the girl said. "I'm sure you'll get a chance—Abdel will at least—soon enough. Irenicus has designs against Suldanessellar, and I've been a friend of Suldanessellar for a long time. I don't want to see harm come to them. I can help you help them, help you help yourselves, help you get to Irenicus. If he gets what he wants, Abdel will lose his soul, and Imoen will waste away to nothing, Suldanessellar will lay in ruin, and Irenicus will be immortal. That's not a world I'd like to live in."

"What are you?" Imoen asked.

"If I told you I was a dragon," the girl said, addressing Imoen with a soft tilt of her head, "would you believe me?"

Imoen let out a breath but didn't look away. "I stopped choosing what to believe in a while ago, thank you."

"What do you want in return?" Abdel interjected. If there was one constant in his dealings with people, elves, dragons, sons of dead gods—whoever—it was what Gorion used to call *quid pro quo*.

"The drow of Ust Natha have stolen my eggs," Adalon said. "I want them back."

Abdel sighed and took a step back from her. "This is madness. This is all madness."

"Eggs?" Jaheira asked. "You have . . . eggs?"

"So I could tell you I was a dragon, and you wouldn't believe me, druid?" Adalon asked, a wry smile playing at the sides of her lips. "Come back this way, where there's more room."

With that the girl turned away and slipped behind an outcropping of rock, disappearing from view. Jaheira made to follow her, but Abdel held out a hand to stop her.

"Please tell me you're not going with her," he said. "If this isn't a trap, I'm—"

"Give it a rest, Abdel," Imoen said wearily, passing them both and following the mysterious girl.

Jaheira offered Abdel a defeated smile and slipped past his hand. From around the corner there was a sound like leather being scraped against stone, but the sound was loud enough that it might have been a whole army clad in leather armor crawling across the floor.

"You're going to walk into a dragon's lair," Abdel said to Jaheira's receding back, "at the very least."

"And if I wanted to kill you, Son of Bhaal," Adalon's voice rumbled from around the corner, "you'd be dead already." Her voice was louder, deeper—the same but somehow larger.

Abdel followed Imoen and Jaheira. As he came around the outcropping, he almost ran into Jaheira's back. Before he could say anything, he looked up and saw the reason the half-elf had come to such a complete stop.

To say that the dragon was the biggest living thing Abdel had ever seen would have been a tragic understatement. He'd seen smaller castles.

The thing's body reflected Imoen's torchlight a thousandfold. Her skin was silver, polished to a high sheen, rippling with muscles and tightly woven scales. The palpable sense of power that washed out from the thing effectively paralyzed all three of the tiny little people who stood before her. Adalon was a creature of godlike beauty.

"You will save Suldanessellar," her voice washed through the cavern from a throat eight times as long as Abdel was tall. "I will give you the way into Ust Natha. You will find my eggs and return them to me. You will defeat the plans of Irenicus there and stop the drow army from invading the glens of Tethir. You will return to me, and I will lead you out of this godsforsaken hole in the ground. You will confront Irenicus and regain your soul from him if it leads you to Hell. You know you never had any choice, Abdel Adrian, Son of Bhaal, Pawn of Evil, Tool of Good."

"I know," Abdel whispered. "I know."

The dragon reared up, and all three of them stepped back instinctively.

"You won't get into Ust Natha looking like that," the dragon said.

The massive creature intoned a string of unintelligible syllables, and Abdel's arms twitched with the desire to attack the thing before whatever spell it was casting managed to burn him to cinders. At the end of the string of arcane words, the dragon waved a huge silver-taloned claw over their heads, and Abdel felt his skin crawl. The sensation was more than a little unsettling.

He looked down at himself expecting to see insects covering his skin, but what he saw was actually more disturbing than that. His skin had turned the color of obsidian. He looked over at Jaheira, who was looking at her own arms. She'd turned black too, and her ears, once gently pointed, were now needle-sharp on top. Her hair had turned white and her eyes violet. Imoen was

131

Philip Athans

looking down her own shirt, her brow wrinkled and black as night.

"That's . . ." Imoen said. "That's just . . ."

"You'll look like drow, sound like drow, be able to understand the language of the drow," the dragon said confidently (she said everything confidently). "You'll have access to the city . . . but only for a short time. The spell will wear off in—"

"This is so bad," Abdel said. "This is insane. We all belong back in that madhouse."

"Abdel . . ." Jaheira said, a warning tone in her voice.

Abdel sighed, thought for a second about being quiet, going along with the whole thing as Jaheira obviously wanted him to do.

"No," he said, turning his back on the dragon, "this is ridiculous. Why would we ever do this? We're going to just stroll into a drow city . . . a *drow* city . . . because we happen to run into a dragon who tells us we should, so we can defeat the plans of someone who, as far as we're concerned, has already been defeated. We're together. I got what I wanted. So this Irenicus is going to attack some elf town I'm not welcome in anyway. That sounds more like their problem than mine."

"Abdel," Jaheira said, her voice impatient but gentle, "I know you don't really believe that. You can't let Irenicus have his way with innocent people."

"And what about all this Bhaal stuff?" Imoen asked. "You think it's all right that we just sort of turn into mindless murdering monsters from time to time?"

"There is very little time for—" the dragon started.

"So you think he's going to just reverse that if we find him?" Abdel asked. "He probably wouldn't even know how to if we could somehow convince him to do it. I'm not even convinced it was any of his doing. My

132

blood has betrayed me in more ways than that, with very little outside help."

Abdel turned on Jaheira and said, "You wanted me to change, so I've changed. Now you want me to go off on a mission of vengeance. We follow Irenicus to this elf town, then what? Kill him? Ask him to reverse that ritual? Beg him to?"

"I'll be more than happy to kill him," Imoen offered, "if you don't want to."

Abdel crouched and put his head in his hands. "So let's kill him, but do we have to—"

He didn't see the dragon pull in a deep, full breath, but he stopped talking when a blast of freezing cold air actually picked him up and blew him off his feet. There was a series of screams from deeper in the cavern. Abdel rolled to his feet, bits of white frost falling off him like snowflakes. He spun in the direction of the screams and saw half a dozen figures quite literally frozen in place, ice hanging from them and pieces of them already snapping off under their own weight. Behind them, another half dozen figures scattered among the stalactites. The torchlight was dim, but it didn't take Abdel more than a second to realize the figures were drow.

Chapter Fifteen

Abdel had seen hundreds of people killed in hundreds of ways, but seeing the silver dragon Adalon rage through the drow was unlike anything he'd ever imagined.

The enormous creature moved forward as fast as a lizard a thousandth its size. She shattered the six frozen drow on her way through, and Abdel could only jump aside and get out of her way.

The sound of crossbows firing echoed through the cavern, and Abdel thought he saw at least one thin quarrel skip off one of Adalon's shining silver scales, but the dragon didn't flinch in the slightest. He heard a number of swords drawn, and that reminded him to draw his own. Seeing the coal black color of his skin as it passed across his face made him pause.

Adalon picked up one drow warrior—a man in glittering chain mail—and squeezed so hard his eyes popped out before he died a bloody, bone-shattered wreck. Adalon tossed him to the floor of the cavern in a splatter of gore that made one of his companions leap aside.

Something like a fireball or some other kind of obviously magical fire exploded near the dragon's head, but she just brushed it off and flicked aside the drow who'd cast the spell. The impotent mage hit the wall of the cavern hard enough to crack his head like an egg.

Abdel looked up into the crowd of quickly scattering drow and saw one of them turn from the dragon. The drow made eye contact with Abdel, and Abdel turned toward the passing foot of the great dragon to make as if to slash at it as it passed him. Something told Abdel he wouldn't have cut through the thing's silver scales anyway, but the illusion seemed to work. When he glanced back at the drow, he was nodding as he turned to run.

A couple of drow warriors made to run with him, but he pushed them back at the dragon and dived behind an outcropping of rock. The dragon's freezing breath descended on the drow warriors in roiling waves of glittering frost and froze them both in mid scream. They were made so cold that when the dragon whipped her tail around it shattered them on contact as if they were made of blown glass.

Go! A voice boomed in Abdel's head—it was Adalon's voice. *The three of you must go—you do not have that much time. Find that drow, the leader, and go back to Ust Natha with him. Go!*

Jaheira grabbed Abdel by the arm, and though he knew it was her, he was still startled by her appearance. She was a dark elf in every way now, as was he, as was Imoen.

* * * * *

"We were the advance party," Abdel said, assuming that if it didn't work, he'd probably still be able to kill the lone drow.

The dark elf nodded and sighed, sitting down on the rough stone floor of the dark cavern like a half-empty sack of grain. Abdel looked over at Jaheira, who was looking back at him with barely disguised wonder. He

knew he'd never have the heart to tell her the ruse was
a wild stab in the dark.

The drow folded his legs into a position that looked
painful to Abdel. A sigh escaped the dark elf's lips—
more a slow, steady exhale. His eyes were closed, and it
was obvious that he was not only trying to calm himself, but succeeding.

"Who's in charge?" the dark elf asked, opening his
eyes and looking directly at Jaheira.

The druid glanced at Abdel, and the drow followed
her gaze. His brow wrinkled, and he seemed confused.
Abdel was about to claim leadership of the party but
realized the drow was finding that unusual for some
reason. Abdel looked at Imoen and tilted his head.
They'd known each other long enough, and Abdel knew
she had a dramatic streak to her that would pick up on
what was passing between them and their reluctant
new friend.

"I am," Imoen said, her voice regal in her new skin.

The drow nodded and said, "I am Solausein, second
to Phaere."

Imoen had no idea how to respond, so she just
nodded.

"I was sent to kill the dragon," Solausein said.

Imoen glanced at Abdel, then said, "We were sent to
offer it one more bargain."

Abdel couldn't help but feel a twinge of pride. Imoen
could really think on her feet.

"Well," the drow said, "with all due respect, it seems
Phaere assumed you would fail."

"Did she assume you would too?" Imoen said with a
tilt of one eyebrow.

The drow looked up at her sharply but quickly
looked away. His legs unfolded, and he stood in a single
fluid motion. Abdel had to work hard to keep from

drawing his sword. Solausein didn't attack, though. His eyes stayed fixed on the ground, and he turned away from them.

"We should return to Ust Natha," he said, not looking at them.

Imoen smirked at Abdel and said to the drow's back, "You take point."

* * * * *

"All this for a diversionary tactic," Phaere said, staring up at the tall archway of the completed gate. "I will say one thing for you humans, you do think big."

Bodhi regarded her coldly and said, "I haven't been human for a long time, young matron."

Phaere turned to the vampire and smiled, letting her eyes slowly crawl up Bodhi's tight, leather-clad body.

"I stand corrected," she said.

Bodhi let the drow woman look at her. The vampire turned her attention to the gate. It was huge—easily big enough to march an army through. Now it was just a plain stone archway, but it still gave off a feeling of power, of magical energy Bodhi could feel from a distance. When it was activated by the dozen drow mages standing by, it would open an enchanted pathway through space and time onto the surface, and into a place Bodhi could never have walked into, let alone a drow strike regiment.

"And it will work," Bodhi said, making sure it sounded more like a warning than a question.

Phaere was still staring at Bodhi when she said, "It will work." The drow turned away finally and shouted a name.

Bodhi's sensitive ears picked up the hissing whispers of the dozen mages, and something told her to turn away from the gate. There was a flash of light that would have been painful to her dark-accustomed eyes. Phaere was holding a hand over her own eyes. When Bodhi turned back to the gate, it was like looking at a rippling pool that was somehow standing perpendicular to the ground. Where she'd been able to see the rounded roofs and tower tops of the drow city of Ust Natha through the archway, now there was only a blue-violet shimmering. There was an audible hum.

"You said you wanted to see it work," Phaere said.

Bodhi smiled at her. "And your army is prepared," the vampire said, again more a warning than a question.

"As much of an army as we'll require, yes," Phaere replied. "This elf city of yours is more like a village. My distant cousins—" and she said the word "cousins" with no small amount of contempt—"have mostly fled to their precious Evermeet. It shouldn't be too difficult to overwhelm them. It's not something they're expecting after all. We don't send armies to the surface. Ever."

"Indeed," Bodhi said, still studying the wall of magic in front of her. "That is precisely what we're counting on. They need to be surprised and . . . occupied, so we can do what we need to do."

"I won't bother asking exactly what that might be," Phaere said, "and I don't really care after all, do I? If I get the mythal, you can have your way with Suldanessellar."

Bodhi nodded and said, "You'll have your mythal."

The drow was looking for the elves' magical engine— called a mythal. Bodhi didn't understand exactly what a mythal was. All she needed to know was that Phaere wanted one badly enough that she'd lead a regiment of drow warriors into the forest of Tethir to get one. The fact that Suldanessellar had no mythal and Irenicus had no intention of getting one for her was something Phaere would have to find out the hard way. By the time she did, Irenicus would be done with whatever it was he needed to do, and they'd be long gone, leaving the elves and drow to work out the rest on their own—leaving them to kill each other.

"The people who followed us will be here soon. They've been to see the dragon by now," Bodhi said.

"Amazing," Phaere breathed. "The lengths . . . I lost warriors getting those eggs."

"Well," Bodhi said, taking a step closer to the humming gate, "good for you. When the three of them get here, they'll have to think they've succeeded in getting the eggs back. They'll want to escape the city and bring the eggs to the dragon, who they think will send them to Suldanessellar. I'll have someone here who they'll think is a friend, who'll nudge them in the right direction—through the gate."

"You'll send them back to the dragon?"

Bodhi smirked. "This gate doesn't lead to the dragon, Phaere. It will bring them where *I* want them to go."

"Humans in Ust Natha," Phaere said. "It's not right."

Bodhi ignored the dark elf and said, "Here he is."

The humming of the gate changed timbre for just the slightest moment, and the color shifted away from violet and more toward blue. A small, round-faced man with the features of an elf but the ears of a human stepped tentatively onto the marble tiles of the square in Ust Natha.

"Yoshimo," Bodhi said.

The Kozakuran looked around himself once, his mouth open in awe, and took a moment to find Bodhi.

He smiled weakly and said, "Bodhi, you have most unusual friends."

"People say the same about you," she replied, "I'm sure."

Bodhi stepped forward, and Yoshimo flinched back. This made Phaere laugh and Yoshimo blush.

Bodhi looked at Phaere and said, "Take care of him for me, will you?"

Phaere smirked sourly and nodded. Bodhi stepped through the gate and was gone.

Chapter Sixteen

"Adalon has agreed to your demands . . . ma'am," Imoen said, her voice echoing through the tall-ceilinged chamber in the alien tones of the drow language.

They'd come a long way through the Underdark and into a deeper cavern, following Solausein yet trying to make it look as if they knew where they were going. The pure brashness of the whole thing was enough to fool the already frazzled drow. His failure with the dragon had shamed and shaken him, and the last thing he suspected was a party of human adventurers disguised as drow. To Solausein they were indeed the "advance party."

They'd learned a lot from Solausein on their way, though it was difficult not being able to ask direct questions. If they showed their ignorance of drow ways, or Solausein's mission, their cover would be weakened or even slip away completely. What they knew by the time they reached Ust Natha was that Solausein worked for the daughter of a drow matron (Imoen in particular seemed enamored with the drow's apparently matriarchal society) who was rapidly gaining power in the city. She was the one who took the dragon's eggs, though he did not know quite why.

Still unable to mark time in any reliable way, Abdel had no idea how long it had taken them to get to the city, but once there, it was almost overwhelming. It wasn't the biggest city he'd ever seen, but the fact that it was enclosed in a single enormous cavern made it seem somehow huge out of all proportion.

For their own part, they told Solausein that his young matron wouldn't know them, that they'd been assigned by one of her people. Solausein didn't press them in any way to know who that person might have been. He seemed accustomed to lies, accustomed to knowing only a small part of anything he might be involved in.

Their drow guide had led them through the remarkable city and straight to the compound that served as his matron's residence. There they'd been quickly ushered into this tall-ceilinged room with arched windows overlooking the skyline of Ust Natha. Abdel had to marshal every bit of his willpower to keep from shaking. His nerves were on edge knowing at any moment he'd surely have to defend himself against an entire city full of trained drow warriors, mages, and priests. He'd never been in a situation where he felt so completely at a loss. A dull yellow haze settled over his vision, and he had to just pretend it wasn't there.

Solausein made the introductions—they'd given him hastily contrived aliases out of simple caution—and it was obvious that the young drow woman was interested only in Imoen, who for her part seemed to be reveling in her position of contrived authority the same way she was reveling in her jet black skin.

Solausein obviously assumed the drow woman he introduced as Phaere knew who they all were—they were the advance party after all—so he went into no details. Phaere didn't seem too concerned with who was who and wanted only to know the outcome of the raid against the dragon.

"I'm surprised," Phaere said, eyeing Imoen up and

down with a surprised but favorable eye. "I was almost thinking it would allow its eggs to be destroyed first."

"Apparently, it . . . uh . . ." Imoen started.

"Its mate is dead," Jaheira said, coming to Imoen's rescue. "Those eggs are its only chance to reproduce."

Abdel just kept his eyes down, waiting for things to require him to lead their fighting retreat. He knew it would inevitably come to that. How could they possibly pull off this insanity?

"Well, then," Phaere said, her attention still on Imoen, "that explains more than a few things."

The drow woman turned to Solausein, who would not meet her gaze. "Are these all?" she asked him.

"Mistress Phaere," he said, "I—"

"You left with twenty warriors," Phaere pressed.

"The dragon overwhelmed them," Imoen said.

Her voice was cold enough to send a chill down Abdel's spine. Was she liking this too much? Liking it at all was too much.

Phaere smiled broadly at Imoen and said, "So it did."

"Mistress, I—"

"Will close your stupid, ineffectual mouth," Phaere finished for him. Solausein stepped back one step and kept his eyes fixed on the ground.

"Jaenra," Phaere said, using Imoen's alias and addressing her directly. "I think I'm beginning to remember you now."

Imoen nodded curtly and offered a wry smile. Phaere stepped closer to her—very close—and said, "You will replace the ineffective Solausein in all his duties."

"Yes, mistress," Imoen answered.

"*All* his duties," the drow emphasized.

"Yes," Imoen answered, more slowly this time, looking the drow woman directly in the eyes, "Mistress Phaere."

* * * * *

"She can be . . . difficult," Jaheira said, doing a good job of sounding familiar with the drow mistress.

Solausein took a deep draft of the strange beverage that Abdel thought smelled a little like beer and forced a smile.

"It is to be expected," he said.

Abdel took a third tentative sip of his own beverage and looked around the tavern room again. Drow taverns, if this one was typical, were quiet, serious places full of quiet, serious people with skin the color of the darkest ebony. It was dark, lit sparsely with candles, and the menu consisted of things Abdel could never bring himself to eat. Live spiders . . . he'd rather starve.

Jaheira had quickly picked up on some of Imoen's more successful lies, and Abdel was honestly happy to see that she wasn't nearly as good at it as Imoen was. Solausein was trying to be stoic about what was obviously a tremendous failure, a major demotion that he might never recover from. Having a female there who appeared even a little understanding seemed to make him feel better, and Jaheira was playing it all very carefully.

"Of course," she said, "you can't be too surprised that she would be disappointed."

Solausein nodded and said, "I failed my mistress."

"But to humiliate you like that," Abdel said, "I would have—"

"Tzvin!" Jaheira barked, using Abdel's drow alias.

Abdel worked at being appropriately chastised and looked away.

"Perhaps," Jaheira said to Solausein, "what you need is a change. There are other houses to serve, aren't there?"

Hopefully, Abdel thought, Solausein won't realize that was not a rhetorical question.

Solausein looked at Jaheira—really looked at her for the first time.

"Others have ambitions," she said, staring directly into the drow's eyes with a look that made Abdel instantly and intensely jealous.

"Ja—" he started to say, but stopped himself before he used her real name. He tried but suddenly couldn't remember her peculiar alias, so he said nothing.

Jaheira faked a chastising glare, and Abdel looked away.

Solausein didn't fail to notice the exchange. He looked at Abdel and said, "It is what men are here for, my friend. It is the natural order of things."

"Yes it is," Jaheira said.

Solausein took another long sip of his beverage, and so did Abdel.

"Speak," Jaheira prodded.

"The eggs," Solausein said. "You want the eggs."

* * * * *

Phaere's bedchambers were rather different than anything Imoen would have expected. Of course she'd heard the tales and legends of the drow since she was just a little girl. Always it was about spiders and monsters and cruel tortures. They were always described as a hideous, even malformed race who kept slaves and reveled in hour after hour of continuous bloodshed and thrill killing.

Her actual experience of the drow was rather different.

First of all, they were far from hideous and not the slightest bit malformed. In fact, Imoen found Phaere quite compelling. The drow's skin didn't glow—it did just the opposite. The blackness of it seemed to draw light into it, never to escape. Phaere's face was long and regal with a pronounced chin and cheekbones. Her nose was small and turned gently upward. Her eyes were big, almond-shaped, and a sparkling violet color Imoen couldn't stop staring at. Her white hair smelled as clean as it looked—even from a distance—and it cascaded down her long neck, over her tight shoulders, and down her slim back nearly to her waist.

Her body was hard from long hours of daily training. Phaere was at least two inches shorter than Imoen, but Imoen knew the drow woman could kill her with her bare hands. Imoen was attracted to her ears as well. They were perfectly shaped, symmetrical, and pointed, the tips peeking out from under her hair. Phaere's hands were lithe and smooth. There was no hint of blemish or imperfection on her at all, and the low-cut, backless robe showed enough of her to make that all the more impressive.

Imoen looked at her own hand and marveled at the deep black color.

"I've had a bath run for you," Phaere said, her voice low and intimate now.

Behind her, a thin-framed drow boy scurried about with a huge amphora of warm, scented water.

"Thank you, mistress," Imoen said, keeping her own voice low as well.

Phaere smiled and nodded toward the curtained room just as the last of the amphora-toting boys passed out of it and scurried off into the corridor beyond.

"Please . . ." Phaere said politely. "Bathe, and we can talk."

Imoen nodded and stepped lightly across the marble tiles to the simple beaded curtain. She passed through into a room easily as large as most of the houses she'd ever been in. The center of the room was dominated by an enormous round marble-tiled tub. Steam rose in gentle tendrils from the water into the cool subterranean air. The bath looked so good to Imoen after countless days of travelling and sleeping on gravel, and the thought of washing away the sweat, the blood, and the fluids of this creature and that monster sounded very appealing.

She'd been enjoying the ruse and would never have trouble admitting that she found the drow attractive— she even found herself more attractive as a drow—but she'd still been rather nervous around Phaere. Now, though, all she could think about was the bath. She shed her torn clothes quickly enough, not even thinking to try to explain them and their state to Phaere. They weren't drow clothes.

Phaere sat down on a low marble bench lined with rich cushions. As she sat, she pulled from a concealed pocket in her robe a long, thin wand that seemed to be made from crushed gemstones.

Imoen slid into the tub and let the water wrap around her. She closed her eyes and let out a long, relieved breath.

"It's been a long time?" Phaere asked. Imoen opened her eyes and saw Phaere twirling the wand between two fingers.

"What is that?" Imoen asked.

"Do you mean am I going to kill you with it?" Phaere asked, not looking at her.

Imoen wasn't sure how to answer, so she didn't. The warm, perfect water was like satin on her skin, and it was quickly making her sleepy.

"It's a wand," Phaere said, almost bored. "Lightning bursts from it on my command."

"Impressive," Imoen said, her voice even lower still.

Phaere looked at her and Imoen closed her eyes.

"Tomorrow is an auspicious day," the drow said.

"Is it?" Imoen asked, not even sure why she needed to keep the conversation going.

Phaere stood slowly and stepped toward the bath. "I truly begin my ascent tomorrow," She said. "I mean to replace my mother."

Imoen said nothing, not even sure what Phaere meant.

"That information would be worth a lot to her," Phaere said. "I'd have to kill you if you sold it to her, though, so please don't."

Imoen opened her eyes and regarded Phaere calmly. "I know who my friends are," she said.

"Good," Phaere answered and let her robe slip to the ground. Imoen pulled in a short breath and opened her mouth too speak, but no sound came out.

Phaere, eyes still on Imoen's, stepped into the tub and lowered herself into the water as slowly as Imoen had. The bath was huge enough that a good half dozen yards of warm water separated the two women.

"Do you know what a mythal is?" Phaere asked.

Imoen shook her head, her body suddenly tense.

"In a few days' time I'll have one at my disposal, and all I have to do is march a few hundred of my mother's all-too-expendable soldiers through a gate into some surface-elf forest. How long have they been expecting that? The arrogant fools actually think we're down here with nothing more interesting to occupy our minds than plans for their meaningless downfall."

Imoen closed her eyes again, willing herself to relax, and said, "So why give them their wish?"

"I must have been six the first time my mother told me never to make a deal with a vampire," answered Phaere cryptically.

The word "vampire" gave Imoen a chill, and her

hand came up enough to disturb the water around her.

"Yes," Phaere said, misinterpreting the gesture. "It's not an easy thing to stomach, I assure you, but I'm getting the better end of the bargain. They have some secret weapon—some unsuspecting humans who carry some kind of curse that's supposed to help them. It's typically ham-handed human conniving—transparent and unmotivated amateurs that they are. The vampire even sent some chubby little human to help lure these others in or send them on their way through the gate for some reason. How this little man doesn't realize his mistress plans to kill him immediately afterward, I certainly don't understand. Not that the vampire's any smarter. I'm sure that bloodsucking bitch doesn't even know what a mythal is—has no idea what she's giving up in favor of a diversion."

"Diversion?"

Phaere slipped closer to Imoen in the bath, sending warm waves lapping against the soft underside of Imoen's chin.

"They have some grudge against one of the surface elves," Phaere said, obviously growing bored with the conversation. "I make this elf think the great drow invasion has finally come, and in all the chaos that follows, Bodhi and Irenicus do whatever it is they've set out to do. In exchange, I get power enough to ascend to the highest position in Ust Natha."

"A good bargain," Imoen said.

When Phaere had mentioned Bodhi and Irenicus by name, another chill ran down her spine. When Phaere touched her, a sensation of an entirely different nature followed.

* * * * *

Abdel was worried about Imoen. She was surprisingly good at pretending to be someone she wasn't, but Abdel realized that every second they spent in Ust Natha brought them closer to being found out. Not to mention the fact that the dragon had warned them that they didn't have much time. If the spell wore off and they were revealed to be human, suddenly couldn't even speak the language, they'd be in serious—very serious—trouble.

Jaheira was getting better at the ruse herself, but she wasn't as good as Imoen. Abdel watched her carefully and took some consolation in the fact that Solausein took his odd behavior to be simple jealousy. The drow thought Jaheira was doing to Abdel what Phaere had done to Solausein only hours before. Let him think whatever he wanted, Abdel decided, it had brought them to the eggs.

Getting past the guards was easy enough. Solausein was their captain, and they deferred to him, not daring to question why he might be there or who his unfamiliar companions were. Abdel had done enough of that kind of work to understand the soldiers' point of view. It wasn't so much that they were afraid to ask, they just didn't care.

"Perfect," Jaheira said, standing in front of the row of enormous eggs.

Solausein, maybe a little drunk judging by the sway in his walk, grinned openly at his new mistress's reaction. "As I promised."

"A fortune," Abdel offered, still reluctant to play along.

"Enough to establish my own—" Jaheira said, stopping when she realized the guards could overhear.

Solausein picked up on that right away and barked, "You men, load these things onto the cart outside, and be quick about it—quick but careful. The mistress has need of the eggs elsewhere."

Satisfied easily enough with the order, the guards hopped to. It took two of them to move each of the eggs, and Jaheira, Abdel, and Solausein stood in silence, watching, until they were done.

When the guards finished, Solausein said, "Leave us, there's nothing here to guard."

The drow guards nodded and took full advantage of their opportunity to stop standing around eyeing a bunch of giant dragon eggs by practically falling over each other to leave.

It was all Abdel could do not to follow them. Outside was Solausein's cart, hitched to a lizard three times longer than a horse. The lizard seemed to make a good enough pack animal. It was surefooted in the cavern terrain and strong enough to pull heavy loads. Abdel judged it to be as strong as a team of three, maybe four horses.

"We should be going, mistress," Abdel prodded.

Jaheira turned and said, "Indeed, we need to—"

"They're being moved?" an all-too-familiar voice sounded in the empty room. Abdel, Jaheira, and Solausein turned simultaneously, and Abdel's head spun at the sight of Yoshimo, flanked by two unhappy-looking drow guards, strolling casually into the room. "I was hoping to see these great dragon eggs for myself."

Jaheira said, "Uh—" and turned away.

Abdel tried to do the same thing without being obvious.

"What is this . . . thing doing here?" Solausein asked the guards.

"It's a human, sir," one of the guards reported flatly. "It's a guest of the mistress's."

Abdel caught the look on Yoshimo's face and realized

the Kozakuran didn't understand what was being said.

Abdel's mind reeled. What could Yoshimo possibly be doing here?

He was in league with Irenicus, then . . . it was all starting to make sense. Abdel realized that it really was important to make sure Yoshimo didn't recognize him or Jaheira. So far, it appeared he didn't.

"This man is known to us," Jaheira said to Solausein, and Abdel felt a short wave of panic wash over him. Jaheira had met Yoshimo in Irenicus's prison but didn't know the rest of it. She didn't know what Abdel knew. "He's of use to me," Jaheira continued. "Dismiss the guards."

She turned her back on Yoshimo, and Solausein, without hesitation, said, "You heard the mistress. We'll take it from here."

These guards were a little more reluctant to be relieved of their duty, but they still bowed to Solausein and left the room. Yoshimo plastered an inane grin on his face. He was surprised by this turn of events and even without looking too directly at him, Abdel could tell he was nervous.

"I did not mean to intrude," Yoshimo said.

Abdel didn't want to look at him—didn't want to show any sign that he understood what the Kozakuran was saying.

"I don't understand this human," Solausein said.

"I must beg your pardon, my black-skinned friend," Yoshimo said, "but I am unfamiliar with the tongue of your underground city."

Abdel felt a tingling feeling shudder through his whole body and was surprised—even a little disappointed—by his nervousness.

"Abdel?" Yoshimo asked, quietly, tentatively.

Solausein said something Abdel didn't understand,

and Abdel suddenly realized the feeling wasn't nerves. He wasn't a dark elf any more.

* * * * *

Imoen quivered lightly from fatigue and nervousness as she tiptoed lightly, barefooted, across the cold marble tiles of Phaere's dark bedchamber.

The tub was drained now, and her tattered clothes had been taken away. She wore a luxurious spidersilk robe borrowed from Phaere's extensive closet, and scared as she was, she felt better than she had in—how long? Days? Tendays even? She was clean; they had eaten, relaxed, and grown intimate in a way Imoen was never afforded in the monastery-fortress of Candlekeep. Her mind was a blur of conflicting emotions, but she was realistic enough to know what she had to do. She couldn't stay a dark elf forever, as tempting as that might be.

She found the wand easily enough where Phaere had left it, and slid it into a fold of her robe. She turned halfway around, but stopped when Phaere spoke.

"Another bath?" The drow's voice echoed in the otherwise silent, empty marble-lined room.

Imoen drew in a breath and said, "You startled me."

"Shall I have the boys draw you another bath?" Phaere persisted.

"No," Imoen replied, "no, thank you. I was just . . . just . . ." she made a hopeless gesture with one hand while keeping the robe closed, and the wand secure, with the other.

"Well," Phaere said, apparently understanding what Imoen was trying to say. "I'll leave you to it."

Imoen nodded, and the dark elf paused briefly, maintaining a long, comfortable eye contact Imoen didn't want to release. Phaere finally turned and slipped back into the darkness of the bedchamber.

Imoen's skin crawled, and she was surprised and ashamed of the sensation . . . until she realized that her beautiful black skin was no more.

* * * * *

Abdel punched Solausein in the face so hard the drow's nose shattered in a spray of blood. He went down fast and hard.

"It *is* you!" Yoshimo exclaimed. He seemed legitimately happy to see Abdel and Jaheira. "My friends, am I happy to have found you!"

"Save it, Yoshimo," Jaheira said, surprising Abdel, who was rubbing bruised knuckles. Solausein didn't stir. "What are you doing here of all places?"

"Why, looking for you, of course," the Kozakuran replied.

Abdel had his sword out and at Yoshimo's throat before he could say anything else. "What in the Nine Hells is all this?"

"I can explain all," Yoshimo said, eyeing Abdel's blade with a mixture of fear and haughty offense. "I think we should be leaving this city of drow elves first, though, yes?"

"Easier said than done," Abdel growled. He turned to Jaheira and said, "We wasted too much time."

"I know a way out," Yoshimo said, "but it will take a while to get there from here."

"We have a cart," Jaheira said. She noticed Abdel's perturbed look and told him, "We need to get out of here. If he can get us to the dragon, I honestly don't care why he's doing it."

"He's working for Irenicus," Abdel said. "I should gut him now."

"Oh, my good friend, I have no idea what you're talking about," Yoshimo said weakly. "I have come to help—that is my one desire."

Solausein grumbled, still unconscious, and rolled slightly to one side.

"He's waking up," Jaheira warned. "We need to get out of here."

"I can get you straight to the surface through a most impressive magical gate."

"We're not going to the surface," Abdel said, glancing at Jaheira with a look of resignation.

"We have to give a dragon back its eggs first," Jaheira said.

"After we find Imoen," Abdel corrected.

"Imoen?" Yoshimo asked.

"We came with another woman—a human disguised as a dark elf," said Abdel.

"Ah . . ." Yoshimo said. "She's with Phaere."

"Still?" Jaheira asked, though she didn't expect an answer.

"And the gate will take you to the dragon," the Kozakuran proffered.

"How's that?" asked Abdel, already pushing Yoshimo to the door.

"It was explained to me that you but think of the destination in your mind, and away you go."

"I can't think of anything better, Abdel," Jaheira said quickly, "and we need to get out of here right now."

Abdel smiled, looked at Yoshimo, and said, "Lead the way."

Chapter Seventeen

Phaere was more than a little unhappy. The young woman Jaenra had disappeared at some point during the night, and Phaere found that disrespectful. She had opened herself and her home more quickly and more completely to Jaenra than she'd ever done before, and though Phaere had a rather thick skin, she just couldn't help but take it personally . . . and take it out on someone.

She slapped the mage across the face with a hard, practiced backhand that sent the drow man reeling. The sorcerer hit the marble tiles of the plaza, and a pouch of spell components he wore on his belt burst open, scattering bits of string, crystals, feathers, and live spiders all over the tiles. He looked up at Phaere in horror, fully expecting to be killed.

"Ready!" Phaere shouted at the man. "Complete! Prepared! These words mean nothing to you?"

"The gate is ready, mistress," the mage said quickly, his voice quivering, "You have my word. I—"

She kicked him hard between the legs, and the man doubled over in pain.

"I didn't ask for your word you little—"

She was interrupted by the roar of a pack lizard rumbling across the plaza floor. She turned and saw something that made her blink several times before she could believe it.

The pack lizard was pulling an open cart onto which the silver dragon eggs were lashed. The cart was being driven by humans, their pale skin positively glowing in the ambient light of the plaza gate. One of them looked familiar—the big one, but how could he? There was a half-elf woman—Phaere had never seen a real half-elf before. She was underwhelmed.

This was Bodhi's crew, though Phaere thought there was supposed to be three of them. She counted two, plus the round-faced human Bodhi called out of the gate to . . . well, to apparently do what he was doing at this moment. The cart was headed for the gate.

Phaere waved a hand signal in the air that made the guards step back from the gate. Crossbows and hand crossbows were leveled at the cart, but the guards were all obedient enough to follow orders and not fire.

Phaere smiled though she was still disappointed. It had begun.

* * * * *

Abdel had stopped trying to keep a count of the obvious set-ups that had been perpetrated on him lately, they were coming so quickly and so regularly now. He saw the drow mistress Phaere standing over some cowering male drow at the edge of the plaza in the center of Ust Natha. She held a hand up in the air and made some gesture. Abdel couldn't understand drow sign language—didn't even know there was such a thing as drow sign language—but he could see the guards lining the plaza withdraw. They all glanced at Phaere, and though they raised their crossbows to fire, they held back. Abdel was running the cart fast and hard through the narrow streets, and the open construction of their vehicle gave them no cover. He'd been relying on dumb luck to get them through the gate, but thanks to Phaere he wouldn't need it. It was as if she was expecting them—and that couldn't be good at all. He said as much to Jaheira and Yoshimo.

"We have no choice!" Yoshimo yelled over the clatter of the cart's wheels on the marble tiles. "It's the only way out!"

"It's a trap!" Abdel repeated.

"What isn't?" was Yoshimo's cryptic reply. "Trust me one time."

Abdel opened his mouth, intending to regale Yoshimo with the full list of reasons why he'd never trust the Kozakuran when a lithe, pale body leaped into the cart behind him.

"Imoen!" Jaheira gasped.

"Don't go through that gate!" Imoen shouted to Abdel, clutching his shoulder to steady herself on the bouncing cart.

That was all Abdel had to hear. He pulled hard on the reins, and the lizard pulled up short. Everything and everyone on the cart slid rapidly forward, and Abdel nearly fell sprawling onto the giant lizard's back. Imoen and Jaheira collided with Abdel from behind, and both of them grunted at the same time. Yoshimo fell against the back of Abdel's seat, bloodying his nose.

"Destroy it!" Imoen panted even as the cart fish-tailed to a stop. "We have to destroy that thing—they mean to march an army through it."

"That's great," Abdel said as he pulled the reins to the left, forcing the giant pack lizard around. In the plaza the drow guards stepped forward but still held their fire. Abdel knew it would take nothing but a wave of Phaere's hand to make pincushions out of them all.

"How do we destroy the thing?" Jaheira asked Imoen. "It's not like you can just—"

"With this!" Imoen exclaimed, producing a crystalline wand out of her shimmering spidersilk robe.

"Don't do this," Yoshimo said, his voice ragged and desperate. "In the names of all our ancestors, I beg of you. It is our only way out of here. You have to—"

Abdel shot one elbow back and connected hard with Yoshimo's temple. The Kozakuran fell into one of the eggs, shifting but not cracking it. He tried to get up for a second, then fell unconscious, sprawled across the silver dragon's eggs.

"Do it," Abdel said to Imoen. "It's as good a day to die as any."

* * * * *

Phaere's heart sank, and she cursed herself silently when she saw the third human run across the roof of a granary at the edge of the gate plaza and jump into the speeding cart. It was Jaenra, and she was as pale as a human. She *was* human.

Phaere's mother had a list of criticisms of her. At the top of it was her weakness for a certain type of woman, a physical weakness that made her make fast, rash decisions based more on passion than cunning. Phaere had always liked to think that passion was as good a motivator as cunning. She'd made some of her best decisions based on it, but . . .

. . . but this was not one of them. Phaere grimaced realizing everything she'd said to the woman in the bath, in bed, whispered into her ears, into the gentle soft curve of her neck . . . by Lolth's malignant teeth, she'd told the human *everything*.

Phaere pulled her own hand crossbow and cocked a poisoned dart as the cart came to a nearly tumbling stop in front of the blue-violet gate. Jaenra, if that was really her name, produced from her robe—one of Phaere's robes—a long, thin, glittering . . .

"Oh gods, no," Phaere murmured. It was the wand. Had she really done it? Had she whispered the command word into Jaenra's ear? She had.

Phaere leveled the hand crossbow at Jaenra and something happened to blur her vision. Was that a tear? Was that what she'd come to? At that moment Phaere knew two things: She couldn't kill the young woman, and everything she'd planned, everything she'd worked so hard for, was shattering before her eyes. It was over. She didn't shoot.

The girl didn't seem to see her, didn't know that Phaere was letting her live, was punishing herself by letting this human woman—who'd managed to manipulate her so well she could have been a drow after all—destroy the gate.

Phaere couldn't hear Jaenra actually say the command word, but a blue-white arc of lightning leaped out of the tip of the wand and met the swirling magic of the gate. The blue-violet gate energy puckered at the point the lightning struck it and coalesced into a churning storm cloud.

Phaere saw the humans leap from the cart, abandoning the eggs in a desperate attempt to avoid what everyone—even the reticent drow guards—knew was coming.

The gate exploded, blasting clouds, and balls of blue-violet energy, and trails of white lightning through the plaza. Phaere put her arm up across her eyes when the cart flashed into a red light that stood out in contrast to the cooler colors of the gate eating itself alive.

The cart was gone in an instant, taking the humans and the dragon eggs with it.

There was a heartbeat of silence and darkness in the plaza, then the gate exploded again.

Chapter Eighteen

They fell from three or four feet in the air onto the cold, rough stone floor of the cavern. When Abdel hit, the air was pushed from his lungs and explosions of purple and red blazed behind his eyelids. He immediately tried to push himself up and roll over, but all he could manage was one quick, dull glance. He saw one of the enormous feet of the silver dragon Adalon and heard a rumbling voice say, "They're safe," before he lost consciousness.

Jaheira shook him awake, and he'd never been happier to see anyone. He sat up, his head spinning for a few seconds before it cleared itself.

"How long?" he asked the druid.

Jaheira shrugged and stood up, turning to face the dragon towering overhead like a living cathedral of liquid silver. The dragon was crying. Abdel's heart swelled from the sound of it, and he knew, all of a sudden and all at once, he knew. Set up or not, manipulation or not, deception or not, there was a time to do the right thing. There was a time to suffer the petty evils of those who came in and out of his life, and there was a time to put an end to all of it—not just for a moment or two but for a lifetime. He'd wanted to rescue Imoen and Jaheira, and he had, but there was more to do. There was Irenicus, and though he didn't understand the evil

161

this man sought to do, he knew it was up to him, one way or another, to stop it.

He looked to one side and saw Imoen, her arms wrapped around herself, sitting against a stalagmite, openly weeping. Jaheira sat down where she stood too, looking up at the massive claw of the dragon hovering over the cart, hovering over its brood. A talon as big as two men came down slowly and caressed the top of one of the eggs with a touch so gentle Abdel couldn't have believed a human could manage it, much less something the size of a decent keep.

Abdel looked away and saw Yoshimo.

The Kozakuran was staring daggers into the big sellsword, not the least moved—barely even aware—of the dragon's superhuman joy.

"That was foolish," Yoshimo said to Abdel, his voice gruff and low. "That was a foolish thing to do . . . for what gain?"

Jaheira turned to look at Yoshimo, and Abdel stood up slowly, reaching for his sword. Yoshimo drew his own blade and faced the son of Bhaal.

"For Mielikki's sake, you idiot," Jaheira shouted at Yoshimo. "Do you have any understanding of where you are and what has been avoided?"

"What has been *avoided*?" Yoshimo sneered. "Do *you* have any idea, druid, what that gate represented? What power that thing . . . You weren't supposed to be so . . . active."

"We were supposed to be good little pawns, is that it?" Abdel asked, surprised by how little anger he felt toward the Kozakuran.

Yoshimo sighed, spared the dragon a glance, and sheathed his sword. "It isn't over yet."

"She was going to kill you," Imoen said suddenly, her voice awash with pain. "The vampire was going to kill you the minute we were sent on our way."

"To what end?" Yoshimo asked her, his eyes betraying his acceptance of what she'd said.

"To what end would she keep you alive?" Jaheira answered for Imoen. "Out of the kindness of her heart? Out of gratitude? She *eats* people like you . . . eats their blood anyway."

Yoshimo's face split with a wholly inappropriate grin, and he barked out a single tortured laugh. "I will not make any sad attempt too argue, young druid."

Abdel sheathed his sword and looked over to see the dragon carefully lifting her eggs from the crumbling cart.

"Yoshimo," Abdel said, "under any other circumstance I'd just kill you now and get it over with, but I've been . . . thinking. You can come with us. You can have a chance to . . ."

"Redeem yourself," Jaheira provided with a smile.

Abdel nodded and said, "Or I will kill you. Believe me that I will kill you."

Yoshimo bowed deeply and said, "I will trust the son of the God of Murder when he gives me his word on that count, my friend, but I am the least of your still considerable worries. You will not be where Irenicus expects you to be, but you are far from safe. Suldanessellar is far from safe. You're forgetting the ritual. You're forgetting what's coursing through your veins and your half sister's. Next time the lovely druid here may not be so lucky as to avoid the things you've both become."

Abdel let a long breath pass out through his nose, then he said, "Yes, I'll need to speak with Mr. Irenicus about that."

"So will I," Imoen whispered.

"You will both have your chances," the dragon said,

her voice loud but gentle in the echoing confines of the cavern. "I will set you on the path that leads up, up to the edge of the forest of Tethir. Find an elf named Elhan, and tell him your tale. You have two battles ahead: one for Suldanessellar and one for your souls. I doubt you can win one without winning the other."

* * * * *

The light was blinding, and they weren't even out of the tunnel yet. Abdel blinked and looked over at Jaheira. Her eyes were red, and tears traced paths down her dusty, cave-grimed cheeks. Abdel assumed the tears were from the light streaming in from outside, but he knew it might be that she was crying with relief at finally getting out into fresh air. Abdel felt like crying himself.

"The dragon was as good as her word," Yoshimo said.

Abdel was almost startled by the sound of the assassin's voice. They were all so quiet from the moment they saw the end of the tunnel, all so relived to see an end to the maddening underground journey. Abdel didn't even care where they were.

* * * * *

Bring your people to Suldanessellar, Jon Irenicus said into Bodhi's mind, *and be prepared to kill them all.*

She was just about to reply when a crossbow bolt punched through the supple, pale flesh of her bare midsection and pushed violently out the other side. The vampire, uninjured despite the momentary mess, looked up to see a group of Shadow Thieves emerge from the darkness behind a large marble mausoleum. In the walled Grave District of Athkatla, the night was overcast and dark, but Bodhi's undead eyesight saw the five assassins clearly enough. One of them was an older woman she'd heard some of her own people talk about. A priestess of Xvim, this one was, named Neela.

She had heard that Neela was dead, but Bodhi had been dead briefly herself once. The priestess had brought only four others with her, a woman and three men in the all-too-familiar black garb of the Shadow Thieves. Bodhi allowed herself a smile at how silly and yet appropriate they looked here, in a necropolis at night.

"Sheeta . . ." Bodhi said, nodding in the direction of the assassin now furiously winding his spent crossbow as his fellows advanced. The sound of Bodhi pulling the crossbow bolt out through her back was almost lost under the whir of the little orc woman's sling.

"Just take them all," the priestess hissed, her quiet voice carrying clearly in the still night air.

The stone left Sheeta's sling, and before the assassins could advance more than half a step, it impacted hard against the top of the nearly cocked crossbow. The string pinged off, sent the quarrel dropping impotently to the dry, stubby grass. The assassin jerked his hand away and hissed in pain, then his eyes bulged as he watched his crossbow slowly fall into pieces on the ground at his feet. Bodhi smiled, knowing Sheeta hadn't hit the crossbow that hard, she just knew where to hit it. Bodhi liked this one.

The priestess hung back, but the three other assassins continued forward. One pulled a short, blunt, pointed thing from under his black tunic. The woman drew two slim throwing knives, and the other man let his scimitar shriek for effect as he slid it slowly out of its scabbard.

"Goram," Bodhi said, "Nevilla, Naris, and Kelvan, join us, please."

The priestess was the only one of the Shadow Thieves not to look surprised when four others stepped from behind crypts and large grave markers behind Bodhi. Naris, himself once a member of the Shadow Thieves, spun a gleaming, razor-sharp bardiche and giggled. Kelvan, also a former guild member, drew two short swords. Goram and Nevilla, Bodhi's vampiric thralls, hissed with bared fangs at the approaching assassins, all three of whom hesitated more than their training should have allowed. The one with the broken crossbow just stood there, confused.

"You're Shadow Thieves," the priestess reminded her people. Two of them spared her a glance, but all three came in faster.

The one closest to Bodhi was the one with the stubby, pointed weapon that the vampire quickly recognized as a sharpened wooden stake. So, they were ready for her. The assassin was fast for a human. Bodhi had to give him that, and even with a wooden stake, it took guts to charge a vampire. If Nevilla hadn't come up to Bodhi's side so quickly, she might have been in danger from the stake. Instead, she grabbed Nevilla roughly by the shoulder and pulled the thrall in front of her just as the assassin stabbed down with the stake. Nevilla apparently realized what was about to happen, because she let out a frightened shriek when the assassin corrected in mid-stab and went for Nevilla instead of Bodhi. He must have figured one vampire was as good as any.

The stake went into Nevilla's chest with a loud pop, and the lesser vampire went limp.

The assassin smiled, an expression that proved to be his last. Kelvan was behind him and crossed his two sharp short swords in front of the assassin's neck, drawing them back and together like scissors. The assassin's head came off in a fountain of blood that Bodhi avoided by tossing the limp form of Nevilla into the decapitated man's falling body, pushing them both away from her.

Bodhi gave Kelvan a pleased smile, a smile the man returned with a wolfish grin before turning to meet the other assassins. She'd been lucky to get this one and had been thinking of making him a thrall. Now that Nevilla was dead, she made up her mind to begin the process sooner. Kelvan and Naris had both pleased her most from among the assassins she'd been luring away from the Shadow Thieves on Irenicus's orders. The Shadow Council, who ruled their petty assassin kingdom like the bureaucrats they were, of course assumed that over the last month and a half Irenicus was forming a rival guild of his own. To some degree this was true, but these assassins would not be sent to kill fat merchants for a pouch of gold coins. These men and women would serve the greater purpose of Irenicus's, a plan the Shadow Council couldn't even imagine if they tried. What confused Bodhi more than a little, and disappointed her when she let it, was that this guild of hers was actually good—getting better every day—and was quickly becoming a real rival for the Shadow Thieves. It had started for her as just another in a long string of favors she'd done for the man she admired most, but she'd started to think about . . . possibilities.

Bringing all these lovely little assassins of mine to some elf city just to kill them, she thought, directing the words to the distant mind of Jon Irenicus, *seems like a waste.*

Oh no, he replied quickly, *not a drop of their blood will be wasted, my dear. These playthings of yours will help me unleash from this child of Bhaal such power . . . I will bring forth the Slayer.*

All that to kill a single elf?

A single elf, yes, Irenicus replied. *A single elf whose death will make me immortal again.*

* * * * *

"That's *fifteen* days," Abdel said. "We've been down there for fifteen days?"

Jaheira and Imoen looked at him, amazed.

"I'm not sure," Imoen said slowly, "if that seems like more time or less time than it actually felt like."

"And you were told to expect us?" Jaheira asked the thin, stern-faced elf who was obviously the leader of the patrol.

"After a fashion, druid," the elf answered in thickly accented Common.

"Who expects us?" Yoshimo asked, suspicious.

The elf looked at Yoshimo blankly, obviously not willing to answer the question. He turned to Jaheira and spoke a sentence or two in flowing Elvish that made Jaheira blush. Abdel felt his hackles raise at not being privy to all of the conversation. Imoen glanced at him and grimaced.

"We'll need to go with them to their camp," Jaheira said.

"Another few days . . . on foot," the elf patrol leader said calmly, as if describing an afternoon stroll.

Abdel sighed. He'd walked longer.

The elf patrol leader slipped off his green-dyed cloak and handed it to Jaheira, who took it with a nod of thanks. The night was cool, and the trees hissed with a chilling breeze. The dark forest was alive with the sounds of a thousand animals of all sizes and descriptions, singing away the very last traces of indigo in the now-black sky and greeting the spray of stars that peeked through the thick canopy.

The stern elf looked at Abdel and said, "It's not usual."

"Nothing about this is usual, sir," Imoen remarked, letting sarcasm drip over the understatement.

"The queen is in danger," the elf said. "Exceptions must be made—even to allow humans into the forest."

"The queen . . ." Jaheira remarked, shooting a stern, surprised look at the elf. "Ellesime."

The patrol leader looked at her for a long time without saying anything, then smiled impatiently and said, "There have been exceptions. We have been told to consider this to be one."

The patrol turned at once, and Abdel, Jaheira, Imoen, and Yoshimo followed them deeper into the forest of Tethir, a place few humans had ever seen.

"We will reach the gate before first light," the elf said, glancing back casually.

"Gate?" Abdel asked.

Jaheira smiled and sighed, a sound as grateful as it was tired.

"We'll be in camp by this time tomorrow night," the elf said.

* * * * *

The assassin with the crossbow finally just turned and ran.

Goram and Naris let him go, keeping their eyes on the priestess. Behind them, Sheeta dropped a stone into her sling and Bodhi eyed the scene with only the necessary concern.

The priestess muttered through a series of seemingly meaningless words and even less meaningful hand gestures. She held something in one hand that disappeared as she coughed out the last word of the prayer. Goram stepped to the side, though Bodhi wasn't sure what he was trying to avoid. Naris leaped forward with the blade of his bardiche straight out in front of him but couldn't get to the priestess before she finished her spell.

Naris pulled back his right arm to bring the polearm to bear and froze that way. Bodhi heard the stone from Sheeta's sling drop onto the hard ground, and the vampire turned to look at her. The short orc woman was also frozen firmly in place. Her little brow was furrowed, and her eyes blazed, but she didn't—couldn't— move a muscle. Goram and Kelvan were unaffected, and they came in faster in response.

The Shadow Thief with the scimitar stepped in to meet Kelvan, and both of them smiled evilly at the sound of steel on steel.

"Make that bitch very, very sorry, Goram," Bodhi said sternly, and the vampire ran straight at the priestess Neela without the slightest hesitation.

When? Bodhi asked Irenicus across the miles that separated them.

When Imoen and Abdel get here, he answered. *Soon.*

Neela produced what was obviously an enchanted mace. She was bringing it to bear on a rapidly charging Goram. Kelvan was engaged in combat with the scimitar-wielding assassin, and Sheeta and Naris were magically immobilized. Bodhi realized the time had come to involve herself.

The Shadow Thief was managing to drive Kelvan back, and Bodhi spared a glance to check on her man's progress. Kelvan's two short swords whirred in the night, striking sparks against the assassin's scimitar. Bodhi turned away when she saw Kelvan accidentally gut the frozen form of Naris.

"Damn!" Kelvan grunted. The Shadow Thief laughed, pleased with the lucky break.

Goram didn't make it to the priestess before he was sprayed with a barrage of throwing knives. Bodhi wasn't worried about Goram—the plain steel blades held no more danger for her thrall than they did for Bodhi—but she was impressed with the Shadow Thief woman's aim.

"Don't waste them, Selarra," the priestess told her charge. "Get the stake."

The young woman scanned the dark ground for the stake and found it still protruding from Nevilla's motionless chest. Bodhi smiled and stepped away. She saw Selarra realize that Bodhi was between her and the dead thrall.

Kelvan finally found an opening in the Shadow Thief's relentless attack and took advantage of the assassin's growing overconfidence. The Shadow Thief was laughing even when Kelvan gutted him, finally realizing he'd lost when Kelvan's second blade slid across the front of his throat.

Bodhi's teasing sidestep brought her to within an arm's reach of the priestess, and the vampire took advantage of Goram's first attack with his strong, claw-like fingernails and scratched out with her own talons at Neela's face. Goram ducked a fast blow from the enchanted mace and had to almost throw himself to the ground to avoid the wild attack. The priestess screamed angrily when Bodhi took her eye in a hard rake of sharp claws. The mace dropped from Neela's grip.

"I could have taken them all, bitch," Bodhi told the Shadow Thief priestess. "I could have had all your assassins—your whole guild."

The vampire turned to Selarra but spoke to her thrall. "You take the priestess," she said. "I want the one with the knives."

Chapter Nineteen

Jaheira seemed especially wistful passing through the forest the elf patrol leader called Wealdath rather than Tethir. She seemed happy and sad at the same time, as if being there stirred that half of her that might have called this place home.

Yoshimo kept passing a hand to the hilt of his sword, and Abdel could see that he was ready to disappear into the dark forest any second. Why would these elves—or anyone—trust a Shadow Thief assassin?

They'd been brought directly from the gate by the elf patrol leader to an enormous tree. As tired as they all were, they were anxious to warn the queen of the dangerous forces still rallying against her. They were led through passages in the tree that might have been natural veins in the wood but for their size. Passing through a beaded curtain, they emerged into a surprisingly huge, tall-ceilinged chamber lit by patches of cold, obviously magical light.

The furnishings were spartan but well-crafted of wood and woven vines. The curved wall of the semicircular room was cut with delicate carvings of leaves sprouting from twisting vines. Against this backdrop stood a slim male elf in simple traveling leathers. At his belt was a sword that made the sellsword in Abdel practically drool. He'd only heard of them, but he was sure the weapon was a moonblade.

The elf smiled and motioned them to seats in the center of the room. Jaheira bowed deeply and said something in Elvish. She didn't look directly at the elf, who returned her bow with a nod of his head.

"We should use Common," the elf said, his accent very thick, "so as to not offend our visitors."

"As you wish, sire," Jaheira said. The five of them sat on deep-cushioned chairs arranged to face a simple wooden stool. The elf, mindful of the long blade at his waist, perched on the stool and raised an eyebrow.

"The queen is in danger," Jaheira said simply.

The elf smiled and said, "I am Elhan. And you are. . . ?"

Jaheira, flustered, said, "Jaheira . . . a druid in the service of Mielikki."

"And the Harpers, of course," Elhan added for her.

Jaheira blushed and said, "I am not here on their behalf." She didn't question how this elf knew of her affiliation with the Harpers. Elf princes, apparently, just knew things like that.

"I am Yoshimo," the Kozakuran said, filling the uncomfortable gap as he so often did. "I am at your service . . . sire."

"I'm Imoen," the girl said weakly. The trip through the Underdark and the woods seemed to have taken an unusually heavy toll on her. She seemed weak and tired.

"My name is Abdel," the sellsword said.

Elhan turned to him and nodded. "You, I've heard of. What brings the son of Bhaal to Wealdath?"

Abdel turned to Elhan and said, "Suldanessellar is in danger. A powerful necromancer, a human named Jon Irenicus is hoping to perform some ritual—"

"Indeed," Elhan interrupted. "Irenicus is known to us. He has . . . my sister—Ellesime—has had a . . . relationship with this human for quite some time. They are

173

linked in a way that I must be honest and say I don't fully understand. Ellesime herself senses only apathy from Irenicus, when she can feel him through this link. She is refusing to believe that he means her harm or even that he is responsible for sealing off Suldanessellar."

"What do you mean 'sealing off'?" asked Jaheira.

"I mean just what I say," replied Elhan with a shrug. "We are no longer able to get into the Swanmay's Glade. Irenicus has somehow barred us from our home."

"What is there to do about this?" Yoshimo asked. "I imagine we must help you return to your city, so you can save your queen's life."

"We will," Jaheira said, scowling at the Kozakuran.

"Ellesime cannot be killed," Elhan said simply. "You'll forgive me for not explaining how this is so. I don't fear her death, but if Irenicus is immortal as well, he can harry my sister for a long time—centuries or more—and cause the gods only know what damage to the city, all of Wealdath, in the process."

"We're not entirely sure why we're here, sir," Abdel admitted. "All we know is that your fate and ours—" he nodded at Imoen— "are tied up with each other in some way connected with Irenicus."

Elhan lifted an eyebrow, curious, and Abdel said, "I am descended from the God of Murder, and I am not the only one. I have a sister, a half-sister who shares that blood. Irenicus means to use that blood to raise some sort of power—if not Bhaal himself then some essence, some avatar of Bhaal. It is this godlike force that Irenicus seems to desire for some unknown purpose."

Elhan smiled and nodded. "I think I can shed some light on all this for you, Abdel Adrian. I think our fates are bound together after all. I'm so glad you made it here. So very glad."

*   *   *   *   *

Bodhi awoke early, as she often did, and stayed in her casket knowing the sun hadn't completely set. As had been the case over that last dozen days or more, she awoke thinking of Abdel. The feel of his hands on her body, his tongue in her mouth, their most intimate embrace, lingered in her in the most delicious way. She would never use the word love, or even desire, but maybe, in whatever was left of the human part of her, she felt both those things and more.

There were so many things Abdel didn't know, but there were easily as many things about him that she had yet to discover. She hoped she would have a chance.

She stretched, and her elbow brushed past several loose pieces of cold metal. Irenicus had told her to keep these broken bits of some antique close to her. She could sense the magic in them and knew it had something to do with the ritual. Irenicus had told her that there was a good chance that Abdel would come to her looking for it. She was happy to keep it in case of just such an eventuality.

She whispered his name just to feel it on her tongue. The hiss of it didn't echo in the confined space. The air, reeking of the soil of her all-but-forgotten home, was too dead to allow for something as graceful as an echo.

"Love," she said aloud into the dead air of her coffin. The sound of it made her smile.

She touched herself and closed her eyes, knowing that that night she would kill all of her assassins in Irenicus's name. She no longer cared that her fledgling guild would never serve her—one way or another, the son of Bhaal would instead fill that role.

*   *   *   *   *

"Irenicus was responsible—Irenicus and Bodhi together—for the worst disaster ever to befall the city of Suldanessellar," Elhan explained.

Abdel settled into his chair, happy to finally get some facts that he might use to make sense of all this mess, happy to feel calmer than he had in a long time. The tree chamber was described as a "camp" and "temporary" by the elves, but it looked permanent enough to Abdel. These elves carried their traditions with them everywhere.

"We didn't know what they were trying to do. None of us would ever have imagined they'd be that . . . I don't know. We didn't suspect," Elhan continued. "Many of the older, weaker citizens died in the initial waves of power that swept through the city. The Tree of Life . . . they attacked the Tree of Life itself."

Jaheira gasped and Elhan nodded at her.

"Ellesime—my sister, our queen," he continued, "nearly died as well. To endanger her, to endanger all of us, to endanger the Tree. It was more than we—any of us— could comprehend. All that, nearly the whole city gone, elves who'd gathered the wisdom of millennia blown away . . . for some petty gain . . . some personal gain."

"And they got away with this?" Jaheira asked, her eyes wide.

Elhan smiled and shrugged. "We didn't think they did. They were punished according to the wishes of Ellesime. They got the opposite of what they desired. Great magic—High Magic—was used to make them human. They were stripped of their elven nature and sent away. Not only were they given mortality, but . . . forgive me," he said, nodding to the three humans in turn, "but they were to have only a handful of years to ponder their crimes before time would execute them for us."

"What was it he was looking for?" Abdel asked.

"Immortality," Jaheira whispered.

Elhan took a long sip from a tallglass of sweet elven wine and said, "Immortality. The simplest, silliest goal of the tiny minded. To live forever in pure arrogance over the master, Time."

"But he didn't succeed," Abdel said.

"He came close," Elhan told them. "He studied spells and rituals that had been shunned by my people for more than one of our very long generations."

"But Bodhi . . ." Jaheira said. "She's managed it, hasn't she?"

Elhan shrugged again and said, "After a fashion. Bodhi is undead. She's not immortal. These are very different things that can easily seem similar on the surface. Once human, Bodhi struggled to find a faster, easier answer. That was always her nature. While Irenicus studied, she acted. Bodhi became a vampire but stayed with the man she called her brother in hopes that Irenicus's continued study would benefit her someday as well."

"I'm not sure I understand," Abdel said. "Irenicus wants to become an elf again?"

"More than that," Elhan said. "He was an elf, and we do live for a long time—long enough that I understand some of your people believe we *are* immortal—but time catches up even with us, eventually. Irenicus was one of our best. Before he descended into mad necromancy, he was perhaps the most powerful mage on all of Faerûn— one of them, at least.

"More than that, he was my sister's consort—as close to the throne as anyone could get. She loved him, and maybe, a long time ago, he loved her too."

"So what turned him?" Jaheira asked. "What could possibly make him betray her?"

"Bodhi," Elhan said flatly. "Though I'm loathe to

attach all the responsibility to her. Still, where my sister and I believe Irenicus once had some pure intentions, I doubt Bodhi ever did. What it is about her that makes her . . . I don't know, and maybe I don't want to. I will be satisfied believing she's simply an aberration."

Abdel suddenly felt the need to stand, so he did. This startled Jaheira, but she didn't say anything. Elhan watched in silence as Abdel crossed to a window and looked out at the forest canopy.

Sensing the stillness in the room, Abdel said, "Go on."

"Bodhi always was Irenicus's most trusted advisor," Elhan said. "She studied with him for some time, helped him, took care of him. They truly were like brother and sister. Ellesime, to her credit, did everything to embrace Bodhi, extending friendship, even a sort of sisterhood, but Bodhi always kept her at a distance.

"Sometimes I believe it's my sister's own wishful thinking that blames Bodhi more than Irenicus . . . that it was Bodhi who forced his hand and drew him into the ritual. They both wanted the same thing, to live forever. Bodhi convinced Irenicus, or he convinced her, or they convinced each other to undertake a ritual so vile . . ."

"The Tree of Life?" Jaheira asked, her voice dripping with incredulity. "The arrogance . . ."

"I have been listening with great interest," Yoshimo said, "and I must ask—what is this Tree of Life?"

"It is the spiritual heart of Suldanessellar," Jaheira said. "It's a force perhaps older than the gods themselves. It has the respect of all gods. Some say it is the source of all life."

"The druids taught you well, Jaheira," Elhan said with a smile. "Irenicus sought to drain life force directly from the Tree of Life. I couldn't imagine anything more abhorrent, more forbidden to us."

Abdel sighed and turned back into the room. "So what do we do about this?" he asked. "They're going to try it again, aren't they?"

Elhan nodded. "I'm afraid that you and your sister have something to do with it this time, Abdel Adrian."

"Well," Abdel said, "I've been the center of an arcane ritual or two before, sir. I don't intend to have anything to do with this one."

"Good," the elf prince said sincerely. "Then there's something you'll need to do for us all."

"Tell me," Abdel said.

"Go back to Athkatla," Elhan directed, his eyes burning into Abdel's. "Find Bodhi, kill her, and bring back the pieces of the Rynn Lanthorn."

Abdel's heart skipped a beat and a yellow haze began to creep into the edges of his vision. He held his eyes closed tightly and calmed himself.

"The Rynn Lanthorn?" Yoshimo asked. "Little pieces of bronze that might fit together to make a whole?"

Elhan nodded.

"I've seen it in the vampire's possession," the Kozakuran said. "Irenicus gave it to her for safekeeping."

"What does this thing do?" Jaheira asked.

"It will put your souls back in order," Elhan said, "not to put too fine a point on it. It will suppress the avatar within you, Abdel, and it will save Imoen's life."

Abdel looked over at Imoen and noticed for the first time that the girl had fallen asleep or passed out. Her breathing was soft and regular, but she seemed pale, her eyes sunken, her lips gray.

"So I'm off to Athkatla," Abdel said quietly, not looking away from Imoen.

"We all are," Jaheira said.

Philip Athans

"No," Abdel said quickly. "This I have to do by myself."

Abdel looked at Jaheira, and she nodded, a tear rolling slowly down one cheek.

Chapter Twenty

Difficult as it was for him to believe, Abdel was actually starting to get used to teleporting.

He never really thought of himself as the teleporting sort. It was something mages, phaerimm, demons, and gods did. He was the kind of man who got paid to guard warehouses or walk next to trade caravans with a big sword in his hand. He traveled the old fashioned way. He walked. Sometimes he'd ride a horse, or in a cart or wagon of some kind, and he'd been on a ship a time or two. Instantaneously shifting hundreds of miles in less than a second in a flash of magical light made him dizzy, and he really felt as if he wasn't in control, which is something that bothered him more than anything else.

But then he hadn't been in control of anything in his life for a long time now, so maybe that was it. Being teleported by one of Elhan's mages was the least of his problems.

He shook off the teleportation afterdaze and looked around to make sure he was in the right place. The ceiling was low, barely brushing the top of his head. The air smelled like stale mead and garbage. It was dark, but he could see the outline of sacks of flour and barrels of ale and wine. He could hear footsteps crossing the floor above his head and the sound of a chair being pulled across it. A mumbled voice clearly said, "All done, Boo," and Abdel knew he was in the right place.

He stood on the exact spot where he had made love with Bodhi. She'd hypnotized him. He told himself that again, though he didn't believe it. The smell and the sounds of the place made the memory clear enough that he couldn't pretend as well anymore. He stepped toward the stairs, and his eye was caught by a square patch of shadow on the floor only a stride or two to his left. His eyes were adjusting to the darkness quickly, and when he stepped a bit closer to the shadow, he saw that it was a trapdoor.

It occurred to him that he was looking for a vampire. It was night, but early. Bodhi would have to be someplace as far away from the sun as possible. A cellar under a cellar—what was that? A root cellar? Not a wine cellar, not in this place—in any case, it was a good bet he'd find a vampire in there.

Elhan's mage seemed sure enough that Bodhi was here. He had some way to feel her or sense her or something. Another improbable force Abdel had to trust.

Abdel knelt over the trapdoor and grabbed the cold iron ring that served as a handle. He almost lifted it open, then stopped himself. He pulled his sword, held its weight, let the creaking of Minsc's footsteps above calm him, and realized he didn't want to kill Bodhi. The elves had told him how evil she was, and there was the fact that she was a vampire and all, but there was something there. Reason enough not to kill her at least. He looked at the blade of his sword in the darkness and realized that it wouldn't kill a vampire anyway.

He slid the sword behind his back, and his right hand found the carved wooden stake tucked into his belt. The elves had given it to him. It was carved from a windblown branch, a branch of a tree in the forest of

Tethir, on the edge of the sealed, doomed city of Suldanessellar. They gave it to him to kill Bodhi because if they were to survive, they needed her to die, and needed the artifact she certainly wouldn't hand over if she were alive.

He squeezed the wooden stake and opened the trapdoor.

The space below was lit by three candles flickering in a very old candelabra made for six. The ceiling was too low to allow Abdel to stand up, and there were no stairs, no ladder. He slid off the edge and dropped to the dirt floor. The place smelled of mildew and rat droppings, and the only thing down there besides the candelabra and Abdel was an empty coffin.

The fact that it was empty filled Abdel with misplaced relief.

* * * * *

Imoen was asleep again, laying under an amazingly sturdy lean-to the elves had woven of vines, sticks, and leaves. Jaheira sat over her, one hand holding her holy symbol and the other on Imoen's forehead. The prayer came to an end, but where there should have been a surge of healing power there was nothing.

Imoen's strength was fading fast. Her skin was pale and cool, and she slept most of the time. This was the third healing prayer Jaheira had attempted, and nothing had helped. The evil in Imoen's veins seemed to be drowning her soul, thanks to Irenicus's ritual. Mielikki was withholding her grace. It didn't seem fair, but Jaheira tried to understand.

"Phaere . . ." Imoen mumbled in her sleep.

"She's dying," Yoshimo said from behind her, startling Jaheira.

"Yes," Jaheira said, not looking back at him.

Yoshimo stepped forward, squatting just behind and next to Jaheira. "What people will do . . ." the Kozakuran mused.

"For immortality?" Jaheira asked, wetting a rag and wringing it out.

"For immortality," Yoshimo said, "for coin, for loyalty to a crown, a flag, or a man."

Jaheira placed the wet rag on Imoen's forehead—knowing it was a silly, futile gesture but feeling she should do it anyway—and said, "Would they kill?"

Yoshimo laughed at Jaheira's obvious stab. "Where I come from," he said, "assassin is an honorable profession."

"It's murder," Jaheira said flatly, "wherever you are."

"A difference of view," the Kozakuran said. "People have killed for less, yes?"

Jaheira gently pulled the rag off Imoen's head.

"Abdel will save her?" Yoshimo asked. He seemed happy enough to change the subject.

"Abdel?" Imoen murmured in her sleep.

Jaheira gently touched her shoulder, and Imoen's eyes popped open.

"Abdel!" she said, her voice clear and loud in the quiet of the elf camp.

"He'll be here," Jaheira told her. "He'll—"

"*Silence!*" Imoen growled, her voice deeper now and coarse. Her eyes flashed yellow, and Jaheira gasped. Imoen sat up in a burst of motion, and Jaheira felt a hand grab her and pull her back. Imoen's jaws snapped in the air in front of Jaheira's face as if the girl was trying to bite her.

"Imoen—" Jaheira said.

"She's not herself," Yoshimo whispered.

Imoen laughed, and it wasn't her usual pleasant

giggle. "Who am I, Kozakuran?"

"Bhaal . . ." Jaheira answered for him.

As if in response, Imoen fell back onto the bed of leaves and was asleep.

* * * * *

Abdel pulled the punch he threw into Gaelan Bayle's midsection, which was the only reason Bayle survived.

"I'd like very much to kill you," Abdel told him.

Bayle's only response was a series of rumbling coughs.

"Oh," Minsc breathed, "I'm sure that did hurt, Boo."

Abdel looked over at the red-haired madman and said, "You need to go for a walk or something, Minsc. The Copper Coronet is closed for the night."

Minsc looked at Bayle then back at Abdel, smiled, and left quickly, whispering, "Looks like we'll need a new job soon, Boo."

"Where is she?" Abdel asked for the third time. "And remember what I told you would happen if I had to ask a fourth time."

Bayle looked up and forced a spittle-lined smile. "All right," he gasped, "all right . . . two thousand . . . gold pieces. That's my . . . that's my final . . . my final offer."

Abdel returned his smile and drew back his arm. Bayle closed his eyes, trying to prepare himself for the blow that was coming soon and would likely kill him.

"I knew you'd come," Bodhi said, sliding out from behind the curtain leading into the back room. "You can let him go."

Abdel turned back to Bayle, who smiled at him and winked. Abdel smashed his fist into Bayle's face and dropped the bartender like a bad habit.

Abdel didn't bother watching Bayle hit the ground. He looked up at Bodhi and took her in all at once. She was dressed in a tight silk dress that shimmered in patterns of vines and spiders. Her hair fell around her pale face and accentuated her gray eyes. Her face was regal and perfect, and Abdel could see that she might have once been an elf. She wore no jewelry or shoes.

She stepped closer to him and said, "You've come to kill me."

Abdel saw her glance at the wooden stake in his belt, and he met her gray eyes. They seemed calm and confident. Abdel knew she was sure he wasn't going to kill her, but of course he was.

"Everyone has been lying to you, Abdel," Bodhi said, her voice as sincere as any voice Abdel had ever heard. "I've lied to you . . . over and over . . . but I'm not the only one. What did they tell you?"

"Who?" Abdel asked.

"The elves," she said, stepping closer still. Abdel's hand went to the stake, but he didn't pull it out. "They told you, what? That I was an elf once? That I did something terrible to them or one of the sacred thises or holy whatses?"

"They told me—"

"A giant crock of horsesh—"

"Enough!" Abdel roared, yanking the stake from his belt but stepping back one stride.

"Abdel . . ." she said, and he looked her in the eyes again. "I'm sorry. I had to do all these things. I had no choice and neither did you."

"I had—"

"No choice," she said again. "Name one thing in the last month you decided to do on your own."

Abdel sighed, and Bodhi's eyes softened. Her pupils seemed to widen, and Abdel felt his jaw relax, felt his grip on the stake relax, then a yellow fog passed over his vision.

"Abdel," Bodhi whispered, "be with me . . ."

* * * * *

Irenicus had warned her that this might happen, and Bodhi had very casually brushed it off, saying she'd seen monsters before. In more ways than one, she was a sort of monster herself, wasn't she?

But what she saw Abdel transform into, she really wasn't ready for.

The stake in his hand snapped in half first, then the link she'd established with him broke all at once, and his body contorted and transformed.

Bodhi was fast, fast enough to stay away from the Abdel-Bhaal thing—the raving, murderous beast. It smashed the bar to splinters and sent stools and chairs hurtling through the air so fast and so hard they shattered the plaster when they hit the walls. White dust was in the air, and the room was full of deafening sounds: roars, the footfalls of something heavier than an elephant, shattering glass, splintering wood, crumbling brick, and disintegrating plaster.

At first the thing was just breaking up the place, lashing out at everything close enough to smash. Bodhi wasn't sure exactly what to do. This was as close to an avatar of the dead God of Murder that anyone alive had ever been, and she admitted to herself that she was well out of her depth.

She knew she couldn't turn and run . . . or could she?

She didn't have a chance to decide before the thing that used to be Abdel turned and fixed its blazing yellow eyes on her.

Chapter Twenty-One

Jaheira was practically panting, and Yoshimo's hand was still on her shoulder for a very long time after Imoen had collapsed back into a deep but fitful sleep.

"She might kill us all before she dies," Yoshimo said.

Jaheira spun out of his grip and spat, "That's enough!"

The Kozakuran bowed his head, his eyes fixed on Jaheira's, and took one deliberate step back.

"She is possessed," he said pointedly.

Jaheira closed her eyes, calmed herself a little, and said, "I wish it was that easy, Yoshimo."

She opened her eyes and saw that Yoshimo was looking down at Imoen, his right hand resting uneasily on his sword hilt. She needed to get the Kozakuran away from Imoen before he tried to do something either cowardly or heroic. She stepped to him and put a firm hand on his chest.

"Let's let her rest," she said.

Yoshimo glanced at her, then back at Imoen, and said, "Wouldn't it be the safest thing?"

"Her soul is being drawn away from her and into the part of her blood that carries the essence of the God of Murder," Jaheira explained. "You haven't seen what she's capable of. A burst of temper and an unsettling change in the tone of her voice . . . you have no idea, Yoshimo."

"All the more reason," he said, looking Jaheira in the

eye. "There may not be another chance."

Jaheira pushed him gently and said, "Let's talk about this outside."

Yoshimo looked down and nodded reluctantly. "You have a few moments, but if she moves again. . . ."

Jaheira sighed, happy to feel Yoshimo step back, happier to see him turn and duck out of the lean-to.

"If I have to," she said to his receding back, "I'll kill her myself."

She followed him out, and they walked a short distance in silence before Yoshimo turned to her and said, "What will convince you that you have to?"

"All hope exhausted," she answered flatly.

"Spoken like a true priestess," was his curt reply.

"Druid, actually," she joked, though her heart wasn't in the banter.

"There's a chance Abdel has already failed," Yoshimo said. "I understand your confidence in him, but Bodhi is no ordinary woman and more than a match for your strong young friend, blood of a god or no."

"I'll have to tell you again that you have no idea what this god's blood can do."

* * * * *

Bodhi's whole body exploded in pain—a kind of burning agony she hadn't experienced since before she'd become a vampire. Things had pierced her flesh before, but weapons of steel or claw never hurt her. A blade had to be enchanted to make her bleed. No fist could bruise her, and no claw could rend her, but here she was, being torn apart by this thing's bare hands.

She'd tried to speak to him, to hypnotize him, to run from him, but nothing worked. The roof had been ripped off the Copper Coronet, revealing the dark, moonless sky. The thing that was once Abdel Adrian had destroyed the tavern, then turned its full attention on Bodhi. She'd even tried to tell him where to find the pieces of the Rynn Lanthorn. She'd tried admitting all her lies and manipulations. She'd even said she was sorry.

It took her leg off, and the pain was literally blinding. It ripped her arm off, and she almost passed out. She could feel cool blood drying all over her.

The creature bit into her chest, and she could feel her heart burst, and more blood exploded out everywhere. One of her breasts came off in its mouth, and she screamed. The sound was as alien in her ears as it was in her throat.

"Abdel!" she screamed, the blood that had filled her throat fountaining out with the name. "I love you . . . I loved you, Abdel. . . ."

The inhuman, wild eyes that had been burning a solid, hot yellow flickered, and the huge, misshapen head tilted to one side.

"Abdel," Bodhi said, and for the first time in more years than most humans could count, she started to cry.

He started coming back all at once, and watching his transformation actually succeeded in distracting Bodhi from the fact that she'd been ripped to pieces. There were few enough ways to kill a vampire, but that was one of them. Her head was still attached to her shoulders though, and at least some part of her heart still quivered spasmodically in her chest. Bodhi came to the nightmare realization that she could live for hours, no days, years, even centuries just exactly like this—in agony.

"Bodhi," he said, in a voice that almost sounded like Abdel's.

"Abdel, please . . ." she said.

His hand came back to normal in the time it took for him to reach for, grab hold of, and lift the sharp half of the broken wooden stake. The yellow faded from his eyes.

"Where?" he asked, his all too human face covered, dripping in blood.

She coughed out another gout of cool red blood and said, "My casket . . . under the soil. In the dirt."

A tear slipped out of one of Abdel's eyes, and Bodhi hoped it would fall on her. It might have, but she couldn't see or feel it.

"Careful," she whispered, shifting her blood-drenched shoulders to turn her open chest to him. The movement sent wave after wave of burning agony through her, but she had to do it. It would be hard enough.

Abdel held the point of the stake over the last remaining fragment of Bodhi's heart.

"I'm sorry," he whispered.

She felt the stake go in, heard something that might have been dry leaves blowing over stone, and there was nothing.

Finally.

* * * * *

Jaheira was about to turn and go back to the lean-to when a blast of hot air blew her off her feet.

She slid to a stop through a bed of dried leaves and came to rest pushed up against the sprawled form of Yoshimo.

"By the long departed," the Kozakuran exclaimed, "she exploded!"

Jaheira got to her feet, ignored her shaking knees, and took one step toward the lean-to before looking up. When she did look up, what she saw made her stop in her tracks.

The shelter was gone—apparently consumed by what looked like a whirlpool of gray, black, and silver smoke. The whirlpool was standing on end, perpendicular to the ground. A man stepped out through the whirling winds still pouring out of the gate as if he was strolling into a friendly tavern for a night of play. He saw Jaheira and smiled.

"Irenicus!" Jaheira sneered.

The necromancer didn't answer, just leaned down, his feet still lost in the whirling magical clouds. He rose with something in his hand—an arm, thin and pale. It was Imoen's arm.

A spell came to Jaheira's mind, and she started her prayer, running through the words as quickly as she could, but finding they fell into their own rhythm, refusing to be hurried.

Irenicus spared her an unconcerned glance before scooping the rest of Imoen's limp form into his arms and simply stepping back.

Jaheira's spell drew to a close the exact moment Irenicus and Imoen faded from sight. A bolt of lightning, easily as big around as Jaheira was tall, crashed into the magical gateway, and Jaheira closed her eyes against the blinding flash. Her hair stood on end, and her skin crawled.

Yoshimo said something in a language Jaheira didn't understand, and she opened her eyes.

The whirlpool was gone, and so were Irenicus and Imoen.

"More than one problem solved," Yoshimo mumbled, "I should say."

Jaheira collapsed to the ground and slammed her fist into the uncaring earth.

* * * * *

Abdel fell more than walked down the stairs into the basement. He was covered in freezing gore and nearly blind with a crushing load of guilt and self-loathing. He found a barrel of water and ripped it open with his bare hands. He spilled it over himself and was immediately drenched. He rubbed the blood off his skin as best he could; his need to be cleaned of Bodhi's gore far outweighing his need to retrieve the pieces of the Rynn Lanthorn.

She'd told him where it was, and he'd killed her—mission accomplished. Abdel knew that back in Tethir, if they knew, they'd be cheering, reveling in their chance to defeat Irenicus. Abdel still wanted to care, but at this exact moment and in this exact place, he couldn't. All he wanted to do right now was go back—crawl back if he had to—to Candlekeep and just hide himself away. Here was more blood spilled because he was the son of Bhaal. More blood and more and more. He could just stay in Candlekeep, behind the walls, in the monastery. What better place? Who better than the monks to find some way to rip this curse out of him or kill him trying?

He looked at himself, and there was still so much blood on him. He saw the water from the barrel running to, then through the trapdoor. The casket was there, and the artifact the elves needed so much—that *he* needed so much—and that Imoen needed so much.

Imoen.

They could go back to Candlekeep together.

Abdel stood and walked purposefully to the trapdoor. He opened it without hesitation. The lanthorn would solve two problems. One more immediate than the other.

He dumped the soil out of Bodhi's casket and heard metal clatter on the wood as the jagged pieces dropped to the dirt floor. Abdel scooped them up in his big, blood-stained hands, and, just as Elhan's mages had promised him they would, the fragments caused a teleport to activate, and the root cellar was gone in a flash of blue light.

Chapter Twenty-Two

"I want to . . ." Imoen whispered, her mind a violent haze of fast-approaching hell, "go . . . home."

She was stretched, magically sedated, across a huge, broken, jagged-edged slab of green-traced marble in the middle of a city elves now long-dead once called Myth Rhynn. All around was the broken remnants of a great elven city, now gone to the wilderness and wandering creatures both benign and hellspawned. The marble slab was tilted on one edge, leaning at a sharp angle. Imoen lay sprawled across it, her tattered clothes gone now, and a hundred twisted sigils traced on her pale, goosefleshed skin.

A ring of elven statues, twice as tall as a real elf, surrounded the slab. The space might once have been a garden or a cemetery. The wind-worn faces of the marble elves looked down at both Imoen and Jon Irenicus with a detached calm no real person of any race could have mustered in that place at that time.

Irenicus himself gagged on his own bile and stepped back. He lost his voice to the shock, revulsion, and twisted, freakish pleasure of the sight of his last desperate hope coming to fruition. He'd chanted himself raw, and his begging with the Weave, with gods whose names no one spoke anymore—to whatever forces would listen—had been answered.

"Yes," he whispered, his voice no more than a painful squeak. "Yes. Change!"

Imoen screamed, and it was the last sound she made as a human. Her face changed first.

There was a loud sound like fabric ripping and the skin of Imoen's pretty, young, smooth-cheeked face fell away in ragged, blood-soaked ribbons. Under it her skull turned the color of old limestone and popped and ground into a different shape with each passing second. Her teeth grew and thinned into needlelike fangs, then grew again when her jaw cracked out and down. Fluid, blood, and some semi-liquid Irenicus pretended not to notice oozed, then dripped, then poured out of a hundred, then a thousand little wounds all over Imoen's spasming body. The girl was trembling uncontrollably, the shaking punctuated by loud, popping cracks that opened new, larger, puss and slime-oozing wounds. Her skin ripped then melted away, and a new arm stretched out of what once was the girl's stomach. The arm was huge, a dozen feet long or more and capped with a dripping bulb of slime that glistened in the encroaching light.

The thing that had been Imoen grew—in one sudden, undulating roll—into a pale gray monstrosity that sprouted thornlike spikes from its back so fast and with such urgency that it was almost flipped off the marble slab.

"Bhaal . . ." Irenicus whispered, his face a twisted rictus of shock and triumph. "It is you. . . . It is you. . . ."

The bulb on the end of the quivering arm broke open even as a second arm unfurled itself from the growing beast. The hand that bulb had formed had more fingers than Irenicus could easily count. The fingers were set on the long, rectangular palm at angles and with joints placed so that it looked like no hand ever seen on

Faerûn. The fingers grew long, curved talons, which shone in the dawn's light in a way that revealed their razor sharp edges.

"The Ravager," Irenicus gasped. "The Ravager awakens."

Another arm exploded out of the writhing mass, then a fourth, the bulbs breaking off to reveal three more multifingered, razor-taloned hands. The Ravager screamed out its birth agony, and Irenicus fell to the gravel, pushed back by the sheer force of the thing's concussive wail. The legs that had once been Imoen's exploded outward and with loud, sickening slapping sounds, bent backward then forward again as new joints formed.

Stripes of muddy brown faded into sharp contrast along the thing's hunched pale-gray back. It opened its eyes, staring blindly at first up into the indigo sky as a red light grew in their pits. When the light reached its brightest, the monster convulsed once in a final jerking spasm, and the slime and blood and fluid were drawn into its hardening, chitinous skin like water into a sponge.

It exhaled in a ragged growl, then drew in a long, sucking breath. Its breathing steadied quickly, and it turned its enormous saurian head toward Irenicus.

The necromancer's knees began to shake, but he managed to stand.

"Obey me," he whispered.

The monster stood all at once and towered over Irenicus. Its hunched shoulders rose easily ten yards above the gravel of the statue court. It reached out one hand as if to steady itself and wrapped its fanlike fingers around one of the ancient statues. It tensed only slightly, and the stone figure burst into a cloud of dust and pebbles, the largest no bigger than Irenicus's hand.

"Obey me!" Irenicus barked at the thing, and its

inhuman eyes burned into him. There was nothing of
Imoen left—nothing human at all.

"Suldanessellar!" Irenicus shrieked. "Ellesime! The
Tree!"

The Ravager roared into the dead morning air of
Myth Rhynn, raged at the rising sun, then turned in
the direction of Suldanessellar and took its first step.
The ground shook, and Irenicus put a hand to his stomach to settle it.

He felt it and watched it go on its way to Suldanessellar, on its way to Ellesime, on its way to his own
immortality, and Jon Irenicus began to cry.

* * * * *

Abdel burst into the forest of Tethir in a blue flash
and just let himself collapse on the ground. The pieces
of the artifact slipped out of his hands, and he made no
effort to hold them, or retrieve them.

He heard Jaheira call his name, and he put one hand
down on the ground, intending to lift himself up to look
at her. He heard her running toward him, and she slid
to a stop next to him in the bed of leaves.

"The Rynn Lanthorn," Elhan said from somewhere
not far behind and above him. "He's done it."

"I've done it," Abdel whispered, his throat tight and
painful.

Jaheira's warm, soft hands touched him, and he
rolled over to look at her, unashamed by the tears
streaming down his face. The tears mixed with traces
of Bodhi's blood.

"Oh," Jaheira breathed, "by the Lady . . ."

"Gather them up!" Elhan shouted, then barked
another series of orders in a language Abdel didn't
understand—Elvish, no doubt.

He crawled away, Jaheira holding him, as a dozen pairs of hands quickly, deliberately sifted through the dead leaves, snatching up the jagged pieces of metal that were worth Bodhi's life.

"Candlekeep," Abdel said, turning his face to Jaheira's. "I'm taking Imoen back to Candlekeep."

Jaheira sobbed once, then gathered her wits quickly.

"Where is she?" Abdel asked.

* * * * *

Elhan stood at the edge of the Swanmay's Glade, the tall trees of Suldanessellar in front of him.

"Do it," he told the mages in Elvish. "Open it."

Elhan was ringed by several of Tethir's most powerful mages, and several of her weakest. Elves as young as twenty years stood side by side with elves who'd seen two thousand summers pass. Though some could wield power others couldn't even imagine, they were all equal now, in both power and purpose. They had but to hold—one each of them—a fragment of the fabled Rynn Lanthorn.

"Suldanessellar must be open to us once more," Elhan said.

He looked up at the typically fair morning sky and saw clouds of deep black roiling against a bruise-purple overcast. Irenicus had sealed them off from Suldanessellar in preparation for this new assault on the Tree of Life, but they'd finally—thanks to a most unlikely ally—managed to gather enough of the fragments of the Rynn Lanthorn to break the back of Irenicus's enchantment and allow them back into the city that had been held captive so long.

Elhan scanned the line of mages around him. Chanting words that were old when humans first emerged from caves to stare in dumb fascination at the stars, the mages brought the fragments together.

The elf prince drew his moonblade and stepped forward. He reached up and touched the tingling, cold barrier. It was a palpable, if invisible thing, and the feel of it, even now mere moments before its destruction, sent waves of nauseous hatred through him.

"Bring it down, loyal ones," Elhan said. "Bring it down!"

The fragments came together in the righteous hands of the elf mages, and a rumbling vibration rippled the ground under Elhan's feet. Some of the mages fell over, a couple of them even dropped their parts of the lanthorn, but it didn't matter.

A wind blasted down from above, and Elhan had to close his eyes against the force of it. He was driven down to one knee.

It'll be over soon enough, sister, he thought, letting his mind touch Ellesime's.

One of the mages screamed, and another shouted, "The lanthorn!"

Elhan opened his eyes and saw that the pieces of the artifact had come together and fused into a still incomplete whole. One of the mages reached out to touch it, and a bolt of green lightning arced out from it, bridging the three paces between it and the mage's hand. The mage was thrown back with a shower of sparks, and there was another louder, stronger rumble that knocked Elhan to the ground.

It's open, Ellesime's voice sounded in his head, *but it's not over.*

* * * * *

Abdel could feel the vibration in the bottom of his feet, could feel the dizzying aftereffects of the teleportation, could feel his friends falling far behind him, could feel an old anger rising in him, could feel that yellow haze that always came before he spilled someone's blood, but none of those things managed to spill through into his conscious mind. He was running to get Imoen. He would take her back to Candlekeep this time and see that the blood of Bhaal was drained from her as it would be drained from him, one way or another.

Irenicus had his back to him, but Abdel was making no effort to quiet his pounding footsteps and gasping, exhausted breathing. The necromancer spun, turning a wild, wide-eyed visage in Abdel's direction. The necromancer smiled, spread his arms wide as if he meant to embrace the charging sellsword. Abdel almost ran him through, then ran him over, but Jon Irenicus blinked out of existence only to reappear a few yards to one side. The necromancer had the nerve to laugh at him.

Abdel fell face first and skidded in the rough gravel, coming to rest against a tilted slab of marble. He stood quickly, ignoring the bleeding abrasions on his forearms. He spun on Irenicus, who stopped laughing and offered up an impatient snarl.

"She dies!" the necromancer screamed. "I will be an elf again. I will win. I will send her to the hells before you join her yourself, and you'll burn there together. Your father's blood can't stop it, your pitiful friends can't stop it, all the elves of Tethir can't stop it!"

"Where is she?" Abdel shouted, his voice low, hard, and commanding. "What have you done with Imoen?"

"Your sister," Irenicus laughed, "has achieved her true purpose. She walks Faerûn in the guise of your father's avatar. Bhaal is dead, but his blood lives on, his power lives on, and I have twisted it, turned it to my will to kill Ellesime of Suldanessellar and rip from that damn tree what I need to live forever."

Abdel, sword in hand, continued his charge at Irenicus.

The necromancer held up a hand and said, "Don't you want to see? Don't you want to see it?" His voice descended into incoherent babbling.

Abdel pulled his sword back, determined to see if the necromancer could live without a head, when something hit him in the chest. It was as if he'd run into a stone wall, and the wall kicked back. Abdel flew backward through the air some immeasurable distance. Wind whistled through the sellsword's ears, then Irenicus's voice: "Don't you want to see your father's face?"

Abdel hit the ground hard, but he held on to his sword. He felt something in his lower back give, heard a crack, and his legs went instantly numb. The word *no!* raged through his mind. The necromancer had broken his back. Abdel lay sprawled on the gravel ground, looking up into the downward-tilted face of a disapproving marble elf.

He managed to prop himself up on both elbows, and there, a good fifty yards away, was Jon Irenicus, waving his fists at the sky and running toward Abdel.

"You'll die before you see it, then!" the necromancer wailed. "I'll see you in Hell where I'll take your soul and meld it with the essence of the tree, and I'll be a god!"

Abdel screamed at the blazing morning sky in incoherent rage, and Irenicus answered with another string of harsh, guttural, chanting words. Abdel looked at the necromancer again, who had stopped a bit closer than half the distance he'd started from and pointed one long, bony, shaking finger at Abdel. Spittle flew from the corner of his babbling mouth.

Abdel felt a wave of overwhelming nausea. A haze of gray fell over his vision, and his head spun. He turned to one side and retched, but nothing came up. He felt a chill run up his spine, and his ears began to ring.

Philip Athans

"Die!" Irenicus shrieked, his voice ragged and shrill. "Die, gods damn you, *die!*"

Abdel didn't die, but it took a long time for the sickness to pass.

"The s-son of B-Bhaal," Irenicus stuttered. "You *are* the son of Bhaal. I've killed a thousand men with that spell . . . a thousand mortals." The necromancer cackled, falling to one knee. His eyes were red, still bulging and looking painful, as if they might burst. "It should have killed you. It has never failed to kill anyone— except Ellesime. Oh, you will serve me and serve me well."

Something popped in Abdel's spine, and sensation returned to his legs in a wave of prickling fire. He stood, tightened his grip on his sword, and fixed his furious gaze on Jon Irenicus.

"You've had all the fun with me you're going to have, necromancer," Abdel growled.

"Abdel!" Jaheira screamed from some distance away.

Yoshimo's voice followed suit, then Jaheira's again.

"Where is she?" Abdel asked Irenicus.

"You can't do anything for her now, Abdel," Irenicus said, his voice strangely subdued. "It's all over. I've won."

Abdel, snarling like a dumb, enraged animal, shot forward. Irenicus said three foreign words and was gone before Abdel could take off his head.

Chapter Twenty-Three

Suldanessellar was already in ruins.

There was smoke everywhere, and Abdel almost choked on the thick stench of burning wood, singed hair, and crisping flesh. Screams of fear, shock, sorrow, and pain punctuated the morning air. All around there was fire, elves running, trees burning, and the visceral death of the elven tree city.

Abdel ran off the effects of the teleport that brought them back from Myth Rhynn fast on the heels of the Ravager. The beast must have flown, run faster than anything on Faerûn, or teleported itself to beat them there. Jaheira and Yoshimo fanned out behind him.

A haze of yellow rage descended over Abdel, and he ran against a tide of fleeing elf civilians into the chaotic hell of the Swanmay's Glade. His eyes blazed bright yellow, and any traces of injury he might have had faded into hard, ready muscle and kill-crazed adrenaline. He came through a wall of thick smoke, and when he saw the Ravager, the yellow haze fell away.

He had to stand in awe of the thing as it hit him all at once. Imoen. This beast was Imoen. This thing was made from the blood that ran through his own veins. This thing could be him. He could be this thing—he had been this thing. It was something just like that that had ripped Bodhi to shreds. His father's name crossed soundlessly across his lips. For the first time, the reality of *who* and *what* he was descended full onto him, and he was simply overcome.

Behind him, Jaheira raised her voice into a keening chant.

The Ravager hung from the side of one of the enormous trees. Its long, taloned feet dug deeply into the ancient bark, and it had all four hands free. With one mighty limb the creature smashed a hole into the hollow tree and revealed the modest home of an elf family who couldn't possibly have done anything to deserve this. An elf woman screamed and all but threw a squalling infant into a bassinet in one corner of the room. The Ravager picked the woman up as if she weighed nothing and squeezed. The claws were as long as the woman's arms, and they impaled her four times from four different directions. She didn't scream again, but she managed a sob before she died. An elf warrior answered from below with a battle cry that set Abdel's heart racing again.

The Ravager heard the cry and bent backward, still holding the tree with its feet, still holding the elf woman in one hand. The elf warrior stepped forward with a wide-bladed bastard sword that only glanced off the Ravager's nigh impenetrable chitin. The beast let the elf think he'd dodged a swipe of one clawed hand, then came down over the warrior with its open mouth. Abdel, in his paralyzed haze, made note of the fact that it was the first time he'd seen anyone, man or elf, bitten cleanly in half.

"Imoen," Abdel whispered, "no. . . ."

The heat and sound of the fireball brought Abdel just one more notch closer to the situation at hand, but he didn't turn to find the source of it. An elf mage stepped a few paces behind what looked like a boulder of yellow-hot lava. A family of elves ran across the fireball's path. The mage showed the fine control she had over her burning conjuration by making it swerve around them so fast and by far enough that the elves didn't seem to see it. The ball was rolling toward the tree, toward the Ravager, and Abdel realized it must have been dozens of spells like it that accounted for all the fires.

Another elf warrior died horribly after trying to even dent the Ravager's armorlike skin. Abdel took a step forward, and he looked at the sword in his hand. He didn't even remember now where he'd gotten it. It wasn't even his sword. It was too light for Abdel's tastes even when fighting only other men. Against the Ravager, it would be no better than a needle. It was poorly made and cheap and certainly not enchanted in any way.

And did he even want to kill this thing? Of course, he had to. The lives of hundreds had already fallen to it, and a beautiful place that deserved none of this was being torn to ribbons, but this was Imoen. Somewhere in there this monster was still Imoen. And Jaheira was here. If he killed Imoen, what would she think? She had tried so hard to turn him away from his father's blood. Any death at his hands was a betrayal of that. Wasn't it?

The flaming sphere rolled to the base of the tree, then up. The Ravager slipped off the tree and almost seemed to willingly fall through the fire spell on its way down. The magical flames merely dissipated around the creature, who paid them no mind.

Jaheira cursed from behind Abdel, and he heard her call on Mielikki and ask her favors before slipping into that arcane tongue once more.

"Imoen," Abdel said again, his feet planted firmly in place.

"Abdel, my friend," Yoshimo said, sliding behind him and coughing once from the smoke. "What is it we're to do here? What can you do from this . . . what, forty yards or so away? Do we attack it? How does a man stop such a . . . such a . . ."

There was a roar, a flash of purple and black, and a tiger the likes of which Abdel had never imagined, much less seen, appeared in the glade in front of him.

"You know what to do, my girls," Jaheira said, her voice as certain and steady as she could make it.

Abdel turned to look at her, and before he saw Jaheira he'd counted six of the huge cats. Standing in front of her were two more. From the mouths of these tigers grew fangs like scimitar blades. A few of the tigers spared Abdel a passing glance, then they loped determinedly toward the Ravager, two of them circling off to the right, two to the left, and four straight down the middle, straight at it.

"I came here for . . ." Yoshimo said to Abdel. "I did not come here for this. It is time for me to . . . go."

The first tiger hit the Ravager hard and heavy, daggerlike claws tried to dig in, to hold, then tear. The monster reacted to the animal's weight with a sense of irritation rather than pain or fear. It took hold of the beast as if it was a mewling kitten and crushed its spine with a single twitch of its massive hand. The second cat was caught in midleap by another of the Ravager's clawed hands. The single backhanded swipe took the tiger's head off. The other cats pulled up short, quickly regrouping in the face of an enemy they couldn't ever have been ready for.

The Ravager waded through the confused tigers and ripped a long, jagged gash in the side of one. The mighty animal's entrails spilled onto the ground, and it died at the Ravager's feet. The other cats each glanced at Jaheira in turn. A tear stained the druid's cheek, but she nodded the animals in. One of them latched onto the monster's leg, sinking its huge fangs through the hard exoskeleton with a loud crack. The Ravager trembled, injured for the first time. It grabbed the tiger and snatched it up hard and fast enough that the animal's head came off, its teeth still wedged firmly into the creature's leg. The Ravager tossed the headless tiger away and grabbed for another, which dodged lithely out of reach.

"I can't . . ." Jaheira said. "I free you. *Go!*"

The four tigers who still lived didn't hesitate to follow Jaheira's advice and withdraw. They scattered in all directions, then simply faded into thin air before reaching the edge of the glade. The severed head was gone from the Ravager's leg, and a thick green fluid oozed from the wound.

"It can be hurt," Abdel said, and Yoshimo nodded.

There was a brilliant flash of blue-white light—a single bolt of powerful lighting—that ran parallel to the ground and was obviously the doing of a young elf, standing defiantly at the base of one of the mighty trees.

The Ravager shook off what little effect the lightning might have had on it and whirled to face the elf mage.

"That elf is going to die very soon," Yoshimo said grimly.

The Ravager took two huge, ground-trembling steps toward the mage, who was wise enough to turn and run. The elf managed to disappear through a doorway that Abdel never would have seen in the base of the tree. The Ravager screamed out its rage and set Abdel's ears ringing.

The sellsword in him noticed a hesitation in the monster's step. The tiger had hurt it more than Abdel had at first realized.

"Yoshimo," Abdel said, "we have to immobilize it."

"Immobilize?" the Kozakuran asked.

"Make it . . ." Abdel fumbled. "Make it so the thing can't move. Make it fall down and not be able to get back—"

"I understand, now," Yoshimo interrupted, "thank you. So, we go for the legs?"

"I think so," Abdel answered, "avoiding the arms. If we can get it to just stop, maybe I can talk to it."

"Abdel—" Jaheira, who had moved up behind them started.

"It's Imoen," Abdel told her. "Imoen's in there somewhere."

"Abdel—" she started to say.

"Don't, Jaheira," he said. "It was you who started this. Before I met you I wouldn't have hesitated—not just now but lots of times before. Yoshimo would be dead now, so would Gaelan Bayle—but they live because of you, because you taught me to fight with my heart—my human heart—not my tainted blood. That thing is Imoen. I can't kill her. I killed Sarevok, but I can't kill her."

Jaheira smiled sadly, then her attention was ripped away by another elf's dying scream.

"Yoshimo?" Abdel asked.

Yoshimo nodded but looked to Abdel to make the first move. "I will try, my friend," the Kozakuran said, "but I will have to go, if I feel I have to go."

It was Abdel's turn to nod. He took the first step, then the two of them were charging.

A wave of fleeing elves covered the bulk of their charge, and the Ravager was still trying to find the elf who'd sent the lightning bolt its way. Abdel got to the thing's leg and made to swipe at the already open wound. The broadsword bounced off the thing's armored skin less than half an inch from the wound. The Ravager took no notice of him.

Yoshimo circled around. The Kozakuran moved with barely a sound, and though it looked as if he wanted to let loose a battle cry of some kind, he held his tongue. The sword bit deeply into the Ravager's leg, benefiting from the Kozakuran's running momentum.

The monster flung its head backward on its hunched neck and hissed into the air. Yoshimo, teeth clamped hard together, began to work his sword back and forth in the creature's leg. Abdel couldn't tell if he was trying to get the blade out or deeper in. Green gore was spraying everywhere, and Yoshimo was quickly covered in it.

"Enchanted," Yoshimo called. "The blade, I mean."

The Ravager reached down for Yoshimo, and Abdel, not sure what else to do, screamed. This distracted the Ravager for only half a second, but that was enough time for Yoshimo to sidestep the thing's multifingered hand.

The Ravager reversed the direction of its arm and swatted Yoshimo away. The enchanted sword came out of the thing's leg, releasing a second torrent of green blood, and Yoshimo was thrown several paces away and to the ground.

"Imoen!" Abdel screamed. "No!"

The Ravager roared and tipped its head down to Yoshimo. The Kozakuran, stunned, shook his head and tried to stand.

"Yoshimo!" Jaheira shouted, "get out of there!" as if the Kozakuran would want to do anything but.

The Ravager brought its mighty head down and impaled the Kozakuran through the small of his back with one of the scythelike horns on the side of its face. Abdel watched this and heard the avatar sniff the fallen Shadow Thief like a dog might test a meal. Yoshimo tried to get up, but the thing had him pinned to the ground. A wavelike shudder went through the

Kozakuran's body, and he coughed on the blood that was quickly filling his mouth. The Ravager almost seemed to grin at the sight of it.

"*Harasu,*" Yoshimo said, his voice breaking, his right hand fumbling vainly in the dirt for the sword. "*Harasu . . .*"

The Ravager slowly brought one hand down over Yoshimo, withdrew the horn, and ripped the Kozakuran to bloody shreds.

Abdel screamed and drew his arm back, forgetting the futility of tapping at this thirty-foot monster with the simple steel broadsword. The Ravager whipped its head around to face him and drew a deep breath through its palm-sized nostrils. The thing tipped its head, reminding Abdel of a dog for a second time. It almost seemed to recognize him. Abdel let his arm drop.

"Imoen," he said. "It's me."

The Ravager roared, and Abdel threw his hands up to protect his ears, dropping the inadequate blade in the process. His already ringing ears ached, and he recoiled at the blast of fetid wind the roar sent his way.

"Abdel!" Jaheira screamed. He barely heard her. "The sword!"

The sword!

Abdel dived for Yoshimo's blade, launching himself farther through the air than even he imagined himself capable. He came down with his hand on the hilt of the sword and instantly felt a burning agony explode on his left shoulder. The Ravager had pinned him to the ground the same way it had Yoshimo. Abdel could feel its hot breath and the smell of it gagged him. The pain of the wrist-sized horn jammed through bone and flesh set Abdel's head spinning in colored lights and brought him to the edge of unconsciousness. The yellow haze came back, and Abdel roared himself this time in rage and frustration.

Abdel flipped himself over onto his side, letting the horn rip through his already numbing flesh. He swiped the sword across his turning body with every muscle in his arm tensed to its breaking point. The blade sheared through the horn, and with the help of his strong twisting motion, it came off the Ravager's face like a branch being shorn from a tree.

The monster flinched back, and Abdel, overcome now only by a desire to kill—an overwhelming bloodlust unlike anything he'd ever felt—reversed the blade and brought it smashing into the Ravager's crocodile-like lower jaw. The whole jaw came off, and green slime drenched the prone sellsword. Abdel blinked but was too far gone to let that stop him. He hacked the thing's head again, ignoring the deep gouges one of the creature's clawed hands made in his right side.

The horn fell from the gory wound in Abdel's shoulder, and without even thinking, he snatched it out of the air before it hit the ground. Without hesitation, he drove it into the monster's blood-soaked throat. The Ravager screamed again, robbing Abdel of his ability to hear at all.

Abdel's whole body twitched, then tightened, and the deep wound in his side closed all at once and was gone. The yellow haze deepened over his vision, and all he saw clearly was the Ravager—his opponent had become the entire world.

The sellsword hacked the thing again, then again, and again. He didn't stop until the huge hellspawned beast fell to the ground with a tremor like an earthquake and a sound only Abdel couldn't hear.

Chapter Twenty-Four

Quiet.

Not silence, there were sounds: the sound of running feet, burning wood, crying children, voices calling out, asking in Elvish if everyone is all right, if anyone has seen my husband, if anyone knows what happened to my family. . . .

Abdel heard all of it, but as one muffled, wavelike hum. He could feel blood trickling out of his ears. His eyes hurt, and so did his head. He felt wet and uncomfortable. The nondescript chain mail tunic and trousers he'd accepted from Bodhi were drenched in gore that smelled sharply of iron and power.

He could see, but his vision was blurred, almost as numb in its own way as his shoulder and side. Jaheira leaned over him, and though he could see her lips form his name, the sound of her voice was buried under the omnipresent dull roar. Elhan was there too, then both of them were dragging him across the uneven, mossy, gore-soaked ground. They got him to the side of one of the trees, and Abdel groaned at the pain that burned through his upper body when they propped him as gently as they could against the rough, but somehow comforting, bark of the ancient tree.

"I killed her," he said, his voice echoing in his own head in dissonant contrast to the muffled sounds of the aftermath around him. "I killed her. . . . I killed her. . . . I killed . . ."

The ground trembled, and a hiss burst out from the morass of muffled sounds. Abdel tried to look at the source of the sound, though he knew it couldn't be the Ravager. His eyes closed and wouldn't open.

"I killed her. . . ." he said again.

"It's the Ravager," Elhan said.

Abdel was surprised at the sound of the elf's voice. The dull hum was fading into a piercing ring, but he was beginning to hear voices over that ring.

"It's still twitching," Elhan added.

Abdel wanted to smile, but his face wouldn't respond.

"Abdel's wounds are already healing," Jaheira said, ignoring the Ravager's death spasms. "It's impossible. He's stopped bleeding, but I can see straight through the hole in his shoulder."

Abdel wanted to say "I killed her," again, but all he could do was let his jaw drop open limply.

"I've never seen anything like that," Elhan admitted. "He was like a madman. Now this regeneration . . . it's not . . . human."

Jaheira shook her head, her face slack with what looked to Abdel like awe. "He's like an avatar now. He's like the Ravager—but stronger. He isn't human. I guess he never was . . . not completely. I should have known he wouldn't be able to deny what he was forever."

Jaheira was touching him. Her hands felt warm, soft, and reassuring against his skin. The numbness was giving way to that sensation, and a burning, nettling itch. Jaheira whispered through a spell, and Abdel could feel the grace of the Forest Queen rush through him, mingling with the blood of a god Mielikki would never have shown mercy to.

Abdel managed to open his eyes, and he smiled at her. The smile Jaheira returned was relieved but tinged with sadness.

"You had to, Abdel," she told him softly. "She was gone before—"

The druid was interrupted by an ear-splitting crack that was answered by the startled shouts of a dozen elves.

"It's cracking!" Elhan called. He fell backward on his rump, sitting next to Abdel, who could only let his head limply hang in the direction of the fallen monster.

A clawed hand—not as big as the Ravager's monstrous claws—burst out of a widening crack in the creature's otherwise still chest.

"Mielikki help us," Jaheira breathed. "It's another one."

The thing that pulled itself out of the Ravager's corpse, like a chick emerging from its egg, was no taller than Abdel. It was shaped, vaguely, like a man, but its body was covered in row after row of bladelike spikes. Its head was a twisted mockery of a bug's—a backhanded slap at the honor of the insect world. It had only two long, sinewy arms that ended in slightly more humanlike hands. Below the thing's arms were two smaller, almost vestigial limbs with a single elbowlike joint. Those smaller limbs ended in bony blades like swords.

Abdel drew in a deep, shuddering breath, and the thing made eye contact with him. Abdel could feel the waves of paralyzing panic practically inundating him from both Elhan on his left and Jaheira on his right.

The creature's eyes flashed violet light at Abdel, and something about that look made the injured sellsword say, "Imoen."

The thing nodded. It made a sound that all who

heard it wished to whatever gods they worshiped wasn't a laugh, and crawled completely out of the ooze-filled chest cavity of the dead Ravager. The thing stood on backward-bending legs and crouched.

Abdel felt for the Kozakuran's sword, but found only a blast of pain from his shredded shoulder. The creature seemed to nod at Abdel again, then it leaped into the air, flinging itself straight up into the heavens like a crossbow bolt. In less than a second it had faded to a point, then nothing against the blazing blue sky.

"Oh, no," Jaheira sighed.

"I'll live," the sellsword managed to croak. The effort sent pain raging up and down his dry throat.

Jaheira put a warm, gentle finger to his lips and said, "Don't. You're healing, thanks to that blood of yours, but you need time."

Abdel forced a smile, knowing full well that time was something they didn't have in abundance.

Elhan couldn't keep his eyes off the tattered remains of the Ravager, even to look at the smoking ruin the proud tree-city of Suldanessellar had been reduced to.

"Where's Ellesime?" Jaheira asked finally.

Elhan spun on her, his eyes wild. He calmed himself quickly, taking a deep breath, then said, "The queen is safe. Ellesime is in Myth Rhynn."

Abdel and Jaheira exchanged a long, pained, exhausted look, and the sellsword began the painful process of trying to stand up.

* * * * *

Ellesime screamed again, and the guards near her cringed at the sound of pure, desperate fear in their queen's shriek.

The link she'd shared with Irenicus for centuries

uncounted had never been one of words or even tangible thoughts. The two were simply aware of each other. Now, for Ellesime to have said that something had changed would be an incredible understatement. The man at the other end of this joining of spirits was at once in mortal agony and riding a cresting wave of self-satisfied triumph. The horror of what Irenicus had become and the feel of his soul unraveling alongside hers was what was making Ellesime scream.

For their parts, the elves who had accompanied her to Myth Rhynn couldn't possibly have imagined what she was going through. The guards were busily fortifying the crumbling structure of what one of the mages had described as a wing of Myth Rhynn's ancient library. The soldiers knew only that the walls were full of holes and there was no ceiling.

They'd heard only pieces, gleaned from magical mind-to-mind communication with loved ones left behind in Suldanessellar, that the creature was dead, but that a new creature was coming. This one had taken to the air, and the guards now looked at the sky above their ring of ancient walls with dread and the simple knowledge that they couldn't keep the thing out, so they'd have to die fighting it.

All of the elves were uncomfortable within the normally forbidden confines of the ruined mythal city, but doubly so the handful of mages they'd brought with them. The elf wizards were busily studying long, time-weathered scrolls and gathering little piles of odds and ends where they'd be in easy reach.

Abdel, Jaheira, and Elhan's sudden appearance in the middle of the crumbling structure made more than one of the elves go suddenly to his guard. One wizard very nearly got a spell off before dismissing it with an impatient grumble, "One less against the beast."

Elhan, dizzy from the teleport, stumbled to Ellesime's side and spoke to her briefly in Elvish.

"I can feel him falling apart," the queen said weakly. "He can't control it."

Abdel, his shoulder now a mass of red, tender skin and his side almost completely healed, squeezed the grip of the enchanted sword. He'd have to choose between this woman, this elf queen who was a vision of such beauty Abdel had never thought possible, and the life of the little girl he remembered playing with in Winthrop's wine cellar.

"How do we k—*stop* it?" Abdel asked the queen. "That thing was once . . . was once a young, impetuous girl, who deserved none of this."

Ellesime nodded, then winced in unseen pain. "I met him here," she said, her voice weak. "It was in this library. I wanted him to come for me here, with this avatar of his. If he saw me here, again, all this time later, maybe . . . maybe . . . At least it's far enough away from the Tree of Life."

"There is another life at stake, your majesty," Jaheira prompted, running as much as all the others on adrenaline, impatience, and sheer terror.

"Your sister," Ellesime said, addressing Abdel directly for the first time, "is not like you."

Abdel drew in a breath and took a step forward that made the elf warriors move to intercept him. He backed away just enough to let them know that if he wanted to get past them, they wouldn't be able to stop him.

"She's enough like me," Abdel hissed, "so that your old lover could turn her into that . . . that . . ."

"It would have been an avatar," Ellesime said, "if Bhaal were alive. Instead, it's just . . . close enough. It can kill me, this new one, the Slayer. Your sister's blood was lying dormant, where yours was given a chance to show itself. What occupation did your foster father allow you to pursue? Sellsword? Mercenary?"

Abdel nodded.

"And Imoen's?" the queen asked.

"Her foster father was Winthrop," Abdel said, "an innkeeper. Not quite as serious a man as Gorion. Imoen was a happy, precocious girl."

"And there was nothing to draw the Bhaal out of her," Jaheira, understanding, added.

"What could all this matter now?" Abdel asked, his brow furrowing in anger. "I have to kill her. You've brought us all here, and now there's only one way to stop all this. To keep this Slayer of Irenicus's from killing you—from killing us all—I have to kill Imoen."

"No," Ellesime said, "there is a chance. . . ."

Chapter Twenty-Five

Irenicus appeared in the center of Suldanessellar in the guise of an elf. Any number of the mages running all around him in a panic to aid in the recovery of survivors could have identified the disguise with a word and the wave of a finger or two. The pandemonium around him was as good a disguise as the illusion. He stood at the base of the Tree of Life unmolested.

He smiled up at it and closed his eyes. He could feel its power pulse through him like a second heartbeat. The tree was life, and for Irenicus, it would be eternal life.

He sank to his knees and touched his forehead to the holy ground. Looking like one of hundreds of elf believers who came to commune with the tree every day, Irenicus started to repeat the words of the ritual.

Her reached out with his left hand, and the tips of his fingers brushed the warm bark of the Tree of Life.

His arm quivered with the power pulsing through it and into Irenicus's heart.

"Forever," Irenicus said, "Forever. Forever. Forever . . ."

* * * * *

The sound Queen Ellesime made was worse than any scream Abdel had ever heard. It was the kind of

219

tortured wail that could only be made by someone who'd lived long enough to understand the true significance of what was happening to her.

"The Tree," she coughed. "Irenicus . . . is at the Tree of Life!"

"Ellesime," Elhan said, following her name with a soothing string of Elvish words Abdel didn't understand.

The queen's body twisted, writhed in pain. "Imoen!" she screamed.

Abdel's flesh crawled.

"It's the Slayer," Ellesime gasped. "I can . . . feel it . . ." Her face twisted into a mask of revulsion so intense Abdel had to look away.

"Mielikki save us all," Jaheira said, dropping to one knee.

Abdel saw the look of resignation pass over Jaheira's face and understood. Jaheira was watching this woman she had known all her life, like all elves, as the immortal symbol of her people. This elf was less a woman than a monument. Nothing could touch her, not time, not even death. Now, here she was, twisting in agony, reeling at the mistake she made before she became that solid core of Suldanessellar, when she was still a girl, seduced by an elf who dreamed of immortality.

Abdel stepped to her and took Ellesime's face in his huge, rough hands. Her eyes rolled into her head, and Abdel felt a stern hand grip his arm.

"What are you doing?" Elhan demanded. "She is in pain. Release her!"

Abdel brushed him off and said harshly, "Ellesime! Ellesime, look at me."

The queen sobbed and closed her eyes, trying to shake her head out of Abdel's hands. "He will live forever now. He will be like you are."

"Ellesime!" Abdel roared.

Elhan stepped back and drew his moonblade. "Unhand—"

"No!" Ellesime said, her eyes popping open to fix on Abdel's. "The link has been made. Irenicus is feeding from the Tree of Life!"

"I understand," Abdel said, though in fact he was still struggling with the sheer impossibility of it all. "Imoen—the Slayer—do you see it? Do you know where she is?"

"It's coming," the queen whispered, not struggling now. Tears streamed down her cheeks.

"How do we kill it?" he asked her.

Her eyes softened, and a look of relief came over them. "You might have a chance."

"Tell me."

"The Rynn Lanthorn . . ." she said, her voice barely audible, squeaking pain and sorrow now mingling with hope.

"The lanthorn will kill the Slayer?" Jaheira asked, standing.

"Breaking the link with Irenicus and the tree will make it mortal. It will not kill it, but it will make it possible to kill it," Ellesime answered.

Abdel let his hands fall from her face, and she looked down and away.

"Mages," Elhan barked, "we will prepare the lanthorn—gather yourselves." He started to repeat the order in Elvish, but Abdel held up a hand, stopping him.

"I cannot kill it," Abdel said, his eyes burning into Ellesime. "That is . . . that was Imoen. She doesn't deserve to die for your mistakes, Queen Ellesime."

The elf queen turned her face up to him, a look of haughty displeasure crossing her brow for the briefest moment before she realized he was right.

"What would you risk to save her?" she asked him.

"Nothing," Elhan answered for him. "We will risk no more lives for this girl."

"No," Jaheira interrupted before Abdel turned on the elves. "Abdel is right. She's only one, but one is enough."

Abdel smiled and turned to Ellesime. "How?" he asked.

"The link I shared with Irenicus was transferred from him to the Slayer the moment he made contact with the Tree of Life. He's bonded with it now and has set the Slayer out along that link to find me," the queen said. "This link . . . it could be transferred from me to . . . to you."

"Ellesime, no . . ." Jaheira said.

"What would that accomplish?" Abdel asked, ignoring the druid.

"You share something with Imoen that goes way beyond . . . well, that . . ."

"Go on," Abdel prompted.

"If the link between her soul and yours is strong enough," Ellesime said, "it's possible that you could destroy the Slayer but anchor Imoen's soul to this plane. The avatar would return to the hell that spawned it, and Imoen would be free."

"Or?" Abdel asked.

"Or," the queen sighed, "it will kill you both."

"Abdel—" Jaheira started to say.

"There's a chance," Abdel said simply.

The queen nodded in response, and Abdel turned to Elhan. "We need this artifact."

The prince nodded and said, "Either way, the Slayer is destroyed?"

"It looks that way," Abdel answered.

"Then let us be off."

"Abdel," Jaheira said, her voice tight. "I can't let you

risk this. With all respect, Your Majesty," she said to Ellesime, "you're not *sure*."

The queen writhed in obvious agony, then shook her head no.

"If I let Imoen die," Abdel asked Jaheira, "let her soul follow this monster's into Gehenna, what have you taught me? Where have I come?"

Jaheira couldn't answer. She knew there was no way to stop him, that she shouldn't even try.

He reached out and touched her cheek. "Maybe I *was* hypnotized," he told her softly. "I would have to have been."

She smiled and let herself cry.

"Jaheira," Elhan said, "they'll need you in Suldanessellar. Go to the tree, but don't engage Irenicus."

"I'm coming with you," Jaheira said to Abdel.

Abdel looked her in the eye and shook his head. She looked away, knowing he was right again. Only Abdel could do what needed to be done.

Elhan helped Ellesime to her feet. Abdel, his eyes still locked on Jaheira's, stepped next to them, and in a flash of purple light, they were gone.

* * * * *

Ellesime had placed it on the rough ground in the center of a ring of standing stones, which might have been the columns of a once-mighty temple, now worn by years of lashing wind in to featureless stubs of their former glory. The elf mages sat themselves in a wide circle around the lanthorn, contorting their legs in a way that confounded Abdel. Ellesime was weakening still, able to move now only when her brother carried her. She motioned Elhan to set her down on the ground near one end of the artifact.

The mages began a grinding chant. They all closed their eyes, and Abdel could see their shoulders sag in unison. It was as if they were pouring every pinch of energy from their bodies into their minds and out through those arcane words.

"Sit across from me," Ellesime told Abdel, her voice thick, quiet, and labored. With great effort she reached out and laid her right hand on one end of the lanthorn. With a nod she told him to do the same.

Abdel set the enchanted sword down reverently next to him and placed one big, callused hand on the lanthorn.

"What now?" he asked.

Ellesime didn't answer. She closed her eyes, and her neck quivered when she tried to shake her head.

"She's dying," Elhan said. He was standing outside the circle, his face gray with exhaustion and fear.

Abdel looked up at him, then had to look away. Elhan was stalking around the circle of mages, trying to look everywhere at once but never managing to keep his eyes from straying to his dying sister.

The Slayer dropped out of the sky five paces in front of Elhan, and the movement startled him. Elhan's hand went instinctively to the moonblade at his belt, and the ancient sword came out of its scabbard and bathed the circle in a blue glow. The Slayer brought its hands up. Two daggers carved from bone seemed to appear in its hands from thin air.

Elhan didn't wait for the thing to attack. He charged at it with brazen courage born of knowing there was no one else there to keep it away from the chanting mages.

Abdel flinched back, and Ellesime hissed, "No!"

The sellsword looked up at her. Her eyes were half open, and her dull gaze lolled over him.

"You must not break the link," she told him. "Just a little longer. I can . . . feel . . . it."

Elhan was a practiced and experienced swordsman, and though the Slayer was faster, the elf managed to swing under its two daggers and sliced hard across the thing's spine-covered chest. The moonblade, as powerful a weapon as had ever been known to man or elf on Faerûn, pinged off the thing without leaving so much as a scratch.

Elhan gasped, never having seen his ancestral weapon fail to cut. The Slayer laughed at him. The sound made every hair on Abdel's body stand rigidly, uncomfortably, on end. The sound was eerily familiar, as if it had a place in his blood. It was his father's laugh. Abdel's eyes began to glow yellow. This was no momentary flash now, but a steady, burning light.

"Everyone's here," the evil thing said. "Your souls will suckle the legions of Gehenna."

The avatar came at Elhan fast, but the elf was just able to dodge back and out of the way of the bone daggers. He brought his moonblade up and knocked one dagger aside, clipping a chip of bone out of it.

Abdel almost took his hand away from the artifact again. Elhan was good, but Abdel could see he wasn't good enough.

"Please," Ellesime said, her voice suddenly stronger. "Don't help him."

Abdel gnashed his teeth but kept his hand on the lanthorn. She was right. The ritual had to be completed. He had to take on this spirit link from her, or Imoen would die. But what of Prince Elhan of Suldanessellar?

The elf prince parried another of the Slayer's attacks, knocking one of the thing's blade-arms away. The parry opened Elhan's left side, though, and the Slayer made full use of it. Moving with such unnatural silence it seemed the thing wasn't even there at all, the avatar sliced in with its other blade-arm and opened a gash across Elhan's stomach wide and deep enough to spill the prince's entrails onto the dead soil of Myth Rhynn.

Ellesime closed her eyes and let out a long, shuddering breath.

When the Slayer laughed as Elhan's body fell lifeless to the ground, Abdel heard it in his ears, but also felt it in his chest. The muscles that he would have used to laugh himself twitched and jerked, and air caught in his throat. He could feel it!

"Not yet," Ellesime warned him, tears streaming down her cheeks now as she cried in unselfconscious abandon.

Abdel felt unfamiliar muscles twitch and looked up at the Slayer. In the air in front of it spun six more of the evil-looking bone daggers. Suspended by some fell magic, the daggers twisted and cavorted in the air, the Slayer eyeing each blade in turn with some satisfaction.

The flying daggers descended on one of the mages still sitting in the circle. The Slayer backed off a bit, as if curious itself to see what was going to happen next. The elf mage was slumped in his position, eyes closed, mind locked into the incessant loop of the empowering chant. The elf had no idea what was coming fast behind him, and Abdel knew he couldn't take his hand off the lanthorn, but he could at least warn—what was this elf's name?

"Elf!" Abdel shouted, then, "Mage!"

The elf mage didn't show any sign of having heard him. The first dagger plunged into the elf's spine to its carved hilt, then tore sideways through flesh and bone. The other five daggers plunged in and sliced out in turn. The elf mage collapsed in a pile of loose skin and pouring blood. Abdel cursed under his breath, struggling to make himself stay where he was.

The elf mage's body twitched violently once, then exploded in a shower of blood and strips of flesh. All of the elf's bones burst up into the air and exploded again in a cloud of sharp, splintered bone. The fragments coalesced, joined the dance of the six daggers, and settled in front of the Slayer. The avatar stood now behind a shield of whirring, razor-sharp bone fragments. Anyone who stepped too close to the creature would be shredded.

And Abdel could feel it. He could feel the cold power of it and could track each fragment in its mad orbit. He could feel it.

"Go!" Ellesime screamed, and Abdel jumped into the air, Yoshimo's sword in his right hand, before that single word had faded into the suddenly silent air.

Their chant at an end, the elf mages all came out of it at the same time and moved quickly away from the Slayer and its barrier of jagged bone. Abdel went the other way, straight at the whirling cloud of blades. Able to feel each fragment, Abdel started tapping them away with the tip of Yoshimo's sword. One at a time the bone chips dropped out of the cloud to bounce harmlessly on the ground. Abdel didn't speak, hardly moved his feet, and his breathing became shallow and steady. The Slayer, if it was capable of facial expressions at all, regarded the scene with a mix of irritated confusion and surprised amusement.

Behind him, Ellesime's exhausted form slumped onto the ground over the lanthorn. She took in one deep, ragged breath and almost managed to open her eyes. One of the mages caught her up in his arms and, nodding to one of the other mages to retrieve the lanthorn, he carried Ellesime out of the circle, putting one of the stones between her and the Slayer.

Abdel wasn't counting the number of bones he knocked

out of the barrier. It must have been nigh on a hundred that hit the ground before the barrier collapsed and showered the ground between the son and the avatar of Bhaal with chips of bone.

Abdel stepped in quickly, but the Slayer, waiting behind the dwindling shield of bone blades, was faster. The thing ripped a deep gash across Abdel's chest with one of its blade-arms. Abdel hissed at the pain but ignored it, dropping his sword arm down to parry the second blade-arm's attack.

"I'll eat your soul raw, son of Bhaal!" the thing shrieked at him. Abdel pretended not to recognize Imoen's voice in the echoing sound of it.

Abdel stepped back, letting the Slayer come in at him, then sliced hard both in and down. The sword took one of the Slayer's blade-arms off at the elbow joint, and the creature recoiled in shock.

It could be hurt, then. It was mortal.

Invigorated by the knowledge that at least that part of the ritual had worked, Abdel came in hard, his sword chopping down in an effort to rid the avatar of another arm. The creature was ready this time, though, and still faster than Abdel. With a hand like an iron vise, the Slayer took hold of Abdel's sword arm and stopped its downward motion so abruptly even Abdel couldn't keep a hold on the sword. The blade flashed in the late afternoon sunlight as it spun far out of the sellsword's reach.

The avatar wrenched Abdel's arm with the strength of a thousand draft horses. His right arm came off at the shoulder with the sound of tearing skin, popping joints, and the hot rush of blood. One of the elf mages screamed, and another turned around and threw up.

Red hot agony flowed through Abdel, but rather than weaken him, it flooded his body with a power he'd never imagined.

Abdel, no longer thinking of this thing as some manifestation of a murder god's power but just an opponent, growled in anger and grabbed the Slayer's other elbow with his left hand. The thing was strong, stronger than any man on Faerûn, but so was Abdel.

The Slayer let go of Abdel's right arm, letting it fall to the ground with a wet slap. The avatar swiped at Abdel, raking cold, sharp claws across the sellsword's already cut chest. Abdel didn't feel any pain now.

He pulled hard on the Slayer's arm, and it jerked toward him. Abdel dropped, took note of the Slayer's surprised, offended expression, and flipped the avatar over him. The creature sprawled across the uneven ground, scuttling to its feet like a crab.

Abdel grabbed his still twitching arm that bled into the ground of Myth Rhynn and was happy to feel its warmth. He jammed the torn end of it onto the ragged stump of his shoulder. A wave of tingling pleasure swept through him, and the arm reattached itself. By the time the Slayer was on its feet and coming back at him, Abdel could use his right arm again as if it had never been ripped from his body.

He scanned the ground for the sword, but the Slayer was coming in too fast. Without ever having thought to do something like this before, he plunged his hand into the beast's wide, spike-covered chest. Abdel's hand sank into the Slayer's body up to the elbow, and the thing screamed in rage.

Abdel knew on some level that was either beyond or not yet at the point of words that if he turned his wrist just so—there! He closed his hand around something warm, soft, and fleshy, and pulled.

The Slayer screamed again when Abdel's hand burst out of its chest. Abdel was holding a length of pink flesh. At the end of it was a hand. A hand with five fingers, no claws, no spikes, no chitin. Green blood followed Abdel's hand out. He was holding a human arm.

"She's mine!" the Slayer shrieked.

Abdel let go of the arm and ignored its groping fingers. He grabbed the Slayer by the sides of its head with both hands and twisted.

"She's no one's" he growled into the Slayer's bulging, incredulous eyes. "She's coming out!"

"No!" it screamed, then tried to scream again, but the sound was cut short in a throat now closed.

Abdel strained with all his considerable strength to turn the thing's head down and to the side. The Slayer answered by grabbing Abdel's head in one huge, misshapen hand. The grip was crushing, and Abdel's jaw clenched tight enough that his teeth started to shatter—each one cracking in turn with a spike of pain worse than the amputation. Blood dribbled down from his scalp. His skull cracked sharply at his temple and flashes of blue-violet light colored his vision.

There was a loud, grinding crack, and Abdel thought he might be dead, but it was the Slayer who went limp. The sudden weight pulled Abdel to the ground on top of it. The human arm still protruding from its chest blindly groped for anything. The hand found Abdel's gore-soaked chain mail and hung on.

The sellsword did nothing to get away from the human hand's grip. He started to claw at the Slayer's lifeless head and another one of the elf mages had to turn around and vomit at the sound it made. He ripped the thing's head open as if he was peeling an orange. Beneath the chitin, slime, blood, and the withering flesh of the avatar was a human face, a girl's face.

She gasped and took in a single, chest-filling breath.

"Imoen," Abdel said, his eyes filling with tears.

"Abdel," Imoen gasped, her eyes not yet able to focus,

but she recognized his voice. "Abdel . . . wh-where are we?"

Abdel smiled weakly and was about to reply when Ellesime screamed, "The tree!"

Abdel turned but couldn't see her. A blaze of hot yellow light filled his vision and burned his eyes. He grunted and something tensed in his chest, and his head exploded in pain.

"Oh, no, Abdel!" Imoen shrieked. "No!"

Abdel felt something pull him downward but couldn't tell where it was holding him. It wasn't his leg—it might have been holding him around the waist. He slipped into the ground and could smell dirt fill his nostrils. His arms tensed, and he could feel them grow. A wave of rage blew his mind away.

Chapter Twenty-Six

Jaheira came awake with a gasp, her head snapping back, and her mouth gaping wide to draw in the unseasonably cool air of Suldanessellar. Her body, suspended in a mass of weblike strands, shook and rocked forward, then back, and came to a vibrating stop over the course of a long, painful minute.

Her eyelids were stuck closed with something, and when she finally forced one open, she realized the other just wasn't going to cooperate. A terrible pain throbbed all up the left side of her body. Her right foot was twisted painfully in the web, and she could feel it swelling.

Her one eye was blurred, but she saw Irenicus kneeling in front of the Tree of Life. She couldn't tell if it was a trick of her fuzzy vision or an actual phenomenon, but she was sure she could see Irenicus's skeleton outlined in bright light that turned his skin and muscles translucent.

The Tree of Life was on fire.

That thought didn't sink in at first. It took the space of two heartbeats, but when it did occur to her what she was seeing and the magnitude of the disaster that meant for not only the people of Suldanessellar, the elves of the forest of Tethir, but everyone and everything in Faerûn, all of Abeir-toril . . .

Jaheira screamed.

She heard the sound echo across the burning ruins of Suldanessellar. Irenicus didn't react at all. He just kneeled there, chanting.

She screamed again, then struggled in the web, which succeeded only in getting her more firmly caught.

"Abdel!" she screamed, between two body-racking sobs.

This made Irenicus turn. His face was as translucent as the rest of his body, and she could see his wildly grinning, mad skull. His eyes blazed a bright yellow she was all too familiar with.

"Abdel," Irenicus said, his voice like the wind rumbling across the Shaar—the voice of a god. "Yes . . . Abdel."

Jaheira screamed again and tried to look away, but her head was stuck, and she couldn't.

Irenicus smiled a toothy, leering, evil grin, and sank into the ground. His body just collapsed into a hole that wasn't really there. The Tree of Life blazed into wild orange flames hundreds of feet high that scalded Jaheira's face, and she screamed again. The webs started to unravel from the heat, and Jaheira's foot shifted painfully, then her head fell sideways.

She screamed, "Abdel, where are you?" in a dry throat with air from burned lungs and fell out of the web into a crumpled pile on the ground.

* * * * *

Abdel was blasted with heat, and it brought his consciousness back from the brink. Physically, he couldn't tell if he was a human or a monster, but his mind came back. Unfortunately, it came back just in time to be burned to death.

Though he wasn't sure it was a really good idea, he went ahead and opened his eyes even though he was afraid they'd be burned from his skull. Oddly enough, they weren't.

At first all they registered was a mass of slowly undulating orange, and it occurred to Abdel that he was submerged in molten lava, but how could that be?

Shadows coalesced in the orange and became figures, then those figures drifted into larger, more solid masses. The shadows were ledges and outcroppings of rock.

Abdel inhaled sharply and felt his jaw open. His mouth opened wrong, sideways, like the monster that Imoen had been before. Against all odds, he'd saved her life. Abdel remembered that clearly. It had happened a minute or so before he'd been pulled down into Hell.

So that was it. He was in Hell, and he was in the body—or his body had become the body—of a hideous, demonic monster. Abdel supposed that made him pretty much right at—

He shook his big giant monster head, not believing that he could be floating in a river of lava in some living Hell just casually thinking about—

Had he come home, then?

He asked himself that question.

Have I come home?

Is this the place I was supposed to be all along?

Do I rule here, then, like my father did?

Is that what I was meant to do?

Did Irenicus in his passionate, blind greed push me toward the destiny that has been mine, has run through my veins, my whole life?

Am I even Abdel now?

Am I Bhaal?

Am I anything? Just the will of murder and death and evil . . .

Am I home?

Is this home?

Abdel opened his mouth, sucked in a breath of hot, brimstone-reeking air, and called, "Father!"

"Bhaal!"

Abdel snapped his eyes shut and waited for an answer.

* * * * *

Jaheira knew she had to just lay there and breathe for a while. She also knew she had to do something. The Tree was still on fire.

She let her tears wet the brittle grass and crawled away from the fire, sweat washing away the rest of the webbing.

She'd come to Suldanessellar to look for Irenicus, and she found him faster and easier than she ever imagined she would. There he was, kneeling in front of the Tree of Life. Jaheira remembered feeling grateful that she hadn't been able to understand the words he was chanting. Of course she wouldn't know this hideous ritual, designed to destroy everything she held sacred.

"Mielikki," she said, not caring that her voice was ragged from the heat, from crying. "Mielikki, sweet Lady of the Forest, please . . ."

She put both hands down on the dry grass and pushed herself up, rolling over onto her left side. Pain made her gasp, then gag, and she sat up. She held her left side and felt wetness that might have been blood or sweat. She didn't want to take her hand away from her side long enough to check.

She looked up in the sky and saw nothing but rolling

black smoke. She saw the Tree of Life giving itself up one soot mote at a time. Jaheira felt as if the whole world was draining up into the sky.

"Mielikki," she whispered, and a tear rolled into her mouth. "Dear goddess, just tell me where he is. Where is he?"

Jaheira's hands shot up to guard her face, and she fell backward, the pain in her side not even registering. She was instinctively guarding her face from the vision that flashed across her eyes.

Orange flames.

Boiling seas.

Writhing bodies.

Souls damned.

He was in Hell.

Abdel was in Hell.

Jaheira screamed again, loud enough to make her own ears ring.

* * * * *

Abdel kept his eyes closed knowing that the sights around him would only distract him. For the first time maybe in his whole life he was going to stop, just let the world go on, and finally demand some answers from the universe. He was going to wait for his father to say something. In his mind's eye he drew a circle around himself, and in his mind's voice he said:

Speak to me.

Tell me.

Where are you?

What do you want from me?

What do I do?

Do I become you? Do I replace you? Do I serve you?

I'll let that tree burn, and the elf city burn, and

Candlekeep itself burn. I don't care. I want to know.

I will know.

You'll come back from wherever you've been, and you'll talk to me.

You'll talk to me, you bastard.

You'll talk to me.

Bhaal.

God of Murder.

Father.

Talk to me.

And Abdel let himself drift in the lava flow of Hell and waited for his father's voice to tell him everything, to tell him what to do. He waited in the pits of damnation for a long time, but his father never spoke to him.

"You're dead." Abdel said, and opened his eyes.

* * * * *

"You come back," Jaheira said, her voice coming in a feral growl that sounded wrong in her ears. "You come back to me."

She rolled back onto her stomach and paused to let pain wash over her again. She waited as patiently as she could, and when the worst of it was over, she forced herself to her feet.

Irenicus had nearly killed her when she confronted him at the Tree of Life. All around them Suldanessellar was burning, and he just started to pummel her with spells. She fought back with spells of her own, and elves came to her defense, but Irenicus's supply of painful, body-twisting magic seemed endless. He smashed her with lightning, burned her with fire, cut her with blades and glass and thorns, and the bastard laughed the whole time. When she finally fell, he hung her in a web to watch. And watch she did.

Philip Athans

She'd watched him suck the life energy out of the greatest source of life energy in the world, if not the entire multiverse.

He drained the Tree of Life and left it so dry the heat of burning Suldanessellar had touched it to flame, and it became an enormous inferno that burned away more than leaves, bark, and branches. Those flames burned away life. They burned away history. They burned away tradition and hope and the brittle dignity of a dying race.

Then Irenicus went willingly down into some hell where Abdel waited—for what? Abdel surely hadn't gone there willingly. They wouldn't embrace there in brotherhood. They'd fight, and even as much as she loved and trusted and was in awe of the Son of Bhaal, Jaheira didn't think he could win. How could he?

How could anyone stand against a man already powerful in his own right but now filled with the essence of the Tree of Life?

"Abdel," she said to the ground around her. "Just run. Get out of there, Abdel. Come back to me. Let him live. Let him live forever in Hell. Come back to me."

She realized she was looking at the point on the ground where Irenicus had sank. She took a step toward that spot, and when her foot touched the forest floor her knee gave out. She fell to the ground and ignored the pain. She tried to get back to her feet but couldn't, so she crawled.

"I'm coming, Abdel," she said.

Chapter Twenty-Seven

"He's dead, you idiot," Irenicus sneered from some-where in the roaring flames of Hell. "Your father is dead, and you'll get no answers from him."

Abdel gave himself over to the rage and reached out for the source of Irenicus's voice. He found something that felt like flesh and clawed through it. There was the sound of a grunt and the feel of blood, then the sound of laughter.

A hand grabbed Abdel's throat and squeezed. Abdel reached up with a viciously taloned foot and ripped Irenicus's stomach open. Irenicus squeezed, and Abdel's head came off at the neck. His vision tumbled and blurred, and Abdel realized that couldn't actually have happened—not even in Hell.

He came back into his body, and it was his body, human and whole, not a monster, not a demon.

"Idiot human child," Irenicus said. "Waiting for orders, waiting for answers. You don't get any answers, child, in the flea speck of a lifetime you enjoy. You don't get to know. You don't get anything but a bit of wan-dering around before a painful, empty, ruthless death. You serve me now as you've served me all along. I brought out the Ravager in you and the little bitch, but it was you who brought out the Slayer. Only you—spawn of Bhaal—could have destroyed the Ravager, and only when the Ravager was destroyed could the Slayer take its place."

"Why?" Abdel asked as he ripped a piece of Irenicus's soul from him.

The necromancer laughed, and Abdel felt the piece of soul slip through his fingers.

"Why?" Irenicus asked. "Idiot man-child. Human speck. Only the Slayer could kill Ellesime. By succumbing to the blood of the god of murder and killing this girl you thought was so important to you, you gave me the weapon I needed. Now, Ellesime is dead. Now, you give me your soul, and I use it and the power of that detestable tree to make myself immortal. I get. I take. I have. You disappear."

Abdel reached out again and felt something he couldn't possibly have any words to describe. He took hold of Irenicus's soul.

"Ah," the necromancer breathed, "there you are."

"Ellesime lives," Abdel said, the words traveling not through air or fire or lava, but through the medium of immortal souls.

There was a silence filled by the roaring of the lava flow.

"You're staying here, Irenicus," Abdel said.

"Neither of us are staying here, Abdel Adrian," Irenicus replied. "There isn't really even such a place as here. I'm going back to Faerûn an immortal, whether Ellesime lives or not. You're going nowhere. You go to oblivion."

* * * * *

The nail of Jaheira's middle finger snapped off backward, but she didn't notice the pain. She dug, clawing into the unforgiving soil under the burning tree where

Baldur's Gate II

Irenicus had fallen into Hell. Jaheira threw out hand-fuls of dirt and had gone maybe a foot down, but of course there was no sign of Hell.

"Mielikki," she said, "Mielikki, help me."

She dug some more though she was growing over-whelmed by the simple fact that she could dig with her bare hands forever and not get where she was going. Abdel wasn't in some place underground. He wasn't on this plane of existence. He was someplace so different from the world Jaheira knew there was no real connec-tion between them. Irenicus had joined the two places somehow—Jaheira knew of more than one way to do that—and dragged Abdel in, then followed him himself. That joining wasn't physical.

"Mielikki," she cried, "help me . . . tell me . . ."

She stopped digging and let herself cry into the dry dirt, gave herself over to her goddess as a small, weak, desperate creature.

"Help me," she begged.

The words called to her—sounded in the wind—and Jaheira sobbed at the sound of them: *Call to him.*

"Mielikki," Jaheira cried, "Lady, thank you."

She pushed her face into the hole she dug and drew in a deep, soil-scented breath.

"Abdel!" she screamed into the ground. "*Abdel!*"

She breathed again, ignoring the pain in her throat, and screamed, "*Abdel!*"

* * * * *

Irenicus was winning.

Abdel could feel his body had changed back to the monster thing—they'd called it the Ravager.

"That's it," Irenicus said, his voice almost a purr. "That's it."

241

Philip Athans

Abdel felt a piece of his soul bitten away, and he let it go. He didn't care anymore. He'd called to his father— his father. The idea was simply ridiculous. He'd called out to Bhaal and got no answer. Irenicus supplied the only thing that seemed like truth, after all was said and done.

"I'll use it well, Abdel," Irenicus whispered straight into Abdel's disintegrating soul.

Abdel felt his legs pop and twist backward, though he didn't really believe he had a body anymore.

"... *del* ..." a woman's voice echoed from so far away, he was sure it was his imagination. He was struck by the fact that he was in Hell and thought that something as simple as the sound of Jaheira calling his name was imagin—

Jaheira.

"Abdel ..." her voice came again, a little louder this time.

Abdel tried to force his twisted, freakish, monster's mouth to form her name. He couldn't.

"That's over now, Abdel," Irenicus said. "She's the past. She couldn't have been yours anyway, could she? A Harper druid and the son of Bhaal? What could come of ... ah, well. Not that it matters now, child."

Abdel felt himself nodding, then Jaheira's voice came again.

"Abdel," she called, "please ..."

That last word burst through the tattered remains of Abdel's soul like lightning, and he could feel her. Irenicus had stripped so much of him away—eaten it in a very real sense—but he'd left one part behind. He'd left the part inhabited by Jaheira. Maybe every part of his soul was home to her in some way.

Abdel felt human again, and it was a human mouth that screamed, "Jaheira!"

242

* * * * *

Every time she screamed his name, a little part of
the fire that was consuming the Tree of Life went out.

"Abdel!"

Smoke was all around her, drifting over the back of
her head and slipping into the hole to tickle her throat.

"Abdel, please!"

There was a flash of light that Jaheira didn't bother
to recognize. It wasn't Abdel—she knew that on a
primal level—so whatever it was didn't matter. Only
Abdel mattered.

"Abdel!"

"Jaheira!" Imoen called from behind her.

"She's calling him out," Queen Ellesime said to
Imoen.

Jaheira felt footsteps approaching her more than
she heard them.

"Abdel!" the druid screamed again, not realizing that
she had very little voice left.

"Help her," Ellesime said breathlessly. "We have to
help her."

Imoen fell to the ground next to Jaheira without hesitation. Tears flowed anew from Jaheira's burning eyes.

"Abdel!" the young girl screamed, her voice louder
than Jaheira's.

"Abdel!" Ellesime screamed.

"Abdel!" Jaheira screamed.

Ellesime and Imoen screamed, "Abdel!" together.

"Abdel!" Jaheira screamed. *"Abdel!"*

* * * * *

"Abdel!" Imoen screamed, and Abdel drew his soul
around him in response.

243

"Abdel!" came another voice—Ellesime. It was Ellesime, then Jaheira again, then combinations of Imoen, Ellesime, and Jaheira. He sent the pieces of his soul up toward them—was it up? It had to be up.

"I'm down here, Abdel Adrian," Irenicus growled. "And so are you. You don't go back. There's no going back."

Abdel focused on Jaheira's voice, and on Imoen's and Ellesime's. He sent his soul reaching up, and his human hands followed. His human eyes turned up out of the orange and toward the bedrock above.

"No!" Irenicus screamed sharply, and the scream took a piece of Abdel's soul away with it, but it was a small piece.

"You *look* at me!" Irenicus shrieked. "You fight me!"

Abdel could feel the desperation surge through Irenicus. The tide shifted that quickly. Abdel had somewhere to go. He had a real future, not the illusion of Irenicus's gloried immortality as master of a single vampire and a madhouse on an island no one had bothered to name.

If all Abdel could look forward to was nothing but nights with Jaheira in his arms, that was more than Irenicus had to look forward to in any number of millennia to come.

"Abdel, I'm here," Jaheira's voice said, and Abdel could feel it now as a point in space above him. He reached up, but it was too far.

"Face me!" Irenicus practically begged. "Fight!"

That was all the necromancer had. He depended on nothing but Abdel's need to fight, the fact that that was all Abdel could do: fight.

Instead, Abdel stepped on Irenicus—figuratively if not literally. Abdel felt as if he had feet, but did he? He might have been in a place where feet were irrelevant.

Still, he stepped on Irenicus, and that sent the necromancer spinning into a mass of incoherent ranting.

Screaming obscenities and threats, Irenicus slipped farther down into the pit, and Abdel didn't care either way. He was getting out. He was starting his life—with no answers, but then, who had answers?

Abdel reached up and felt a hand touch his. The skin was smooth and warm and familiar. Irenicus's raving fell away into an echoing silence, and Abdel's face filled with dirt. It was in his eyes, in his nose, in his ears, and in his mouth.

He coughed and felt his head return to some kind of solid reality. He could feel his body again. He could move again. He was real and alive again, and when his face came out of the ground, he coughed out dirt, shook it out of his eyes, and pulled in a deep, shuddering breath.

"Abdel . . ." Jaheira's voice sounded rough, raw, but closer now and real, not a distant echo from Faerûn to Hell.

"Jaheira," he said into her face, which was only inches from his own.

Jaheira touched him. She was crying, but she was happy. Imoen was there, wherever there was, and so was Ellesime. He looked around and saw a tree bigger than any tree he'd ever imagined. The tree was blackened, but the black was falling off in clumps to reveal healthy bark beneath. Brilliant green leaves grew, and as the Tree of Life surged back to life, Abdel was sure he could hear Jon Irenicus screaming.

"Abdel," Jaheira said, "you're alive."

He looked at her, smiled, and said, "I want to go home." He glanced at Imoen. "To Candlekeep."

The Cormyr Saga
Death of the Dragon
Ed Greenwood and Troy Denning

The saga of the kingdom of Cormyr comes to an epic conclusion in this new story. Besieged by evil from without and treachery from within, Cormyr's King Azoun must sacrifice everything for his beloved land.

Available August 2000

Beyond the High Road
Troy Denning

Dire prophecies come to life, and the usually stable kingdom of Cormyr is plunged into chaos.

And don't miss . . .
Cormyr: A Novel
Ed Greenwood and Jeff Grubb
The novel that started it all.

Sembia
The Halls of Stormweather
A new FORGOTTEN REALMS series

In the mean streets of Selgaunt everything has a price, and even the wealthiest families will do anything to survive. The cast of characters: the capable but embattled patriarch of the Uskevren family, a young woman who is more than just a maid, the son who carries a horrifying curse, a wife with past as long as it is dark, a servant with more secrets than his master could ever guess, and much more.

Seven talented authors introduce the FORGOTTEN REALMS to a new generation of fans. Featuring novellas by Ed Greenwood, Clayton Emery, Richard Lee Byers, Voronica Whitney-Robinson, Dave Gross, Lisa Smedman, and Paul Kemp.

Available July 2000

Sembia
Shadow's Witness
Paul Kemp

Erevis Cale must battle ghosts from his own dark past if he is to save the family he dearly loves. The first full-length novel in this exciting new series—your gateway to the FORGOTTEN REALMS !

Available November 2000

R.A. Salvatore
Servant of the Shard

The exciting climax of the story of the Crystal Shard

In 1988 R.A. Salvatore burst onto the fantasy scene with a novel about a powerful magical artifact—the Crystal Shard. Now, more than a decade later, he brings the story of the Shard to its shattering conclusion.

From the dark, twisted streets of Calimport to the lofty passes of the Snowflake Mountains, from flashing swords to sizzling spells, this is R.A. Salvatore at his best.

Available October 2000

A new series from Elaine Cunningham!

The Magehound

Counselors and Kings • Book I

In the south of the magical continent of Faerûn lies the hot, humid land of Halruaa. Mysterious figures come and go on strange errands and unspoken deeds. In this land of intrigue, only the society of Counselors, impervious to the effects of magic, can bring order. Yet among them there may be one in whom the magic spark lies hidden. And there is one who can ferret out this spark and destroy it: the Magehound.

Available April 2000

And don't miss . . .

Elfshadow

Songs and Swords • Book I

The half-elf Arilyn Moonblade seeks to learn the secret power of her sword.

Elfsong

Songs and Swords • Book II

A mysterious curse is affecting the Harpers of Faerûn. To stop it Danilo Thann must join forces with his worst enemy.

Legend of the Five Rings®

The Clan War

A legend of the Emerald Throne of the emperors. Of a struggle among the clans for power. And of a war that would devastate all Rokugan.

The Scorpion
Stephen Sullivan
Available July 2000

The Unicorn
Allison Lassieur
Available September 2000

Live the legend!